MW01060682

Keeping Silent

A Caleb Knowles Mystery

by

Carla Damron

For Ray—
a great fellow writer!
Best Wishes,
Carla Damron

A Write Way Publishing Book

This is a work of fiction. Names, characters, locales and incidents are either the product of the author's imagination or are used fictitiously, and any resemblance to actual persons, living or dead, is entirely coincidental.

carladamron@yahoo.com

Write Way Publishing
PO Box 441278
Aurora, CO 80044
staff@writewaypub.com
www.writewaypub.com

First Edition; 2001

ISBN 1-885173-90-3

1 2 3 4 5 6 7 8 9

I would like to thank:
Jim Hussey, a wonderful husband and supportive friend;
Pam Knight, my patient editor/sister;
the rest of my mystery-loving family for keeping the faith;
the Inkplots Writers Group
and the SC Writers Workshop
for cheering me on;
Stephanie Thompson and Jane Schwantes,
"best women" always;
and especially the people with mental illness
whom I have known over the years.
You have been my teachers in so many ways.

CHAPTER ONE

Caleb Knowles ignored the insistent buzz of his office phone as he studied the client in front of him. Ellen Campbell grinned wildly back–it was a wide, toothy smile that had little to do with what danced around in her head. Schizophrenia works like that on people.

"So you think you're ready to get a job. That's a big step. What exactly do you have in mind?" he asked.

Carefully opening a brown paper bag she had crumpled in her lap, Ellen pulled out a tattered sheet of paper and proudly handed it to Caleb.

He laid the paper on his desk, pressed it out with his hands, and scraped off a piece of banana peel. "Let's see. It's a job application for Burger Heaven. You put down your name and address, phone number ... looks okay, Ellen." She had printed her responses in smeared, child-like block letters. Caleb smiled and said, "Now this part's interesting. Under 'Work Experience' you put 'I worked at Hardee's. I own Hardee's. I own all the Hardee's in the world.' You think that's accurate?"

The woman who also believed she'd had nine children by Mel Gibson nodded enthusiastically, thrilled with this new venture.

Caleb raked a hand through his auburn curls that needed a pruning and thought out his next move. Five years as Ellen Campbell's therapist had been a long, challenging journey. Whenever her reality collided head-on with the real world, it was his job to intervene. Ellen believed she once quarterbacked for the '49ers and spent a summer bartending with Elizabeth Dole. Then there was Caleb's favorite delusion–she believed she had three million dollars stored somewhere at Westville National Bank. She'd tried to withdraw the money more than once, after missing a few doses of her medicine.

"This question, 'What skills do you have that would qualify you for this job?' You put down, 'I can sing, I speak Norwegian, and I own a gun.' You don't keep a gun, do you, Ellen?" he asked, caution leaking into his voice.

The phone buzzed. "You have a call on line one," his secretary said.

"I'm with a client," Caleb answered, his attention shifting from the speaker phone back to his client. "Ellen?"

She scowled, tugging at her faded black Aerosmith T-shirt. It needed washing, as did her blond hair, which she'd gathered into three lumpy braids. Ellen wore faded cut-off jeans and fur-lined vinyl boots that felt hot in South Carolina's scalding July weather.

"You taking your medicine?" he asked.

She squeezed her eyes shut and said, "I feel mosquitoes in my brain."

Caleb leaned forward, studying her puckered face. "Did my question make you angry?"

"The pills turn into mosquitoes in my brain," she muttered, which of course explained it. Once again, she'd stopped taking her medication, which accounted for her fetching outfit and imaginative résumé.

Caleb regarded her with a mixture of sympathy and admiration. Screaming voices and bizarre thoughts constantly swirled through Ellen's mind, yet she somehow muddled through each day. It was hard to take problems like the rising cost of gasoline too seriously, thinking of Ellen's struggles.

"Ellen, the pills don't turn into mosquitoes in your brain. I think sometimes you don't want the medication. But when you stop taking the pills, you end up back at the hospital, which you hate."

She squeezed her eyes shut again. "Too many bugs there."

"You're scheduled to see the doctor right after me. You plan on seeing him?"

One eye popped open and looked at him. "He have any candy?"

"Peppermint, I think." Caleb pointed to the bag in her hand and asked: "Now, back to my other question. Do you have a gun?"

"Excuse me, Caleb," his secretary's voice on the speaker phone insisted. "There's an emergency call on line one."

Caleb stared nervously at the phone, then back at his client. "Ellen?"

She opened the greasy brown bag before handing it to Caleb. Reluctantly, he reached inside and lifted out a bright green water gun. Firing at a thirsty fern hanging in his window, he said: "Nice pistol, Ellen. Why don't you hold on to it while I take this call?"

He handed it back to her as he lifted the receiver. "Who is it, Janice?"

"A police officer. He said it's a family matter," she said.

Caleb punched the line. "This is Caleb Knowles."

"Mr. Knowles? This is Officer Rowley, with the Westville PD. We've got a situation over here at your brother's house. We need you to get over here right away." His drawling voice was barely audible over a cacophony of banging sounds, muffled voices and radio static coming through the phone.

"What's happened?" Caleb asked.

He heard more confusion over the line and what sounded like someone shouting. The officer said, "I can't tell you more. Detective Briscoe gave me your number and said to get you here right away."

"Let me talk to Detective Briscoe," he said, glancing at his client.

"The detective can't talk now. She said to tell you it was urgent."

Caleb glared at the phone. He knew Claudia Briscoe well enough to know it had to be something serious. He heard more commotion on the other line as someone yelled out: "Bag those fragments."

"Where is my brother?" Caleb demanded. The officer didn't answer before the line clicked dead.

Ellen said: "My brain has bugs again. I can feel them." She closed her eyes so tightly that her top lip drew back, exposing again the random line of teeth. This was her way of shutting out tension. She clearly felt the panic in the room.

"Uh ... I know, Ellen. It's okay, really." He tried a reassuring smile but it fell apart at the edges. "I'm afraid I need to end our session early. But you wait for Dr. Rhyker, okay?"

He grabbed his keys from his desk before ushering her out. He herded her to Janice, muttered he had an emergency, and bolted out the door.

Adrenaline pushed his foot against the accelerator and the truck lurched into traffic. What the hell had happened? he wondered, his mind racing with possible scenarios. Maybe Sam had been robbed. No, it sounded more serious than that. But how serious? Maybe Sam had been hurt, or worse ... He shook his head to dislodge that image. Don't go there, he told himself.

His hands trembled against the steering wheel, every nerve

on alert. Maybe Sam had witnessed something, and they needed Caleb to work as interpreter. He'd heard so much chaos on the phone, his deaf brother wouldn't know what to do. Yeah, maybe something not so serious. He tried hard to convince himself, but his panic only escalated.

The traffic didn't comply with his need for clear passage. At the intersection of Lake and Haynesworth, the light turned red as the Mustang in front of him veered left. Ignoring the on-coming cars, he laid his hand on the horn and swerved onto Sam's street. Better to ask forgiveness than permission.

His Toyota pickup climbed the curb in front of the restored two-story mill house that served as Sam's home and sculptor's studio. Several police cars, with blue lights strobing, were wedged between the porch and the narrow brick street. Caleb leapt from the cab of the truck, maneuvering between the cars, the police officers, and the on-lookers who had gathered in the yard.

He didn't feel his legs carry him, and he ignored the calls for him to stop, instead racing through the front door.

The studio was even more chaotic than the yard. Uniformed officers and men in jumpsuits wore latex gloves as they poked through broken glass fragments and pieces of wood, while a policewoman stretched yellow plastic tape across the far corner of the room. Caleb scanned the faces for his brother.

At last he spotted Claudia Briscoe, notepad in hand. Her mahogany skin glistened with sweat. She waved a crimson-nailed finger at two officers to check out something on the floor.

Caleb rushed to her. "Claudia? Where is Sam?"

Her sharp black eyes studied him for a second, then softened as she cocked her head toward Sam's office. There, bent forward and still as a stone, sat his brother.

"Thank God." Caleb rushed to him. Right away he saw the blood on Sam's shirt, a mass of brown spattered against the gray. Sam's hands, propped on blood-speckled knees, clutched each other tightly. His dark eyes stared blankly at the activity around him.

Caleb stooped down and touched Sam's shoulder. Sam looked at him, looked through him, then turned away.

Caleb grabbed his arm more forcefully and, using his hands, signed "Are you hurt?" He surveyed Sam's chest and stomach, where the bloodstains were, but saw no injuries. Caleb shook Sam's shoulder and waited for Sam's eyes to find him. When they met his, he brushed his right fist, thumb out, against his forehead, signing "Sam!"

He watched him carefully, alarmed by what he saw. Sam's face contorted and his brown eyes searched Caleb's, then he looked back down at the floor.

"Jesus, Sam."

"He's been like that since we got here. I guess he's in shock." Claudia had slipped up behind him. She eyed Sam with a mixture of frustration and sympathy.

"What the hell happened here, Claudia?"

"We found a body. Tentative ID is Anne Farrell, from a purse we found in a desk. You know her?"

"Anne? Anne's dead?"

Claudia nodded. "How do you know her?"

"She's Sam's fiancée. What happened?"

Claudia turned her iron eyes to Sam again. But he was far away, oblivious to them. "I think he knows. I've tried to talk to him, I know he reads lips quite well. But he hasn't answered me." She turned again to Caleb. "I hope you can get him talking, Caleb, because we need answers here. And we need them fast."

Caleb crouched down and touched Sam's massive hands. "Talk to me, Sam," he signed. But his brother's eyes, his window to the world, would not meet his.

"Where's Anne?" Caleb asked Claudia.

She looked at him "We do need an ID. But I'm not sure you want to see her. The murder was brutal."

He nodded, but he had to see her—maybe then he'd believe that this was real and not a nightmare.

He followed Claudia to the front of the studio, turning toward the far left corner of the room. They passed a line of Sam's sculptures, centered in splashes of light from an angled track system, but the order of the display gave way to disaster as they neared the corner. Plaster fragments and jagged pieces of wood covered the floor. Two toppled columns, broken and nudging against each other, were strewn with yellow tape. Anne Farrell's body lay on top of them.

"Dear God," he whispered. She didn't look real, she looked like some twisted, broken doll. She was tilted on her side, her pale arms splayed out at odd angles from her slender frame. Her eyes, wide empty beacons, held no sign of life.

He'd never seen so much blood. Her brown hair was matted with it. Her pale blue dress had drunk it up like a sponge, but a pool had still spilled over beside her. Splotches of brown sprayed the walls, the pillars, and the wood sculptures that encircled her. Caleb tried to cross over to her but Claudia stepped in his way.

"Not too close, our lab guys aren't finished yet. You okay, Caleb?" She touched his arm and he jerked back.

"Yeah. It's Anne." He didn't feel okay. He felt sick. He wanted to run, to bolt from that room, but he couldn't move. He couldn't tear his eyes from the body.

"What do you make of this?" With her pen, she pointed at Anne's hands. Both were positioned the same way, with the index and middle fingers squeezed into the meat of the thumb.

"No." His hands reached out toward hers. "She's signing 'no.' Anne was deaf, too. I guess she was screaming at the killer, the only way she could."

Claudia added this to her notes. She motioned a uniformed officer over, explained that Anne had been identified, and told him to call it in to their captain.

"No need. Captain Bentille just got here," the young officer replied.

"Terrific," she muttered.

Caleb stepped back unsteadily. His head felt clouded. He looked over at his brother, now understanding his withdrawal.

Claudia leaned over to Caleb and whispered, "Shit. Here comes Bentille. He's gonna want a statement from your brother. If not here, then at the station. I know he's deaf, but he reads lips and he talks more articulately than I do. You know how Bentille is, Caleb. Sam better be ready to cooperate." She rushed past him to where her boss huddled with his entourage.

Caleb couldn't care less about the police and their politics. He knew Sam couldn't talk now, he had shut down. When reality hurts this much, you turn off, you push it away. He remembered other times when Sam had pulled into himself. Right after the accident that had deafened him at sixteen. After the fights, again and again, with their drunken father.

He went back to his brother and pulled a chair over in front of him. Sam didn't seem to notice. Caleb reached out and took his hands, feeling the rigid tension in them. It took a while, but slowly, Sam's eyes made their way to his.

"How you doing, Sam?" he signed.

Sam looked puzzled, and stared at him for a long time. Finally, he asked aloud, "Where's Anne?"

Caleb felt words freeze in his throat. With his right fist, he stroked his cheek, then extended both hands out, one palm up, the other palm down. Slowly, he rolled his hands over; "Anne's dead," his hands said.

"Dead?" Sam asked out loud, disbelieving.

"Yes," Caleb struggled to find his voice. "She's dead. I'm so sorry."

"No," Sam said, his gaze slipping back to the silence of the floor.

Caleb glanced around until he spotted Claudia again. He crossed over to her and said, "I need to get him out of here."

"Did he tell you what happened?"

"I don't think he knows. He's in bad shape. Let me take him home with me."

She shook her head. "You don't understand. So far, he's all we've got. He's got to answer some questions."

"Look at him. What do you think he could tell you?"

"Listen to me. We got a call at two p.m. from a neighbor. She hears a ruckus over here but decides to ignore it. Neighborhoods like this, nobody wants to meddle. Then Sam comes running over to her place, yelling for her to call an ambulance. When the EMTs got here, the woman was dead. They radioed for us and the coroner. The lab guys got here about an hour ago."

"And no one else was here?"

"No one but Sam." She motioned at Captain Frank Bentille. "He's gonna insist Sam come downtown with us." Caleb glanced over at the police captain. He'd met him last year during a child abuse case and quickly decided Bentille was too politically minded to ever be trusted.

Bentille looked over at Caleb and tried a smile, but it came off as a quick, shallow, TV evangelist's grin. Claudia leaned into him whispering, "It's not my call. Sam will have to come in."

"Is there a problem, Detective Briscoe?" Bentille had maneuvered in beside her. He was tall, almost matching Caleb's six-foot-two height, but thinner. He wore an almost tasteful beige suit that revealed more wrist than it should.

"Yes, there is," Caleb interjected. "The detective says you

plan to question my brother. Since no one on your force knows sign language, you'll have to have an interpreter. Sam may read lips well, but that means he gets maybe sixty percent of what's said. If you're going to question him, he'll need to get every word. Until arrangements are made for an interpreter, I think Sam should stay with me."

Bentille studied him up and down, assessing, but then the camera-ready smile returned. He laid a hand on Caleb's shoulder. "Sorry, Knowles, I know this is upsetting. But we do have an interpreter lined up. He's on his way to the station right now."

"Who is it?" Caleb asked. He knew all of Westville's registered interpreters, and some were better than others. Sam would need the best.

"I think you'll approve of this one. Reverend Stewart Brearly."

Caleb nodded, relieved. Stewart was the best. He was also Sam's closest friend.

A commotion at the front door attracted Bentille, who quickly busied himself barking orders at his legions. Soon the door swung open and a man and woman rolled in a gurney. They heaved the body onto the stretcher with little care. After strapping in Anne's body, they covered it with a sheet.

"*No!*" a voice boomed, sounding not quite human. Sam sprung up and started after the stretcher.

Caleb rushed to Sam, fending off the officers who tried to restrain him. "Easy now, Sam. They have to take her."

"No," he said again, with less muster. Caleb held his shoulder, but couldn't bring himself to look at his brother's face.

The medics wheeled the gurney past Sam, past the bloodstains, past the officers, and out into the torrid summer air.

CHAPTER TWO

Caleb's caffeine addiction roused him into consciousness the next morning. He could smell coffee coming as Shannon climbed the stairs, inched open the door, and paused at the foot of their bed. Squeezing his eyes closed, he said, "If you tell me it was all a dream, I'll pay you cash."

"Wish I could," Shannon said. "You awake?"

He opened his sluggish eyes to the tray she held in front of him. A huge mug of coffee–French Roast, with a hint of cinnamon–and two slices of black-edged toast made up Shannon's version of a home-cooked breakfast. He went straight for the caffeine, hoping for a direct hit. "What? No paper? And where are my slippers?"

Shannon bent over and kissed him. A gauze gown trickled over her like pale blue water. Dark curls escaped a silver barrette to bob and dangle around her face. Caleb stroked them back behind her ear.

"Careful, honey, or those slippers may find themselves shoved up some posterior body part. As for the paper, it can wait. How do you feel?" she asked.

"Like I'm hungover." Caleb gulped down some more coffee, closed his eyes, and tried to clear his head. Last night had seemed endless: he'd spent three hours squirming in a cold metal chair outside the closed interrogation room where the police had questioned Sam. Captain Bentille finally released Sam and told him not to leave town, sounding like a sheriff in a Gene Autry movie. Sam refused to come to Caleb's and refused his company as well, so Caleb drove himself home and crawled into bed. Sleep came much later, bringing dark storm dreams that made his slumber more exhausting than restful.

"Those stress hangovers are the worst." Shannon plopped in bed beside him. "You didn't sleep very well."

"No." He blew into the coffee cup and the steam rose, heating his face.

She lifted his arm and pulled it around her, nestling in. "I wanted to let you sleep in, but I know you have a long day ahead of you." Shannon reached for his mug and took a sip. "Matthew called."

"Did you tell him what's going on?"

"I filled in some missing pieces. He wants you to call when you can."

He nodded. Dr. Matthew Rhyker was his boss and colleague and friend. Caleb started working for Matthew six years ago at the Westville Counseling Center, a non-profit agency that took care of most of the mentally ill citizens in Westville, South Carolina. The small but bustling practice consisted of Matthew, Caleb, a secretary, and a part-time child psychiatrist. Shannon had worked there, too, up until four months ago.

After Caleb survived a tumultuous divorce and bitter two-year custody battle over his daughter, he had pretty much concluded that he'd rather be drawn and quartered than entangle himself with another female. But then Matthew hired a new social worker, Shannon McPherson. For six months, Caleb tried to ignore how her smile was always half-mischievous and how her lightning-quick wit came out at all the right times. But Shannon was not a woman to be ignored. One day when Shannon asked him out, the shock caused Caleb to dump a soda in his lap. It only took a few months before Shannon moved into Caleb's small cottage and they decided sharing both a home and an office might pose a risk to their young relationship. One of them needed to move on, they concluded, and Shannon had easily found a more lucrative position at a managed care company.

Matthew had been understanding, but Shannon's departure had disrupted the team, and the extra work nearly overwhelmed the remaining clinicians. It made for tight schedules, long hours and, sometimes, irate customers. Client emergencies could send them in a tailspin, but somehow, they persevered.

Caleb grabbed the phone, punched the auto-dial number, and heard Matthew answer on the second ring.

"It's me. I don't think I'll be in today."

"I didn't think you would, Caleb." The voice was quiet and serious. "Is there anything I can do?"

"Well, if you could reverse time by about twenty-four hours, that would be a help."

"Like you always remind me, a doctor isn't God. But is there anything else? Like of the human realm?"

"Nah. Have Janice cancel my appointments. And Ellen Campbell ... I was with her yesterday when the call came. She was pretty anxious, but I had to leave. Did you see her?"

"Yes. I put her back on injections. She doesn't like taking the pills. She says they make her breasts too big."

"Well then. Our Miss Universe has to be careful. Thanks for seeing her."

"Caleb, let me know if I can do anything. For you or Sam."

"I will. I'll talk to you tomorrow." He hung up the phone and turned to Shannon.

"Maybe I should stay home today," she said.

He shook his head. "You have a new job and you don't

need to be taking time off. Besides, you're in cold corporate America now, my dear. They may not be too sympathetic."

"I don't care if they're sympathetic or not. If you need me—"

He lifted her hand to his lips and kissed it. "If I need you, I'll call you. But I have a lot to do; I'll probably be too busy to even think. You go on to work."

Her nod was reluctant. She headed for the bathroom and a minute later he heard the shower running.

He thought about walking in on her. He could lean into the water, letting the warm torrents pound the tension out of his neck and shoulders. He could wrap himself in Shannon's arms, holding on so tight that not even water could come between them. Maybe then, he could escape this dark, new truth, if only for a moment.

No, he couldn't lean on Shannon that way. Not now. Not when there was so much to be done.

He looked out the window. Two tall oaks, unstirred by any breeze, stood at attention against the hazy July sky. With no clouds in sight, the day promised to be another scorcher.

He rubbed his face, pondering the morning ahead. He would go over to Sam's. Maybe help clean the studio. There were people to be called, arrangements to be made. Soon would come the funeral, then the burial.

Caleb thought about yesterday. It had started like any other day: Sam had been busy in his workshop when he decided it was time for a break. He'd stepped into the studio and stumbled over the body of the woman he'd loved more than life itself. It must have been surreal to him. It must have felt like his whole world collapsed in that single frozen second.

After a two-year, erratic, long-distance courtship, Anne had moved to Westville to live with Sam a year ago. Christmas came and Sam dragged Caleb to every jewelry store in Westville, looking for the perfect ring. On New Year's Eve, Anne had accepted his proposal and Sam had been ecstatic. At last, someone who fit wholly into his world.

Sam had never fully immersed himself in the deaf culture, which had a social system of its own. The world of the hearing wasn't always comfortable for him either: because of his exceptional lip-reading and clear voice, hearing people tended to forget he was deaf. And the little things, like speaking too fast or talking when his head was turned, easily alienated him. So Sam limited his world to his family and a few close friends. And of course Anne. And now she was gone forever.

Caleb took a final gulp of the lukewarm coffee. He heard the creak from the door opening and the click of nails trotting across the floor. Quickly, he shoved the half-full mug on the nightstand and dropped a pillow below his waist. He saw the approaching gray and white head and stiffened as Cleo launched herself from the foot of the bed, landing squarely on Caleb's chest. The blurry mass of gray and white fur wiggled her way up to his neck to lap at the stubble on his chin.

Shannon came back into the room and let out a laugh. "Now there's a picture."

"You haven't seen Cleo, have you?" Caleb asked. The sheepdog, her large clueless eyes staring adoringly, licked him again.

"No. She must be here somewhere." She reached over to rub Cleo's head, who plopped back down on the floor and licked Shannon's toes as she tried to make her way to the closet.

When Caleb crawled out of the bed, it felt like he was moving through Jell-o. He stumbled over to the mirror and flinched at his reflection. His almond-colored eyes had new shadows hanging beneath them. An auburn shadow had sprouted on his chin. His hair looked like birds had nested in it overnight. He needed a shower, a shave, and maybe five more hours of sleep before he could face the hellish day ahead.

The shower and shave helped a little, but he still felt sleep-deprived and bone-weary when he plodded downstairs and allowed himself to be herded over to Cleo's empty food bowl. After feeding her and refilling his coffee mug, he made his way over to the paper on the kitchen table. Tuesday's headline screamed at him: DEAF WOMAN FOUND MURDERED IN ARTIST'S STUDIO. The article milked the tragedy for all the sensationalism it could get: "Local deaf sculptor, recent recipient of Southeastern Artists' Guild Award, was held for questioning by police." A photograph showed Claudia Briscoe talking to an officer in Sam's front yard while behind her, Anne's body was being loaded into an ambulance.

"Terrific," Caleb muttered. It was ludicrous that anyone might think Sam had killed Anne. How could the newspaper get away with that crap? He glared at the photo of Claudia. Reaching for the phone, he dialed the number to the police station. "Detective Briscoe, please."

"Detective Briscoe's in interrogation. Is there a message?"

"There sure is." Caleb took in a deep breath that did little to quell his frustration. "Tell her Caleb Knowles called. Tell her I need to talk with her as soon as possible."

The operator said she'd relay the message, but the detective would probably be tied up for several hours. Caleb promised he'd be waiting for her call.

Shannon came up from behind, wrapping her arms around him. "You sure you don't want me to stay home?"

He breathed in the sweet scent of her shampoo. He didn't want to let go of her. "I promise I'll call if I need you," he said, walking her to the door. She kissed him before heading out to her car.

For the next hour, the phone rang a dozen times with calls from concerned friends and curious acquaintances. Caleb had no interest in talking with any of them. He wished he could turn off the ringer, but he couldn't afford to miss Claudia's call. When the doorbell rang, he checked through the peephole and opened the door to find his brother and Stewart Brearly on his front porch.

"Thank God," Caleb signed, ushering them inside. "Are you all right? Where have you been?"

Sam stood in the doorway, his large frame filling it. His face had more age on it than Caleb had ever seen. A shadow of whiskers covered his thick jaw. In Sam's wheat-colored hair, Caleb spotted flecks of sawdust from yesterday's work. And Sam's eyes, his main access to the world, stared at Caleb with the same flat expression they had held last night.

Stewart slipped past him and motioned that Sam should sit. "How are ya, Caleb?" Stewart grabbed Caleb's hand and shook it. He wore his usual gray shirt with a clerical collar, jeans and running shoes. His silver hair and beard, dusted with white, gave him a wise, kindly look. During his three years as rector of St. John's Lutheran Church, Stewart had developed a strong reputation as a community leader.

"How I'm doing is irrelevant," Caleb signed. "I'm worried more about my brother here."

"I've been at the police station most of the morning," Sam said aloud.

Caleb pulled his chair closer. "Again? Why?" he signed, touching his head, then pulling his hand away, index and pinky extended.

"Stewart went with me," Sam answered.

"How did it go?"

Sam replied by turning away. Caleb could tell he was on the verge of shutting down again and couldn't really blame him.

Stewart forced a weak smile and said, "It was a little better than yesterday. But I don't think they're done with us yet."

Sam suddenly stood, towering over Caleb. "I need to get out of here."

"Hold on, Sam. What do you want me to do? I'd like to help."

Sam opened his mouth as though about to speak, only to clamp it shut. He slid his hands in the back pockets of his jeans, then pulled them out again, staring down as though unsure what to do with them. Finally, he said: "Could you run some errands for me? Anne's parents are coming in tonight. You could make reservations for them at the Avery Inn. And we may need help with the arrangements. I think they'll want to have the funeral up in Rock Hill."

Caleb knew how much Sam cherished his independence; he'd asked this small favor because the one thing Sam couldn't do was make a traditional phone call. And even asking this had been hard for him. "Okay. I'll take care of all that." Caleb glanced over at Stewart and back at Sam. "But Sam, talk to me! You've been through hell ..." Caleb's voice trailed off and his signing ceased. His brother turned away again, ignoring him.

Caleb touched his shoulder. Sam slowly turned to him, his face glazed over with indifference.

"Let me drive you home," Caleb offered. "Maybe I can help you get things cleaned up."

Sam shook his head. "My bike's in the back of Stewart's truck. And I can't clean up anything because the police have barricaded the studio. I can't go near there." He left without looking back.

Stewart stayed behind. "He's been like that since it happened. I can't get through to him any better than you."

"What happened yesterday, Stewart?"

Stewart dropped into a chair. "Sam said he was back in the workshop, finishing up a piece for the fall opening. He'd left Anne in the office off the studio, working on some books she'd brought home from work. Sam got hot, decided to get a soda. He thought she might want one, so he went into the studio and found her. No one else was around. He felt for a pulse, but she was already gone." Stewart paused, his gray eyes searching the floor for a long moment. He cleared his throat and continued, "Sam ran to a neighbor's and had them call an ambulance, then went back to the studio. The rest I think you know."

"What are the police saying?"

"They don't say much. From their questions, I can tell that the only fingerprints they have are Sam's. And Anne's, of course. They have the murder weapon, one of Sam's pieces. I'd never seen it before–it must be something new. Some kind of winged figure, maybe two feet tall."

Caleb nodded, remembering the day Sam had finished the "Gabriel" and how proud he had been. He'd experimented with a more abstract style and the result was magnificent. The arched, delicate wings, made of pale oak, reached almost a foot on either side. Its head, bowed down reverently, held only a suggestion of a face. The muscles of its torso had been carefully articulated to give a quality of both tremendous power and gentle grace.

The Gabriel would have been a gift for Stewart's birthday.

"There was a partial fingerprint on the statue, and it matched Sam's," Stewart added.

"Big surprise there. Pretty hard to create something without touching it." Caleb let out a frustrated sigh. "Maybe the murderer wore gloves or something. What else did the police say?"

"It's not so much what they said, it's their attitude. They were almost sarcastic with Sam's responses. They made him tell the story again and again, like they're trying to wear him down until he tripped up or confessed or something. Detective Briscoe was more compassionate, because she's your friend and knows Sam. But even she says they've seen this many times before. A couple gets into a fight, tempers get out of control, et cetera."

Caleb shook his head in disbelief. Maybe it was a common scenario, but it sure didn't fit his brother. Sam, for all his mass and strength, was one of the gentlest people he knew. Sam rarely got angry, and when he did, he'd swallow the rage, dissecting it into self-effacing bits. He might say something to the person who'd angered him, but this was always followed by a long, heartfelt apology.

"You have any ideas, Caleb? We need to get the police looking in another direction."

"Maybe it was a robbery or something."

"Nothing's missing. Anne had two hundred dollars in her purse, and it was still there. Her jewelry was still on her, including the engagement ring." Stewart shook his head. Tears brimmed in the corners of his eyes and he turned away to hide them. "It's so unbelievable. She was such a vibrant, beautiful woman."

"Yes, she was," Caleb said.

Stewart stared out the window for a tense moment. "I called the Farrells last night and told them about Anne," he said. "I hope I never have to make a call like that again. Monroe Farrell took it especially hard."

Caleb nodded. "I met him once. His dislike for Sam was obvious. He didn't think Sam was good enough for his daughter. He made snide comments about Sam's work, like he didn't think Sam could support a family."

"Sam makes twice as much as you or me," Stewart said. "The police asked me about Sam's relationship with Anne. I told them what I knew. That he's the kindest person I know and he could never hurt anyone. But hell, they didn't really care."

"At least it's something."

Stewart arched his bushy gray brows at Caleb.

"What? Is there something else?"

"No. It's just that I noticed some tension there recently, maybe not between them, but tension in Sam's house. Wish I knew why."

Caleb glared at him, disbelieving. "I don't think you know what you're talking about."

"Take it easy. I didn't mention it to the police. And maybe I'm overreacting. But Anne had been—nervous, edgy. It was unusual for her."

"Hell, Stewie, they were getting married. I was a basket case before my wedding."

"I remember." Stewart grinned. "Sam and I went camping a few weeks ago and we talked about Anne. She'd been through so many changes. Moving here, taking that job at the accounting firm, getting engaged. Sam was worried about how she was handling everything." Stewart leaned forward and looked at Caleb with some intensity. "Look, you and I both know Sam didn't hurt her. But somebody did. All those hours at the police station, I've had time to think about this. Maybe something else was going on with Anne. If there was, we need to find out." He rose, arching his back, stiff from sitting. "And we need to get your brother a lawyer, Caleb. And fast."

Caleb walked him to the door, saying he'd work on it and that he knew a good attorney. As Stewart's truck pulled out of the drive, the phone rang. Caleb grabbed the receiver, hoping it was Claudia Briscoe—he definitely needed to talk to the detective.

"I hate to bother you. If it's a bad time—"

"What's up, Matthew?"

"Heard from a patient of yours, Melanie Carson. She seems to be in crisis. What can you tell me about her?"

"What's the crisis?"

"She wouldn't say. She was upset on the phone with Janice, said she had to see you. Janice told her you were out, she said she had to see someone."

"Mmm. That's unusual for her. I've been seeing her for about eight months. Anxiety, moderate depression, dysfunctional family. All in all, though, she's a bright lady. Great sense of humor. Her chart's in my desk."

"I was afraid you'd say that," Matthew commented. "Your desk always scares me a little."

"It's not so bad. Janice exaggerated when she claimed something bit her. What time is Melanie coming in?"

"Eleven o'clock. Anything else you can tell me?"

Caleb thought about it for a moment. "Tell you what. I'll see her. I could use the distraction."

"You sure?"

"Yep. Be there in a sec."

CHAPTER THREE

Twenty minutes later, Caleb pulled his sputtering Toyota pickup beside Matthew's sleek new Volvo behind the Counseling Center. The office was housed in a rambling old brick house built in the 'thirties. Huge, antebellum live oak trees provided a green canopy over the parking area and the walkway leading to the porch. Clay planters lined the steps up to the Center, each crowded with petunias and impatiens that somehow survived the scalding South Carolina heat. On either side of the heavy oak entrance, long panels of stained glass glimmered in the summer sun.

Caleb broke out in a sweat before he reached the front door, sun beating down on him with merciless force as it pushed the temperature up through the nineties. Caleb predicted a three-digit day by noon. He swung open the door and felt instant relief as he stepped inside to breathe in cool, life-sustaining air conditioning.

He glanced around the reception area. Wide plank floors, polished to a mirror shine, led to a curved staircase. Janice's desk lay to the right of the stairs and, beyond it, French doors opened to the waiting area. He noticed most of the chairs were occupied, but couldn't tell if his client had arrived.

Caleb found his stack of messages on Janice's desk and sifted through them, hoping Claudia Briscoe had phoned here. But the calls were from a few colleagues who were inquiring about the newspaper article. He didn't feel like dealing with any of them. After all, he'd come to work to escape his own problems.

When he heard Janice in the breakroom, he slipped in to see her. She immediately reached up to hug him with plump arms. "How is Sam? And you? Can I do anything? I brought a casserole for you, it's in the fridge."

Caleb smiled into her bright green eyes. Her monochromatic blond hair was tucked in tiny blue bows that belied her fifty-four years. She wore a skirt and blouse printed with swirls of every Easter egg hue. Her shoes matched the hair bows, so did a chiffon scarf tied loosely around her neck. Janice had been with the clinic since its beginning twelve years ago.

"What is it about casseroles?" Caleb asked. "Someone dies, and all over town, females pop casseroles into ovens. I just don't get it." She couldn't seem to tell if he was serious, so he winked at her. "Melanie here yet?"

"Yes, but she's early. You could get a cup of coffee if you want. I just made some. Industrial-strength, just the way you like it."

He poured himself a cup and took it back to his office. He switched on the brass floor lamp, opened the Venetian blind in front of his window, and dropped into the leather desk chair. The desk itself couldn't be seen. Stacks of journals, reports, and charts lay scattered among dirty coffee cups, a Slinky, and his daughter's latest Play-Doh sculpture. He rummaged through the mess until he found the phone book. After looking up the number to the Avery Inn, he called the reservation desk and asked to reserve a room for Monroe and Louise Farrell. He was about to pull out a credit card when the clerk told him that the Farrells had already arrived. Did he wish to be "rung through" to the Farrells' room? Caleb declined and hung up the phone. He wasn't ready to deal with Anne's grief-stricken parents. Not yet.

***

Melanie Carson took the chair by the window. She shifted in her seat, crossing her legs, then uncrossing them, folding her arms before dropping them in her lap. Her hazel eyes were red and swollen; the flesh on her angular face looked blotchy and older than her twenty-six years. A shaky hand tugged at short tufts of copper-colored hair.

Caleb had never seen her like this. "Can I get you some coffee or something?"

She shook her head, tears flooding her eyes.

He handed her a tissue and slid his chair closer. She dabbed at her face and looked embarrassed. "Sorry ... I seem to keep falling apart," she said.

"It's okay to fall apart. We'll put you back together again."

She tried to smile, but the tears kept coming. "I don't even know where to begin."

"Has something happened?"

She nodded, her bottom lip trembling. With the tissue squeezed in a tight ball, she tried to dam up her tears.

"Take your time, Melanie. You don't have to talk about it until you're ready."

She rubbed her reddened nose with the tissue, then began unsteadily, "It happened last night. I was working late, the books had to be reconciled because it's the end of the month and there's a board meeting next week."

"At CarolinaCorp?" He knew she was a bookkeeper for the non-profit corporation.

She nodded. "The books were out of balance–which sometimes happens–and it was driving me crazy. I decided I'd stay there until I figured it out, even if it took all night. So it gets to be about ten-thirty, and I hear the front door unlock."

Caleb's eyes widened. "A break-in?"

"No, no. It was Mr. Edinger, the director. It really surprised me–at that hour. He comes in, and he's acting real weird. His tie is hanging loose around his neck. His suit's a mess–the jacket's all wrinkled and has a big grease spot on it. I couldn't believe it. This is a man who knows that 'anal-retentive' has a hyphen–you never see him with a hair out of place." She tossed the balled-up Kleenex into the wastebasket and reached for another. "So I know something's wrong. He comes into my office, leans over my desk to see what I'm doing. He commends me for my devotion to the agency. His breath is all hot and boozy, I can tell right away he's drunk."

"That must have been unnerving," he said.

She drew her thin lips in tight. "Well, it wasn't exactly a foreign situation. But I would have never expected Mr. Edinger ..." her voice trailed off.

"What happened then?"

"I try to ignore the fact that he's drunk. I make small talk, tell him about my bookkeeping problems, but he isn't interested, or he's too drunk to understand what I'm talking about. He says he'd rather talk about my career plans, my future in the company. He asks me to come sit beside him on the other side of the desk. And like an idiot, I do it."

Caleb studied her, unsure whether to probe or support. He opted for probing. "What made you move over to him?"

Headlight eyes met his. "I–didn't have a choice. It's ridiculous, thinking back on it, but I just got up, went over to him. His eyes were glassy and he stumbled over his words when he talked. He went on and on about the agency, how much it meant to him and his family, how he'd given it his whole life. How nobody understood how much he'd given up for it. He wasn't sure it was all worth it, he said. It had turned him into someone he didn't like," she nodded in slow rhythm with her words. "I listened, hoping he'd sober up enough to drive home."

"Why didn't you leave?"

"That's what I keep asking myself. I wanted to, but I guess I thought he might get behind the wheel and get himself or someone else killed. I'd have felt awful if something like that happened."

Caleb nodded, understanding. No, she couldn't leave. Yes, she had to obey him. With this man, she was a young child frozen in that strange, sick mixture of fear and loyalty. This man could have been her father.

Melanie had endured a troubling childhood with a drunken, rageful father and depressed, passive mother. Her first ten years included several ventures into the hell of foster homes. Her mother would pull it together enough to get her kids back, then sink again into depression. Melanie did her best to hold the family together, taking care of her sister, mom, and dad.

"So you thought you should stay with him until he sobered up."

She nodded. She lifted a shaky hand to her face, lowered it. "But then he changed. He wasn't just a drunk whining about his life. He got mad. 'What do they expect? What do they all expect?' He kept screaming. He started pacing around the room, banging on the desk. His hands are huge, you know, so he made this thunderous sound each time he hit it." She flinched as though hearing it again.

"What did you do?"

"I was so scared. I never would have thought he ..." Melanie's voice slid to a whisper. She seemed to be struggling with some painful memories from last night–and probably, from years before.

"You're safe now, Melanie. Take your time."

Her eyes fell to the floor. "He locks the door. I hear the deadbolt click, and the jingle of his keys as he puts them back in his pocket. It sounds so ... final." She swallowed, and kept her eyes fixed on the floor, like she was watching it all again. "He's red and sweaty, and he breathes so hard I can hear it. It's an ugly sound, like a panting animal.

"I tell him I have to leave because it's so late. When I try to get to the door, he grabs me." Her trembling hand touched her arm, remembering, reliving.

"You're okay." Caleb leaned forward and said, "You're here, in my office, and you are safe. Do you hear me?"

She lifted her head and looked surprised to see him there. "He touched my face and said I was beautiful. He said he'd never really noticed that before, that he'd never let himself see me that way. His face moved real close to me. I could feel his breath on my neck. And smell him–that disgusting smell of booze and sweat. It made me want to vomit. He took my arm. He wouldn't let go."

Suddenly, the image of Anne's murdered body flashed across Caleb's mind. The picture was so vivid and so utterly grotesque, as though burned permanently on the retina of his brain. Had Anne been cornered, like Melanie? Had her last moments been filled with the same terror? Caleb took a deep breath, he needed to focus on his client.

Melanie continued: "He didn't rape me. Or really even hurt me. But he held me there for a long time, and I was ... trapped." She seemed to be reliving it. She sat still, breathing.

He watched her, concerned. "What else, Melanie?"

"I– He squeezed my arm tight–I have a bruise where he held it." She fingered the inside of her arm.

"Anything else you remember?"

She started rocking, her body swaying as she wrapped her arms tightly around her midriff. Her eyes stared out, trance-like.

"Melanie? Can you hear me?"

"Yes. I ... don't remember anything else. Just him holding me."

"How'd you get free?"

She blinked a few times. "I said I had a friend expecting me, which was a lie. I pulled my arm free, gathered all the books from the desk like I was going to finish them at home. He said I was a very dedicated employee, taking work home like that. Finally, he unlocked the door. As I was leaving, he said he enjoyed our meeting and hoped I did, too." She let out a forced, nervous laugh. "Can you believe that?"

Caleb shook his head. "You went home?"

"I drove around for awhile. I was afraid to go to bed because I knew I'd have nightmares. I stayed up all night, then called you first thing this morning."

"And I wasn't here. Sorry about that."

"It's okay, you got here. I was nervous about seeing someone I didn't know." She leaned back and stretched out her neck. "The weird thing is, nothing really happened. I wasn't raped, I wasn't hurt. So why am I such a wreck?"

"It's understandable. When you think back on last night, what comes to mind?"

She squinted at him for a long moment before her gaze shifted to the wall behind him. "How helpless I felt. I didn't know what he would do. I was terrified he would hurt me or even rape me. He had that fearless look in his eyes, and he was out of control. You never know how far someone can go when they get like that."

"Which is real scary." He glanced down at her hands; they had stopped shaking. "Can you remember another time you felt like that?"

She nodded. "Sure. A thousand times, when I was a kid. I'd hear Mom and Dad fighting, and then something would break, and Mom would scream. I was afraid he'd kill her, you know? My sister and I would be in my room, huddled against the door, listening. We'd want to go and help Mom, but we were so scared we couldn't move."

"You were paralyzed?"

"Yes. Paralyzed. Like last night." She looked at him. "I get your point. More 'scar tissue,' right?"

He nodded. Yes, it was an emotional scar. The incident with Edinger was a blow to a mental wound from years before not yet healed all the way. "You've been through a lot, Melanie."

She gave him a quick, half grin. "No kidding."

"Listen, this has been a trauma for you. You need to give yourself time and space to heal."

"How do I do that?"

"Some simple things. Be careful to eat regularly, do things to help you relax. If you have problems sleeping, or find yourself feeling too overwhelmed, we can help with medication."

She shook her head. "When I think of pills, I think of Mom. I won't turn into her, Caleb."

"I don't think there's any threat of that."

"But what about my job? I couldn't go in today. Every time I think about Mr. Edinger, all I can think of is how he smelled when he was breathing all over me."

"Call in sick. You need some time off. And maybe dust off your résumé. Down the road, we need to talk about your rights concerning this incident. At the very least, he committed a serious act of harassment. You may decide to hold him accountable."

She sighed, taking that in. He could tell it felt impossible now, because she believed Edinger held all the power. But with healing, that might change.

"I want to hear from you later this week. If you're feeling

okay, then call and tell me that. If you need to come in, just let me know. Otherwise, let's schedule again for next Monday. That okay with you?"

She nodded. "Thanks, Caleb. For being here."

Caleb stared at his office phone and thought about calling the Farrells at the Avery Inn. He glanced out the window. Sam had only asked him to book the Farrells' reservation, but he wouldn't want them to be alone. And who else did they know in Westville? With a sigh, he turned off the desk light, buzzed Janice and told her he was leaving for the day, and locked up his office.

Plump clouds had drifted in, filtering the wafer of sun that continued to pour searing heat on the small city. Caleb yanked off his tie and tossed it on the dashboard of his truck before climbing in. He turned the air conditioning on high, pointing all the vents at his face. Though the air was still warm, the breeze helped a little. He backed the truck out of the lot and headed to Main Street.

The Avery Inn was on the outskirts of Westville, bordering on the larger city of Carrolton. Beyond it, Caleb could see towering office buildings where men and women wore three-piece business suits, carried fat briefcases and pecked at computers all day—Caleb's definition of corporate hell. But the Bed and Breakfast didn't match its surroundings. Instead, the Victorian structure had turrets, a slate roof, and a gazebo surrounded by a small garden. It was a reminder that Westville was still The Old South. Caleb parked under a magnolia and plodded up the wooden steps to the front porch.

The twenty-something year old man standing at the check-in desk wore a crisp tie and a huge white smile that advertised the fortune his parents must have spent on orthodontics. He was happy to inform Caleb the Farrells were here and he'd gladly ring them up. He handed Caleb the phone extension.

Caleb had met the Farrells only once, when he and Sam had visited Anne in Rock Hill. They lived on a sprawling farm that had been in the family for three generations. Monroe Farrell managed the farm and taught classes in farm industry at the local technical school. Louise Farrell had been a full-time mother until her children had grown and had always helped her husband with the farm. The family lived a close-knit and isolated rural life. Caleb remembered Mr. Farrell's intense scrutiny of Sam, the invader who had come to woo his beloved daughter. He wondered how Mr. Farrell felt now.

It took five rings before a woman answered the phone.

Caleb took in a deep breath and said, "Mrs. Farrell? This is Caleb Knowles. I'm downstairs in the lobby."

She didn't respond right away. He could hear her breathe in long, faltering breaths, like someone who had been sobbing. "Come on up, Caleb. Third floor. Room Fourteen," she said. Caleb handed the receiver back to the smiling desk clerk, then took the stairs up to the third floor. When he found room fourteen, he rapped lightly on the door.

Louise Farrell looked embarrassed about her swollen, red eyes. She rubbed them with a tissue and kept her head down, motioning Caleb inside. "My husband isn't here. He went to the police station to find out what happened to our Anne." Mrs. Farrell covered her face again with the tissue as tears ran down her face. Her voice quaked as she blurted out, "I just can't believe she's gone. She was my baby and now she's gone."

"Is there anything I can do for you, Mrs. Farrell?" She was a short, plump woman with soft, silver-colored hair that made a cloud around her head. She wore a nylon sweat suit covered with flecks of shredded tissue. "Can I get you something?"

She shook her head and made her way over to a chair beside a table that held an overflowing ashtray. Caleb took the other seat and laid a hand on hers. She grabbed his fingers and squeezed hard, crying, "I just want my baby back, you know?" Her hungry eyes locked on him. "We called the funeral home. They don't have her body yet, the coroner's got her. I want to see her, just one more time. Maybe then it will be real to me. I'll know she's really gone." She shrugged, tilting her head to the side in a curiously child-like gesture.

"I'm sorry for your loss. My brother's having a hard time with this, too."

Louise stiffened and drew back her hand. "He should have never brought her here. This place is too big, there's so much violence here. He should have left her with us, where she was safe."

"I understand how you feel, but Anne loved Sam and wanted to be with him."

Mrs. Farrell took the last cigarette from its pack and, as she lit it, the smell mingled with the stale stench of old smoke that already permeated the small, musty room. She turned her head away from Caleb, "You probably think we were too protective of Anne. People always told us that. But they didn't understand. She was six months old when we found out she was deaf. She was such a precious, dear little baby, and she couldn't hear a thing. She couldn't say 'Mama,' or 'Daddy,' and these strange little sounds came out of her mouth.

"But she did talk to us. She talked with her eyes. Those eyes took in everything, even when she was tiny. She was such a sensitive, loving child. Monroe and I looked into those eyes and knew we'd do anything and everything we could for her. We wanted her to be safe. And we wanted her to be happy." She turned to face Caleb again. "Do you think she was? Happy, I mean."

The question startled him. "Yes. She loved Sam. I think she loved their life together."

She pushed the cigarette to her lips, took three quick puffs, and lowered it. "I want to believe that. But lately, I don't know. When she'd write us, there was something different about her. She tried to cover it up like everything was all right, but I'm her mother and I could tell something was wrong. I never mentioned it to Monroe, because I knew it would upset him." She twirled the filter between her fingers and studied the pale cloud of smoke. "I did ask Elaine, my other daughter, about it. She said Anne was just nervous about the wedding and all, but I think it was more. I think something was wrong." Tears brimmed again. "And now she's dead. My baby's dead."

Caleb watched as she let out quiet sobs, wishing he could say something that could help her.

There was a noise behind them and the door swung open. Monroe Farrell walked in and dropped his keys on the bed. He was older than his wife and moved as though weighed down by some unseen burden. His thick hair was creamy white against his tanned, farmer's skin. His unshaven face had become a roadmap of wrinkles from five decades of labor under an unforgiving sun. He moved around the bed and glowered down at Caleb.

Caleb stood to face him. "How are you doing, Monroe? I'm very sorry about what brings you here."

"Are you?" Monroe Farrell's lips moved like he wanted to say something else but thought better of it. He glanced over at his wife and nodded. "You doing okay, Lou? I brought you the cigarettes you wanted." He dropped a pack of Salems on the table.

She stood and came over to him. His arm slipped around her, wanting to protect her. "What did the police captain say?" she asked.

Monroe kissed the top of her hair. "Captain Bentille said he had his whole department working on Anne's murder and he'd have an arrest very soon." He shot a defiant look over at Caleb.

"Did he say who he suspected?" Caleb asked, dreading the answer.

"I think you and I both know, don't we?" Monroe closed his eyes as if looking at Sam's brother was physically painful for him. His wife started to cry again. "Shhh, now," he whispered to her. "You've got to get some rest, Lou. You're gonna make yourself sick."

"Monroe," Caleb said, "I know the police have questioned Sam. But he didn't kill Anne. You have to know he would never hurt her." Caleb fought to keep the anger out of his voice because Monroe clearly had his mind made up, thanks to Captain Frank Bentille.

Monroe's eyes peered out at him from over his wife's bowed head. "What I know, Caleb, is my daughter is dead. That sweet lovely child is gone forever from this world and we'll never see her again. Look at my wife. Can you imagine what this is doing to her?"

Caleb swallowed, shaking his head.

Monroe grit his teeth. "It's all in God's hands now. Sam will have to face it." He stroked the back of his wife's head, then added, "I think you'd better leave now, Knowles."

Caleb made his way to the door, but hesitated. "I don't care what the police told you, Sam didn't kill Anne. I understand the loss you feel, but we have to do whatever we can to find out who killed your daughter."

CHAPTER FOUR

That next morning, Caleb found a note from Shannon which said she'd left early for a ride on Sundance, her horse. She often reached the stables by six AM for a trail ride before work, claiming that Sundance was "like therapy" for her. Caleb himself hadn't seen a pre-dawn hour since his daughter's infancy.

He sipped his coffee while searching the paper for more news about Anne's murder. On the front page of the metro section, a photo of Frank Bentille had a caption that read: INVESTIGATION CONTINUES, POLICE AWAIT CORONER'S REPORT. Caleb set his cup on Bentille's shit-eating grin and read the accompanying article that merely rehashed yesterday's account. It looked like there was no new information, and he wasn't sure if that helped or hurt his brother.

He had just finished a few slices of toast and his second cup of coffee when the phone rang. "I need your brother. Know where he is?" Claudia Briscoe asked, tone blunt.

"Last I heard, he was staying with Stewart Brearly. You got that number?"

"Yes. No answer. I called the church and Reverend Brearly said Sam took off early this morning. You think he left town?"

Caleb didn't like Claudia's tone, and he couldn't believe he was having this conversation about his brother. "Of course not, Claudia. Christ, he just lost his fiancée."

"Let me know if you hear from him." The line clicked dead.

Caleb thought about dialing her number back, but realized from Claudia's attitude she wasn't about to tell him anything useful on the phone. He sighed, called the office to say he'd be in late, and headed out to his truck.

He needed to warn Sam about Claudia's call, maybe get him to the police station before his situation got any worse. He headed down Haynesworth, took a right on Lake, and pulled into Sam's drive. Yellow police tape zigzagged across the front porch of the mill house, a grim reminder of what had happened there. Sam lived in a two-story apartment that comprised the back half of the home, so Caleb pulled up to the back door and pushed the button that lit up the flashing door light inside. No answer. He hopped off the back porch and checked the garage behind the house. Sam's bike was gone.

Caleb climbed back in his truck, but didn't put the key in the ignition. He wondered if he should wait for Sam. There was no point. Sam wouldn't surface until he was ready.

Sam liked to isolate himself when things got stormy in his life, a pattern since the accident that tumbled him into the silent, mysterious world that was now his home.

Caleb closed his eyes and let the too familiar images from that night flash through his mind. At sixteen, Sam had been the star athlete and straight-A student. Their mother had hoped Sam would be a surgeon, like her father had been. Sam Knowles, Sr., planned for Sam to pitch for the Braves and make him famous. A year younger, Caleb stumbled through adolescence in his brother's wake, an awkward, sullen teen who resented his stellar sibling almost as much as he revered him.

Caleb remembered Sam's friend from the baseball team at the house that rainy afternoon. Sam climbed on the back of his friend's new motorcycle, much too cool to wear a helmet. The call came a half hour later. His mother screamed, his dad ran out the door. Caleb and his younger sister, Bess, waited by the phone, both breathless and terrified that Sam was dead.

His dad called around midnight, saying Sam was unconscious because of some bleeding in his head. A day later Sam woke up, unable to hear a thing. His parents had him sent to every specialist they could find, but nothing could be done.

When Sam finally returned home, he'd become a very different brother. He brooded and isolated himself because he had no access to the hearing world. Their mother finally enrolled him in a private school for "handicapped and special needs children."

Caleb had found a sign language class at a local Baptist church and arranged some private tutoring from a sympathetic teacher. He had spent evenings in Sam's room, practicing his signs, desperate to get through to the silent stranger who was still his older brother.

Then, like now, Caleb hated to be shut out.

He twitched the key in the ignition and backed the truck out of the drive.

Ten minutes later, he pulled into the parking lot in front of the Westville Police Department. It had been almost a year since Caleb's last visit, and nothing much had changed. He saw the gray-green walls, stained with grease and dirt. The dank linoleum floors, scarred by age and neglect. The dark, torn vinyl furniture that smelled like twenty years of accumulated sweat and cheap cigar smoke. Most of the faces were the same, too, though few seemed to recognize him.

He approached the front desk, where several loud uniformed officers squabbled about the plight of the Westville Pirates as they sipped coffee. The return of an injured outfielder should turn around their dismal season, a naive teenage-looking officer asserted. Two more cynical seniors argued the only thing that could save the Pirates was divine intervention. Caleb had to agree.

At last one of the older, familiar officers looked over at him, squinting a bloodshot eye. "You that psychologist fella, ain't ya?"

"Social worker. Caleb Knowles." He reached over and shook a warm, sticky hand.

"You helped on that child abuse case last year. That was a gruesome one. Remember, Jake?"

Another officer nodded solemnly, then came over to take Caleb's hand. "Can I help you with something?"

"I need to see Detective Briscoe."

"She expecting you?"

"I think so." She should be, he thought, after their phone conversation.

The officer gestured up the long, poorly lit hall. "Third door on the left."

Claudia sat in front of a computer, her lethal-looking crimson nails clicking away at the keyboard with rapid precision. She wore a cream-colored sleeveless blouse tidily tucked into a navy skirt. A heavy gold necklace complemented her skin, matching gold clasps gathered her coal black hair behind the ears. She looked every bit the razor-sharp, ambitious professional that she was.

Caleb had been her counselor once, several years ago. Then, she'd just completed the university with a degree in Criminal Justice, and been recruited to join the ranks of Westville's finest. She was a bright, competent, but insecure black woman. She was the police department's answer to Affirmative Action and she knew it, which didn't lessen her anxiety.

She'd been an easy case for Caleb. Progressive relaxation training took care of the anxiety symptoms and her own fierce tenacity overcame the self-esteem problems. When her colleagues noticed she was damn good at her job, the gender and race issues lost steam. She became Officer Briscoe, a part of the team. When Caleb met her again last year, she'd been promoted to detective.

"What do you want?" Claudia's ebony eyes bored holes in him.

He grinned and did his best to look charming. "Easy, now. I just thought I'd stop by so we could finish our chat."

She sighed. "What's to finish? I called to find out where the hell your brother was. You said you didn't know. That change?"

He shook his head. God knew, he was beginning to wonder.

"Look. I gotta get this report in to Bentille by noon or he'll have my butt," Claudia grumbled. "Thanks for stopping by."

Caleb took his time about sitting down, stretching out his long legs, folding his arms across his chest. "So Claudia, tell me who you think killed Anne Farrell."

She rolled her eyes over the computer terminal. "This is not a conversation we are going to have."

He ignored her as he continued, "I realize that you know my brother. But I'll bet you don't know that he won the Southeastern Guild Sculptor's award this year. Or that he's on the vestry for St. John's Lutheran Church. Or that he's a founding member of the Council for the Deaf. Pretty impressive, don't you think?"

Claudia nodded. "Oh yeah. You know, this is a great story. I know you'll get to the point any day now."

"Sam needs to arrange Anne's funeral. Of course, we don't know when that will be, because of the autopsy and all. Then he needs to get on with his life, which can't happen until Anne's killer is found, which brings me back to my original question ..."

"Thanks for stopping by," she said, pivoting her chair back to the computer.

"Claudia, give me something. This–this is making me crazy." He was surprised by the edge in his voice and apparently, so was she.

Her expression softened a little. "Caleb. You know how grateful I am for what you did for me, back when I was just starting out. But right now, you are the over-involved brother of a murder suspect. There isn't a thing I can say to you."

Murder suspect. The words resonated like a bell in his head. What had seemed impossible, even surreal, abruptly came into stark, black and white focus. Sam could be arrested. He could be tried, and maybe even sentenced.

And this police department had no interest in clearing him.

"You know my brother, Claudia. He couldn't–" Caleb could barely get the words out. "You know he couldn't do this."

"I know he needs a lawyer," she muttered. "Got one yet?"

"He wouldn't need a lawyer if you would do your damn job," he blurted out. "Look, Stewart Brearly was the interpreter when you questioned Sam. He told me Sam's fingerprints were on the murder weapon. Well, it's his sculpture, so of course his fingerprints are on it. What else do you have? Bentille talked to Monroe Farrell. Monroe thinks you're ready to arrest Sam, and you and I both know that's bullshit.

"We know Anne was in the studio when somebody came in, they struggled, and he killed her. Sam–of course–didn't hear it. He came in and found her. So my question is, what are you doing to find the real killer?"

She shook her head in exasperation. "Okay. You want something. Try this on. You told me Anne Farrell's hands were signing 'No,' remember? Seems to me that proves whoever killed her was more than likely deaf, too. Does that describe anyone we know?"

He cocked his head back. The ceiling tiles held no answers

for him. After a moment he answered: "She was dying. She was screaming out, the only way she could. Signing was her language. That doesn't mean her assailant understood her."

"Your pal Phillip Etheridge is a good attorney. He knows sign language, too. I'd suggest you hire him real fast."

"You brought him in for questioning, Detective?" a voice boomed from behind them. Captain Frank Bentille leaned against the doorjamb and stared at them. Gray and black tweed pants and a gray shirt hung loosely on his gangly frame, making him look like a greyhound long retired from the track. The striped tie had a red spot from some recent meal. His close-set eyes were dwarfed by the dense brows that nearly met each other over his nose.

"No, I just dropped by. I'd better be on my way." Caleb stood to leave. Just looking at the police captain stirred up even more fury and he didn't need to make a scene.

"Before you go, I have news that may interest you." Bentille's voice was uncharacteristically buoyant. "I got a call from our pathologist. She's completed the autopsy on Ms. Farrell. Her remains are en route to Duncan Funeral Home. I know the Farrells are anxious to make arrangements."

Caleb nodded. "Thanks."

"And you will let your brother know we need to see him right away. I'll have to issue a warrant if he doesn't turn up soon."

His daughter's daycare was only five minutes from the station. Caleb parked under a tree beside the chain-link fence that contained the squealing preschoolers, all out for recess. He spotted Julia right away. Loose tendrils of long, curly red hair escaped from the barrette his ex-wife had probably put on her with great care. Julia wore denim overalls, a green T-shirt, pink socks, and her favorite red high-top sneakers. Caleb and Mariel learned long ago there was no point in fighting it; Julia insisted on dressing herself. To see her in an actual dress required financial payment. To see her in matching clothes, one had to dress her while she was asleep. Julia had her own unique fashion statement to make.

From his truck, he watched her line up with the other four-year-olds as her teacher instructed them. They held hands, forming a long line opposite another group. Soon, the "Red Rover" chant began. Julia swung both arms and tilted her head back, screaming with great gusto until, at last, her turn came. She freed herself from the line, stepped forward, and leaned over like a sprinter beginning a meet. Then she ran, hair flying, arms pumping, feet kicking up sand in her wake. She burst through the line and threw her hands in the air while her team squealed cheers of victory.

Caleb loved this child. She was the best of each of them. She had Mariel's quick mind and lithe little body. She had his sensitivity and, God help her, sense of humor. Not having Julia with him all the time had been torturous when he and Mariel first separated. But gradually, Caleb had acclimated, learning to cherish the Wednesdays and weekends he had with his daughter.

Soon he would have to tell Julia about Anne. How did one explain murder to a four-year-old? He wanted so much to shield her from it, from all the darkness and death that was spreading in the world. She adored her uncle, and Sam loved her.

Sam wouldn't be having children, at least not for a long while. He'd hoped to start a family with Anne right after his marriage. Caleb remembered a conversation a month or so ago, when Sam had said: "I'll need your help, you know. We'll probably have a hearing child so you'll need to coach him for us. I want him to say 'Daddy' before he says 'Uncle Caleb,' you got it?"

Caleb felt tears in his eyes, and quickly blinked them away. He saw Julia's teacher gather the kids into a line. Julia, dawdling with her friends, was the last to join. He wanted to call out to her, to take her in his arms, to escape into the amazed innocence of her four-year-old world. And though this was his day to have her, she didn't need what this day would bring.

He climbed out of the truck and waved at the teacher as he opened the waist-high gate.

"Hey, Mr. Knowles!" Her teacher smiled at him. "You getting Julia early today?"

"No, but I'd like ten minutes with her, if you don't mind."

Julia spotted him. She bounded towards him, full throttle, and jumped into his arms. "Man, you're getting big. I think you grew three inches since last weekend."

She giggled and dimples appeared in her freckled cheeks. "Are we going to your house?" she asked.

Your house, he thought. Not our house. Not our home. Yet another scar left by the divorce from Mariel. "No, Sweetie. Not today."

She scrambled down and, thrusting her fist against her hip, stared up at him. The gesture was a perfect mimic of her mother. "I promised Cleo I would play with her today," she said.

"I know. Cleo's mad at me, too. But honey, something's come up and I won't be able to take you."

She pursed her lips at him. "You said you'd see me on Wednesday. You said Cleo and me could go to the park. You said we could have a cookout and go see Uncle Sam."

He winced, hearing his words from their last phone call coming back at him like pellets. "And you're disappointed. I sure don't blame you." He knelt down, getting eye-to-eye with her. "I'll call you tonight. And we'll do something extra special this weekend."

Her eyes rolled to the side as she thought it over. "We could go to the stables," she said finally.

"It's a deal. We'll go see Sundance. Maybe Shannon will even let you ride him."

"Can Uncle Sam go, too?"

He slid his arms around her, lifting her and squeezing tight. "We'll see, honey. I love you."

When Caleb pulled into his drive, he noticed a ten-speed bike propped against the back porch. Sam stood beside it with his head down and his hands buried deep in trouser pockets. Caleb approached him and tapped his shoulder. "Hey, brother," he signed.

"Hey yourself." Sam looked up at the sky. Fat, gray clouds were rolling in, threatening a summer squall.

Caleb watched him carefully, wondering what was sinking in. Did Sam picture Anne crumpled on the floor, in porcelain death? Did he imagine the pathologist taking her body apart, extracting her organs with tweezers, examining each piece under a microscope? Did he understand, completely, that Anne was gone forever?

"I need a favor," Sam said.

"Okay," Caleb signed. "What?"

"Call the funeral home up in Rock Hill, make sure they're arranging services for Friday."

"Sure. Anything else?"

Sam shook his head.

"How are you doing, Sam?" Caleb twisted his fists against each other, thumbs and pinkies extended. He noticed the veins throb in his brother's jaw.

"Don't."

"Don't what?"

"Don't play therapist."

Caleb stepped back, a little stung. "I'm not playing therapist. I just saw Claudia Briscoe; she wants to see you. You need to hire a lawyer."

Sam shrugged, grabbed the bike, and climbed on. Caleb watched as he wheeled onto Sims Street and out of sight.

CHAPTER FIVE

William Percy Elias, Caleb's Friday 10:00 appointment, liked to be called Percy. William had been his grandfather's name and his father's name, and Percy estranged himself from that name and those men long ago. He had dyed orange-sherbet hair and pasty white skin. A heart entwined by a snake had been tattooed on his wrist. The lavender silk shirt, plum-purple jeans, and snakeskin boots he wore today were actually sedate for him. When he'd first come to Caleb four years ago, Percy wore a blond Marilyn Monroe wig, leopard-print stretch pants, and three-inch heels. He claimed the costume was traditional daytime attire for a Professional Drag Queen.

Percy had been known then as "Percy Plastique" and worked a circuit of rather scuzzy gay bars in seedy parts of Carrolton, Savannah, Atlanta, and Charleston. The money was great, the drugs were rampant, and Percy soon developed himself a nice little cocaine habit. That, coupled with the bi-polar illness he'd inherited from Mom, first brought him into therapy with Caleb.

For Percy, the disease meant manic episodes of dangerous proportions. He could go weeks without sleep, in perpetual motion, quickly spinning out of control. Then he'd spiral down. The depression often led to extreme–and deadly–suicide attempts. Pouring cocaine on his mental illness was like tossing gasoline on a fire.

Caleb case-managed Percy through two and a half years of

drug and prostitution arrests, hospitalizations, and drug rehabilitation. Percy finally gave up the crack. And now, eighteen months into recovery, he'd adapted to a calmer, less "stimulating" lifestyle. Reluctantly, he'd hung up the heels and false lashes and taken a job his uncle had found for him as a mail courier for CarolinaCorp, the same place Melanie Carson worked. Evenings, he pulled a shift at a local French restaurant. Staying busy was critical for his sobriety and helped him work off his effervescent manic energy.

Caleb had decided to work a few hours this morning. Anne's funeral wasn't until two, and Shannon would pick him up around noon. They would grab a bite to eat before the hour drive to Rock Hill, where Anne had been born and would now be buried. A short life gone full circle.

"I saw him last night, Caleb," Percy was saying, batting his eyes and punctuating the "him" with fluttering, bright red lashes.

"Who?"

"Snake, of course. My *ex*. My downfall! He was standing outside the Void, that sleazy place off River Drive. He was cuddled against this old guy who had the *ugliest* toupee I've ever seen. No kiddin', we're talkin' a little black squirrel curled up on his head! The guy was loaded, in more ways than one. Big gold chains, big rock on his pinky." He absently picked at his own little finger, perfectly manicured, but unpolished.

"How did it feel, seeing Snake?"

"No big deal. It's over, *finis*! Didn't phase me."

Caleb raised his brows, waited.

"Well, okay, so it hurt a little. A pang, you know? I gave that man five *years* of my life! Good years, too, back when I was young and *virile*!"

Caleb suppressed a grin. "Feeling old for your thirty-two years?"

"Feeling ancient. Too many lost years, really. Lost on Snake, lost on the powder."

"Why were you down that way? Near that bar?"

He smiled coyly. "Caught me! I just happened by. Maybe drifting down memory lane. Remembering the wild times, the good times."

"That's a dangerous road for you, and you know it." Percy's old lover dealt cocaine for a living. He used and manipulated Percy into holding his stash for him, running drugs for him, and getting arrested for him.

"Eighteen months, Caleb! Substance-free for eighteen months! You don't think I can breeze by an old hangout without getting a hit? Have you no faith in me?" Both hands drummed fingers against his chest.

Caleb leaned forward and scrutinized him. "Be straight with me, Percy."

"No! No, I didn't get high. Yes, I wanted to. God, how I wanted to, seeing him with that old fart."

"A little crack to ease the pain?"

"Yes. It would, too," he said, defiance oozing in his voice. "But then you'd jump all over me."

"We've covered this before, you know. The hardest thing is facing situations that hurt, really hurt you in your gut. That make you really, really want relief from cocaine. You tempt fate when you go back to the Void, or anywhere else where you'll run into him."

Percy pivoted his head, pretending to be chastised–ever the performer. Caleb grumbled with exasperation. Four years of counseling him, he knew all the games.

"Is my shrink frustrated?" Percy asked.

Change of strategy. Caleb tilted his chair back and reached for the coffee that had gotten cold. He took a slow sip, looked into the cup, then took another. He waited. He set the cup down and leaned back in his chair, lacing his fingers behind his head. He waited some more. He could wait like this the rest of the hour, if he had to. And Percy knew it.

Percy returned the stare, at first with flamboyant lip pursing, then with a furtiveness that looked more genuine. He looked at Caleb, then out the window. Gradually, his eyes melted. A tear found its way down his pale cheek.

"I know it hurts to see him," Caleb said.

"It shouldn't. He just screwed up my life before. I thought he needed me, but all he needed was my paycheck." Percy brushed the tear away.

"I'm proud you're letting yourself feel the pain. It shows strength. I knew you had it in you."

"You are a piece of work. I'm here sobbing like a baby and you tell me how strong I am. And *I'm* the one on medication," Percy said.

Caleb handed him a tissue, and he blew his nose so boisterously that it honked. They both smiled, cutting the tension.

"Okay. No more visits to the Void. No more Snake. I can't fix him. And he can do me in."

"Yep. And you miss him."

He nodded. "I'll get over it. I got over a coke addiction, I can get over him. Hell, they're the same thing–both get me high as a kite, but the crashing later really sucks. Like a Hoover." Percy stretched his long, thin arms, making a steeple over his orange head. After a moment, he said, "I read in the papers about your brother. You haven't said anything. You guys okay?"

It took Caleb by surprise. "Getting there. I'm leaving in a few minutes for the funeral."

"That explains the suit! I didn't think you were all dressed up just for me! I was so sorry to hear about Anne. Such a nice lady."

Caleb squinted at him. "You knew her?"

Percy nodded. "She worked at the accounting firm my company uses, Skolnick and Bagardis. They were doing our audit, so I was bringing lots of records over to her office. A nice lady. Real class."

Caleb nodded.

"Most of those auditor types give me the willies, you know? They like numbers more than people. The last auditor we had was this Queen Bee Bitch, I think her panty hose were made of bonded steel.

"But not Anne. She was shy, and hard to talk to–we had to write everything down–but she was so nice. Sweet. Even Mr. Edinger, who seems to hate everybody who isn't related to him–he even liked her."

"She was easy to like." But hard to really know, Caleb thought.

Caleb felt Percy's gaze on him and could tell he was looking through the nodding therapist façade, searching for the human. After four years, the professional distance between therapist and client was more of a mirage, and like it or not, their connection sometimes transcended it. Caleb needed to change the subject. "Well, Percy. You mentioned your boss. Everything okay at work?"

"Everything sucks at work! Edinger's been on a real tear. Did you know Melanie's been out sick for two days? I know about patient confidentiality and all, blah, blah, blah, but I referred her to you so I can tell you. Man, the place falls apart when she's not there."

"Well, you know the formula. When work gets tense, do your best to stay out of the conflict. Your recovery is too important and doesn't need the added stress."

"Caleb, honey, my work isn't stressful. I pick up mail from

one office, drive it to another. Sometimes–on a big day, mind you–I get to make copies or order supplies. Yee-hah. Stress ain't the problem. Boredom is."

An hour later, Caleb turned off the lights in his office and headed out the door. Shannon waited in the car with hamburgers to eat on the road. She wheeled Esmerelda, her restored baby-blue 1968 Impala, out of the drive and eased her onto Highway One. With the burger in her lap, Shannon was soon comfortably cruising at seventy miles per hour. Caleb liked to comment that Esmerelda got about three gallons to the mile and could sleep twelve, but he had to admit she had enough leg room for his long frame. It wasn't long before his eyelids gave up the fight with gravity and Caleb drifted off into a turbulent car nap.

One hour later, Shannon turned onto a gravel road and Caleb jerked himself awake. He glanced out the window as the car wound its way through a lush hardwood forest. The trees stretched tall into the bright blue sky like proud old soldiers. The underbrush was painted every hue of green, with dabs of orange and purple where the wildflowers peeked out. The unencumbered sun splashed light on the forest, on the road, and on the blue car winding its way to a funeral.

Another turn took them to a small white chapel with a crisp slate steeple etched against the horizon. Caleb could see the black funeral canopy behind it, an ominous reminder of why they had come. After Shannon eased Esmerelda beside Stewart's Bronco, Caleb climbed out and glanced around the small cemetery. Old headstones mingled with new in family clusters, all shaded by the arms of massive oak trees. He could hear the leaves rustling, stirred by a nice breeze and by a squirrel bounding from limb to limb. Life among the dead, he thought, grateful Anne would have this resting place.

Stewart Brearly presided over the small, graveside service. Anne's parents sat in metal chairs directly in front of Stewart. Louise cried silently, leaning on Monroe's arm. Caleb tried to imagine their grief. If he ever lost Julia ... he shuddered. Instinctively, Shannon's arm came around his waist.

"This sort of tragedy," Stewart began, "is the hardest for us. We say goodbye to someone we loved, someone who touched us all. We ask God, 'How can you take her from us?' We have grown to count on her to fill an empty space in our lives. We are intolerant of goodbyes, even those willed by God." His voice and signing hands trembled with emotion. "And the hardest part is there is no concrete answer. We can look at Anne's life and see that she had accomplished so much. She had a successful career as an accountant. She was about to enter into the most beautiful bond, the covenant of marriage." His hands spoke to Sam's unwavering eyes.

Caleb glanced over at Anne's sister, Elaine. He'd only met her once before and remembered liking her. She had been the only one in Anne's family who supported Anne's move to Westville, helping Anne fight it out with her parents, helping her pack, and even helping her drive down to Sam's in a rental truck. He remembered her tearful goodbye, as she left Anne to Sam and their new life. Was she regretting it now?

Elaine was taller than her sister, with darker hair, but the same small nose and serious mouth. There was nothing repressed in her mourning; she sobbed loudly, leaning into her husband's side, her shoulders quaking with each wave of grief.

Caleb looked back over at Stewart, who seemed to be struggling with the service. His gray eyes looked overwrought–this man of God trying to console the inconsolable. Stewart cleared his throat and continued: "So our task is to accept that Anne's life is over, too soon, too horribly. Our task is to accept that she is gone from us and we must return to our lives without her. How do we do it? How do we move on? We do it because of Anne. We do it because we know she is with God now. In heaven, there is no separation between the deaf and hearing world. In heaven, she'll have peace we cannot know in this world. As we feel our pain and our loss, we can close our eyes and imagine our Anne, content, held in her loving Father's arms," he gracefully drew his arms in, signing both "hold" and "love," as he looked at Sam.

As the short service drew to a close, the family, one by one, approached the casket, each placing a single white rose across the top. At the end of this procession came Sam; he laid a red rose with the white ones, then gingerly fingered the lid of the casket. His face showed nothing–no sign of loss or grief. No sign of life. His soul seemed as dead as the body in the coffin.

Gradually, the mourners scattered into clusters, whispering to each other in muted voices. Caleb followed Shannon as she approached the Farrells. The grief-ridden parents nodded curtly to them and turned away, an older gentleman taking Mrs. Farrell's arm and guiding her out from under the canopy.

Elaine Halloway remained. Her mourning was primal, guttural sobs exploding from her throat, tears cascading down her inflamed face. Shannon eased in beside her and laid a comforting arm over her shoulder. Elaine soon grabbed her, holding on tight, her anguish spilling out.

Caleb looked at the casket. It seemed quite beautiful. A spray of yellow roses draped over the graceful contour of the ivory lid. Soft relief carvings of flowers covered the side between the simple brass handles. It might have been a work of art, a still life–like the corpse inside.

He searched the remaining faces at the gravesite and soon spotted Monroe Farrell. With Louise at his side, he stood behind the metal folding chairs at the back of the canopy. Grief had aged him even more these past two days. It looked like gravity was working harder on him, pulling him down. There was a new sag in his shoulders. Folds of skin around his mouth drooped down, sacks the size of pockets hung below his eyes. He stared darkly at the pale coffin holding his daughter's remains.

Monroe leaned down, whispered something to his wife, and pulled away from her. His knee clanged against a metal folding chair and the sound rang out, drawing everyone's attention. Slowly, Monroe limped toward Sam. Caleb inched closer to his brother as Monroe maneuvered around the remaining mourners and came directly in front of them. He stood there, staring, for a long moment.

His eyes had shed their grief. They locked on Sam like they could bore right though him. "I'd like to have a word with you," he said.

Sam nodded. Stewart crossed over to Caleb and the two kept a close eye on the exchange.

"I need you to look me in the eyes," Monroe signed. "And tell me what you did to my daughter."

Sam didn't respond.

"I never wanted Anne to leave our home. But you took her away from us. And what did you make her do? You made her live in sin with you. We didn't bring her up that way, we're God-fearing people." He signed "people" with a clipped jab of three fingers. "And now, she's gone. You took her. I pray and pray about it, about how God could let you do this."

Sam opened his mouth like he was about to speak, but instead, turned away. Again, his eyes rested on the coffin.

Monroe stepped closer and jabbed a finger into Sam's chest. Stunned, Sam pulled back from him.

"Don't you look at her! How dare you even be here, after what you did?" Monroe's voice rang out hotly, and his wife rushed over to him.

She took his hand and said, "Not here, Monroe. We're burying our girl."

Approaching from the other side, Stewart Brearly said softly, "I can't imagine the loss you feel, Monroe. But I know the kind of woman Anne was. She was a loving, gentle spirit. So let's say our goodbyes to her the same way, with love and gentleness." Stewart's voice faltered.

"You're a man of God."

"Yes. And I'm Sam's friend." Stewart wiped his eyes, embarrassed. "Look, we're all in pain here. Let's not make things worse."

Monroe looked over at Sam and at Caleb. After a long moment, he slipped his arm around his wife and returned under the canopy. Stewart glanced nervously at Caleb, then followed them.

"Hello there, Knowles."

Caleb stiffened at the voice. He turned and nearly collided with Captain Frank Bentille. Bentille wore a shiny, dark suit that seemed to change color from black to deep purple when he moved in the sunlight. It looked to be made of some form of flame-retardant polyester that would never decompose, even in the event of a nuclear incident. An efficient and completely tasteless suit–Bentille's best effort at making a good impression.

"I'm surprised to find you here. A bit out of your jurisdiction, isn't it?" Caleb muttered.

"I wanted to pay my respects. I met the Farrells. Nice Christian people. Deserve better than this," he said, gesturing with a toothpick toward the casket. "I assured them we'd have an arrest soon."

"That still doesn't explain your coming all the way up here."

"Doesn't it?" He looked over at Sam without a hint of subtlety.

Caleb eyed him squarely, not containing his rage. "Not here, Bentille, don't start that crap. This isn't the time. These people ... my brother ... are grieving."

Bentille returned the toothpick to his mouth and wiggled it around with his blubbery lips. Caleb watched him, focusing on those silvered eyebrows that badly needed thinning. If he had a weedeater on him right then ...

"I had to make sure your brother doesn't disappear on us again." He made a sweeping motion with his toothpick toward the small, dispersing crowd. "Always interesting to see who shows at the funeral."

"Interesting's one word for it."

"He'll need to come in first thing in the morning. We got the coroner's report, and there are a few new things I need to go over. Have him there at eight, or we'll come for him."

"No problem. He'll be there. With his attorney."

Bentille winked at him, flicked the toothpick, and walked away.

Caleb crossed over to Sam and signed the message from Bentille. Sam shrugged noncommitally. Caleb added: "I want you to come and stay with us for a while. Julia's coming tomorrow and I think she might be good for you."

Sam's response jolted him. He closed his eyes, as if fighting to stay in control. "I don't think so," he said, and walked away.

Shannon came up beside Caleb and slipped her arms around him. He could tell she had been crying. He kissed her forehead.

"Elaine wants us to stop by her house. I think she needs to talk. That okay with you?"

He nodded, holding her tightly. "You okay?"

"I just want this day to be over with. And I want Sam to be all right. And I want to get back to our normal life, whatever that was."

Elaine and Trip Halloway lived in an upscale subdivision outside Charlotte, North Carolina. Large, elaborate homes sprawled across lots that were far too small for them. Street signs held names like "Quail Haven" and "Mourning Dove Trace," a bird theme that began with a hideous copper goose at the entrance. Elaine turned on Sparrow Lane, then again on Turkey Summit, then into her drive. Shannon parked behind the Mazda and the two of them followed Elaine inside.

"Trip had to go in to the office," Elaine said. "That's why we took separate cars."

"He works in Charlotte?" Caleb asked.

"Yeah. He practices family law, and there's an ugly divorce case going to court tomorrow. He'll be tied up 'til after dinner, I suspect." There was an edge in her voice. She showed them into her den and they sank into a plump overstuffed sofa that seemed to mold itself around them. Elaine took a seat in a rocking chair beside the stone hearth and scarcely filled the seat. She was waif-thin, the way some models are, with pronounced cheekbones that made her eyes look sunken in their sockets. Perhaps her thinness was the result of illness or an overactive metabolism. Or maybe she was one of those women obsessed with their weight, who feasted on lettuce and exercise in pursuit of a skeletal frame.

"Can I get you something? A drink?" she asked them.

"No. We still have a bit of a drive ahead of us," Shannon said, leaning out of the sofa's grasp. "Elaine, you said you wanted to talk to Caleb. You said it was about Anne."

Elaine folded her hands together across her middle and

started to rock. "I can't believe we just buried her. My little sister."

"I know," Caleb said.

She studied him. Her dark eyes were like her father's, and held on with the same intensity. "You know what it's like, don't you? I mean, having a disabled sibling."

"I suppose. You feel protective. And maybe a little lost in the shuffle."

Elaine nodded. "Anne was three years younger than me. When my parents found out she was deaf, it changed our whole world. It was like they built our family into a little cocoon to keep her safe, to shut everyone else out. You've seen how my dad is. He loved her so fiercely, I worried he might suffocate her."

"How was it for you, Elaine? Did you feel left out?" Shannon asked, and Caleb heard her therapist's voice coming out.

"Yes. I think that was normal, given the situation. When Anne turned six, Dad didn't even want her to go to school, but the law said she had to go. I remember the first day we rode the bus together. I think that was the first time we were ever alone, you know, without our parents. I finally got to know her then."

"I think she was lucky to have you. She knew she had a big sister in her corner," Shannon said.

Elaine nodded in rhythm with her rocking. "My parents meant well. But I think their over-protectiveness made her fearful. She never handled change very well."

"What kind of change are you talking about?"

Elaine rocked some more, her hands kneading each other in her lap. "Any change. Going to college. Meeting Sam. Moving down to Westville."

"Sam said you and Anne were pretty close," Caleb said. "He said you were the only one who supported her move to Westville."

"Dad hated Sam. Hated everything about him–especially how he makes his living." She shook her head. "Dad isn't exactly one to appreciate abstract art."

"But you helped Anne. If you hadn't encouraged her relationship with Sam, she may never have left home," Shannon said.

"Yes, well, I'm not feeling very proud of that right now. Maybe if she'd stayed with my folks, she'd have lived a sheltered, repressed life. But at least she would still be alive." A spark of anger flashed in her eyes and she looked away from them. After a moment, she started rocking again. "I guess like you, I want to believe Sam didn't do it. For purely selfish reasons. I encouraged Anne to move in with him, and now ..." She took in a deep, staggered breath.

Shannon reached over and squeezed her hand.

Elaine rocked again, the movement pulling her away from Shannon's grasp. The rocking seemed to help her get her composure. After a moment, she said, "There is something you should know, if you don't already. I can't understand why no one has mentioned it so far."

"What is it?" Caleb asked.

"Anne was pregnant."

"What?"

"She told me last month. She e-mailed me and said she had to come see me. It was a strange visit.

"I could tell something was wrong because she was real nervous. But I couldn't get her to talk. She paced around the house, like she always did when something had her upset. Finally, I got her settled down and she blurted it out."

Shannon looked over at Caleb, not hiding her shock. "How far along was she?"

"Just a couple of months." Elaine sighed. "So you didn't know. And Sam?"

Caleb shook his head. "No. God, this will make it so much harder for him."

"Did Sam want kids?"

"Yeah. He was always talking about it, about how they were going to start a family right away. He joked that Anne might have to hit the alarm on her biological clock."

"You're sure?"

"Sam loves kids. This baby would have meant the world to him." Suddenly, Caleb felt very hot. The tie that had been around his neck for way too long seemed to be tightening on its own. He jerked it loose, then over his head. "Do you think anyone else knew about the baby?" Caleb asked, remembering Bentille's comment about some new information.

"No. And I pray Mom and Dad never find out." She shuddered.

"Your father thinks Sam killed Anne. He's made some threats. Should I be worried?"

"I don't know. I can't get through to him. He's out of his mind with rage–I think he stays like that so he won't have to feel his grief. It gives him something to do."

Shannon nodded. "If he says anything to you, will you let us know?"

Elaine said she would. Showing them to the door, she hugged Shannon and promised to stay in touch.

CHAPTER SIX

"Daddy, who put the ribbon around Uncle Sam's house?" It was a Julia Saturday and Caleb's daughter had insisted on seeing her Uncle Sam.

Julia, dressed in coveralls and cowboy boots, stood in the walkway leading to Sam's studio and pointed at the yellow "Caution" tape webbed across the door.

"That's not ribbon, honey. I mean, it's not a ribbon like you put on a birthday present," Caleb answered, hoping she'd move on to another subject.

Julia cocked her head to the side, her red curls tumbling down over her tiny shoulder. "Who put it there?" she persisted.

Caleb took her hand, prodding her around the back where Sam lived. "They're doing some work in there," he lied. "We have to leave it alone so we won't mess up anything."

"Who's in there?" she asked, pulling away like she planned to scamper up on the porch and peer inside.

"Nobody's in there right now!" Caleb grabbed her, one hand on each side, and lifted her up onto his shoulder. He could feel her hands tangling themselves in his hair. "Let's see if we can find Sam."

As they circled around to the back of the property, Caleb could tell Sam wasn't there. Though his van was in the drive, his bike was missing from the rack in the garage. Caleb lowered Julia, who trotted up the steps and pressed the door signal four quick times, the special code she and Sam had worked out when she was only two. No one answered.

"Where'd he go?" Julia asked.

"I don't know, Sweetie. We'll e-mail him when we get home." He reached out his hand and she wrapped hers around two fingers. As they climbed down the steps, they heard tires crunching on gravel and a large white car pulled into Sam's drive.

"Maybe that's him!" Julia said, grinning up at him.

A car door squeaked open and Monroe Farrell stepped out. He moved slowly, holding on to the door as he straightened to his full six-four frame. "Knowles," he said, nodding curtly at Caleb.

"Hello Monroe. Sam isn't here."

"Know when he'll be back?"

"No. Was he expecting you?"

"My wife e-mailed that I was coming down. To get my daughter's things."

Caleb felt Julia climb around behind his legs like she did when something scared her.

"That your girl?" Monroe asked.

Caleb nodded. "This is Julia."

She peeked around his knees. "Julia McElroy Knowles," she corrected.

"She's a pretty little thing," Monroe said. "Annie used to wear coveralls like that. She said she was gonna grow up to be a farmer like me."

"Julia wants to pilot the space shuttle." He gave her hand a little squeeze.

Monroe dropped down on his haunches with surprising agility and winked at her. "She know what happened?"

"No. Not yet."

"Just as well. You want to protect her from that kind of

truth. That's how I felt about my girl. I wanted to protect her from everything." Monroe's eyes misted over and he cleared his throat, looking embarrassed.

Julia stepped out from behind Caleb's legs. "You have a little girl?"

"I had two. Cute as you are." He reached over and pinched her nose, which made her giggle.

Caleb squeezed her hand again. "Julia, can you wait for me by the truck? I'll just be a second." She nodded and trotted over to the pickup as Caleb turned back to Monroe. "Sam may not have opened any e-mail lately. He's still not doing very well."

"Can't say that surprises me. They arrest him yet?"

Caleb felt a quick flash of anger. "No! He didn't do it, Monroe."

He took a step closer to Caleb. "That's not what I hear. I hear he picked up a piece of wood and smashed it against my child's head. How would you feel, something like that happened to your girl?"

Caleb felt a chill climb up his back. He stepped away from the man, unsure what to do or say next. Monroe shrugged, turned around, and walked over to his car.

Caleb looked over at his daughter. Julia had climbed into the cab of the truck and was mouthing engine noises as her hands tried to turn the steering wheel. No, he didn't know how he'd feel if anything ever happened to his child. But he knew he wanted her away from Monroe Farrell.

That Monday morning, Caleb was the last staff person to arrive at the Westville Center. The waiting area was empty, which Caleb took as a good sign. Some Mondays, folks lined up at the front door, ready to offer their weekend crises, medicine problems, and drug relapses to their beleaguered therapists. He remembered the time Ellen Campbell greeted him in the parking lot, carrying a sack of penny candy and a three-page document declaring her mother president of South Carolina. Ellen had decided to stop in on Caleb before she visited the governor, which was a good decision. Sadly, a trip to the hospital interfered with her lobbying plans.

Caleb stopped in the breakroom and poured a second cup of coffee, draining the pot. Then he trudged up the stairs and noticed Matthew's office door was open. When he stopped to peek inside, his boss motioned him into an empty chair.

Matthew was nodding therapeutically into the telephone and jotting notes down on a pad. Eight-forty AM and Matthew could handle a crisis. Impressive. He looked spry and energetic and probably felt it. Typically, Matthew started his day with a six AM run through five miles of Sidney Park. At forty-eight, he had the disgusting physique of a thirty-year-old. Only his receding hairline, silver mustache, and Bob Dylan record collection betrayed his age.

Caleb leaned back in the opulent leather chair and stared at the floor-to-ceiling windows looking out on Calhoun Street. The windows faced north and provided good light to Matthew's forest of plants, greenery so dense that Caleb once hid an eighteen-inch stuffed monkey and Matthew didn't notice it for over a week. Matthew's revenge had been to hang a noose around it and suspend it from Caleb's door. A note pinned on it read: "If you don't catch up on your records, this could happen to you!"

"Okay, I can work you in at twelve," Matthew said into the phone. "I'll see you then."

"Great. No lunch for you again."

Matthew smiled, cradling the receiver. "Who needs lunch when there's a borderline in crisis?" He fetched his pipe and tobacco pouch from his pocket, packed the pipe, and lit it. The smell of Matthew's special blend, sweet, with a hint of hickory, wafted through the office. "So. How are things with you?"

"Okay. Considering."

"Considering you just buried your future sister-in-law. Considering your brother–one of the most private people I've ever known–has been questioned by the police and had his name in the headlines for the past six days."

"Yeah. Considering all that." Caleb offered an evasive smile, wanting to change the subject.

Janice appeared in the doorway to interrupt them. "Hate to bother you,"she said sweetly. "But I've got a problem." She waved a manila record folder at Matthew and he took it.

"This is Caleb's client," Matthew said, scanning several billing sheets.

"What is it?" Caleb asked.

Janice shook her head. "Melanie Carson's here to see you. But there's a problem with her insurance coverage."

Matthew handed him a claim form from the file. "It looks like they terminated her mental health coverage."

"What?" Caleb glanced down at the CLAIM REJECTED stamp imprinted on the form.

"They terminated her effective April first. Does she know?"

"I'm sure she doesn't. She'd have mentioned it to me."

"Does she have the resources to self-pay?" Matthew asked.

Caleb shook his head. "She probably brings home twenty thousand. Look, Matthew, she's going through a real tough time right now. I can't spring a big bill on her now."

Matthew turned to Janice. "What's her balance?"

Janice ran a finger down one of the sheets. "For nine sessions at full fee–around six seventy-five."

"No way!" Caleb's voice rose. "This is not the time to bring this up. Believe me, she's too fragile."

Matthew lifted the pipe to his lips and blinked through the smoke as he puffed. “If you had your way, all of our clients would pay two dollars a visit.”

“And medications would be free, too,” Janice added with a laugh.

“Not true. I’d charge the managed-care companies twice our full rate,” Caleb retorted.

Matthew chewed on the pipe as his gaze shifted from Caleb to the papers in his hand. After a long moment, he said, “Janice, get back to the insurance company and make sure this isn’t some sort of computer error or something. If she isn’t covered, drop her fee down to twenty a session, back date it to April.”

“Thanks, boss,” Caleb said with a grin.

“Sometimes I don’t think I can afford you,” Matthew replied.

Melanie Carson didn’t look quite right. She drifted into the office as though she’d never been there before and looked around like she couldn’t remember where to sit. Caleb gestured to her usual chair across from him. She sat down, crossed her legs, and carefully folded her hands on her knees. Vacant eyes fell on Caleb.

He waited. She generally didn’t take much prompting because she always brought her own agenda into each session, using their time together with efficiency and insight. But not today.

She wore a loose-fitting green dress, belted at the waist, which she’d filled out better a few weeks ago. That color would have looked good on her then, too. But not today. She looked thinner, gaunt, shrunken, like a child in a grown-up’s clothes, trying to play a grown-up’s role. It wasn’t a good sign.

“Melanie, how you doing?”

"I ... don't really know. I started not to come. I didn't know what we'd talk about."

"I'll get us started then. You still away from work?"

She shook her head. "I had to go back. They called, they said they really needed me. So I went back on Thursday, worked overtime on Friday. I'm supposed to go in at noon today."

He sighed and hoped she didn't hear it. "That's a lot of hours. How's it been?"

"Okay. Not as bad as I thought. One of our contractors is real late on a project and we're trying to negotiate a bridge loan with the bank. I've been pretty busy."

That wasn't exactly what he was asking. He wanted to know about her boss, if he had touched her or intimidated her or hurt her again. But something in her expression told him to stay away from that subject. "Staying busy helps then?" he asked.

"It keeps my mind off other things." She looked at him, as if hoping he wouldn't bring up those pesky "other things."

He weighed it. He could see her defenses were gone. And personally, he had a new awareness of how that felt. Still, she was spiraling down–he could see it in her weight loss, her denial, her dead affect. She looked much worse than last week, and he had to do something. "Have you seen Mr. Edinger?"

She squirmed, her eyes searching the ceiling, the walls, the floor. He leaned toward her and asked, "Has he bothered you again?"

She shook her head. "No, not at all. He came to see me at my house Wednesday afternoon."

"What?"

"No, no. He wasn't like before. It was like nothing happened. He was very nice and said he was concerned that I was out sick. He mentioned how much he depended on me, how they all did. I told him I was still working on the books at my house and he said I was a very dedicated employee. He told me he didn't want me to try to come back until I felt up to it."

"Were you afraid of him? Having him there at your house?"

"At first I was nervous. But he acted so normal." She looked down and studied her hands, which vibrated against each other. "He acted like nothing happened."

Which is exactly what he wants you to think, Caleb thought. "Mel, Mr. Edinger's probably very ashamed of his behavior last week. Maybe he doesn't even remember all of it, because he was so drunk. But that doesn't mean it didn't happen. I want you to be very cautious around him."

"I'm still not sure exactly what happened. I mean, he didn't really hurt me."

"He abused his power with you. He harassed you. He knows you could sue him." He wasn't sure if it was sinking in.

She looked around the room again, as if lost. Poor kid. "Abused ... seems exaggerated ..." she said.

He mulled over his next move. She wasn't budging, but he needed to be gentle. "It's gotta be confusing for you. He was so intimidating the other night. Now he's acting so nice, trying to be helpful. Does it make you want to forget what he did?"

"He didn't do anything! Nothing happened, really. What I remember was being so scared. But everything turned out okay." Her eyes widened at him. "Didn't it?"

Caleb laced his fingers together and leaned forward. "You ever been through something like this before? Maybe when you were a kid–someone hurts you, then later acts like nothing happened?"

Her bony shoulders rose and fell. "No! Look–can we talk about something else?"

He thought about it. He'd struck a nerve in her and was beginning to wonder what else may have happened–with

Edinger, or with someone in her past. But now wasn't the time to pursue it. Doing anything intrusive might feel like another violation. "I'm sorry. I put words in your mouth, which wasn't fair. Mind if I change our focus a bit?"

She looked at him.

"Okay. Let's talk about your weight. You seem mighty thin to me. You eating okay?"

"I don't have much of an appetite. I try to eat and it makes my stomach hurt. I had some diarrhea." She flinched with embarrassment.

"Well, sometimes our stomachs talk to us, you know? Yours is saying it's had enough stress. How are you sleeping?"

She shook her head. "I go to sleep okay, but then I wake up about two or three and can't get back to sleep."

"You having nightmares, Mel?" he asked, anticipating the answer.

"I don't remember any." Her voice was almost a whisper. It seemed like she'd exhausted herself on their fifteen minutes of conversation.

"You don't remember. But do you wake up scared? Or nervous?"

She nodded, the movement so slight it was hardly noticeable. "I wake up screaming."

"That must be frightening."

She looked over at the door. She'd have bolted right then if she'd had the energy. But at that moment, she looked nearly catatonic.

"I have another question for you, Mel. You having any problems concentrating?" He leaned forward and poured as much energy into his voice as he could, hoping to spark life in her. Sometimes it worked, the client unconsciously responding to the tone, the spirit, the therapist conveyed. But not this time.

"I do okay when I'm busy. But I can't watch TV, or read. I still can't balance the books from work. I brought them home that night and I told Mr. Edinger I was working on them." She shrugged. "But I can't. The numbers all sort of run together."

"You know where I'm going with this?"

"You think I'm depressed?"

He nodded. Again, the blank stare in return. "You've been depressed before, Melanie. You know it can sneak up on you. Your appetite problems and sleep problems and concentration—these are all symptoms, right? Now I gotta ask. Are you having any thoughts of hurting yourself?"

She shook her head and answered quickly, "No."

"Sometimes when people get depressed, they sort of wish they could go to sleep and not wake up. You feel that way?"

He could feel her fear. He tried to coax her with his face, to convince her to let it out.

"I told you I don't really sleep. I'd love to close my eyes and sleep for days. But I don't want to die."

"Okay, Mel. I'm glad to hear that. And I think maybe we should give you something to help you sleep."

"Medication?" She sighed. He could tell she wanted relief—a week of no sleep can wreak havoc on your internal systems, not to mention your mental health. But she was scared to death of medicine, of needing medicine. Of becoming her mother.

"Look, Mel, I'm not saying you're like your mom. The symptoms you're having right now are trauma-induced. So I'm thinking you need something short term. Like a month or two. Just to help you get back to yourself."

"You think it will help?"

He grabbed the phone and buzzed Matthew, who said he could work her in right then. He turned back to Melanie. "You've seen Dr. Rhyker around here, haven't you? Tall guy, wears a tie all the time?"

She nodded.

"He's our doctor. He can see you now. I'll be glad to go with you, if you want." He read reluctance on her face. "Look, he's a regular guy–you're gonna like him. You can talk to him."

Matthew put her on Zoloft, an easily tolerated antidepressant with minimal side effects, and Benedryl to help with sleep. She was instructed to call if she had any problems, and agreed to come for group that Wednesday. She had a long road ahead of her.

CHAPTER SEVEN

When Caleb's four o'clock appointment canceled, he decided to sign out for the day. He needed to talk with Sam or, more to the point, he needed to talk some sense into Sam. He pulled into Sam's drive and parked behind his van. After climbing the steps, he nearly fell over Sam's bike, which lay on its side directly in front of the door. This was strange, Sam had ordered the ten-speed from Sweden and shelled out over a thousand for it. He usually treated it with great care–he'd even built two special racks for it, one over the wainscoting in the living room, and the other on the wall of his garage.

Caleb lifted the bike and leaned it against the porch rail before pressing the door signal. He knew Sam was probably inside, and even if he didn't want company, the flashing door signal would soon annoy him enough to come to the door. He pressed the button a dozen more times until he finally heard movement on the other side.

The door swung open. Sam swayed against the door frame, stepped back unsteadily, then caught himself. Bleary eyes struggled to fix on his visitor. "I don't want company," Sam blurted out.

Caleb glared at him, disbelieving. His brother was drunk. Stone drunk. Bracing himself, Caleb stepped inside.

He'd never imagined Sam's place looking, feeling, like it did at that moment. Sam had always been a neat person, as neat as a carpenter can be with sawdust and tools of his trade following him home each day. But that evening, his home looked like a frat house after a revelry. Flies buzzed above a half-eaten hamburger laying beside a pair of muddy Reeboks on the table. In the kitchen, an overturned bottle swam in a puddle of spilt beer on the counter and mounds of filthy dishes covered the sink. A pile of clothes on the floor bumped against the overflowing trash can, which lent a rank smell to the air.

The stench of alcohol and garbage permeated the place, the stale odor of a neglected life. For Caleb, it immediately triggered powerful memories of their father: The sleeping drunk on the couch. The angry drunk hurling insults and blows at his children. The guilt-ridden drunk, muttering thick-tongued apologies. Caleb fought a strong impulse to bolt out the door.

Sam staggered over to the fridge, retrieved two beers, offering one to Caleb. Caleb shook his head in disgust, tossing a pile of newspapers from a kitchen chair so that he could sit down.

Sam slid a chair out from the table and barely managed to sit. He popped open the can, took a long swig, then glared at Caleb with glazed-over, droopy eyes.

"What the hell's going on here, Sam?" Caleb asked aloud.

"Use your ans, Caluh!"

"You, too. You're so damn drunk, your pronunciation's horrible."

"Fuh you. I'm nah druk," he replied, both hands wrapped tightly around the beer can.

Caleb fought the urge to knock the can from Sam's grip. He signed slowly: "Have you been back to the police station?"

Sam squinted a bleary eye at Caleb, as if not understanding. "Carrie's house?"

Caleb shook his head. He thumped a curved hand over his chest, signing "Police." The sign for Sam's agent, Carrie, was a curved hand swept across the chest. Sam wasn't paying attention.

"Oh yeah. I was back at the police station. Again."

"What happened?"

"What do you think happened? Questions. More questions."

"Was Phillip with you?"

Sam squinted again, as though not understanding.

"Watch me carefully," Caleb signed, with slow, deliberate motions. "Was Phillip with you?" he letter signed.

"Yeah. Phillip was there. Good man, Phillip." Sam raised his can in a toast to his lawyer, before downing the rest of his beer.

Caleb watched, a sour feeling spreading in his gut. Both Knowles brothers had grown up with a keen awareness that too much alcohol was a dangerous thing. Their dad drank more when times were tough–self-medicating, Caleb supposed, to feel no pain. He'd crawl inside the bottle, daring anyone or anything to challenge his choice, oblivious to the damage it inflicted on his family. Caleb took a hard look at Sam, who'd apparently made the choice of following in dear old Dad's unsteady footsteps.

"I'm worried about you, Sam."

"I'm okay."

"Right. Your place stinks. You're drunk as shit. You're in a hell of a legal mess and you aren't doing a damn thing about it."

"None of which is your business." Sam's eyes narrowed in a searing stare.

Caleb had never seen this brother before and hoped their acquaintance would be short. "Funny, it feels like my business."

"Fuh you. Get the fuh out of here. Get the fuh out of my life!"

Gladly, Caleb thought, but knew he couldn't leave. He was hearing the ramblings of the alcohol, he reminded himself–Sam was buried somewhere deep below.

Sam stood, swayed a little, and weaved his way back over to the refrigerator. He grabbed another beer, popped it open and drank.

Caleb crossed over to him. "What do I do to sober you up? Coffee? Cold shower?"

Sam tilted his head back, opened his mouth wide, and bellowed. It was an ugly, inhuman sound.

Furious, Caleb grabbed his shoulders and yelled, "What the hell's wrong with you?"

Sam jerked away, stumbled back, and knocked over a chair. His wild, flailing arms shoved at Caleb, and reflexes Caleb hadn't needed in years kicked in as he ducked under the arms and maneuvered to the other side of the table. He took a quick inventory of the situation. Sam was a strong, determined man, which made him a strong, determined drunk. And right now, his brother was way out of control. Caleb had no choice but to get out of there. He tried to slip around the table and out the door, but Sam stepped in front of him.

"Why the fuh are you here? Be my fuckin' therapist?" Sam leaned forward, his rancid breath hot on Caleb's face.

Caleb fell back, winded. Suddenly, his anger slipped away, taking with it all of his defenses. It was like he was twelve years old, staring in his father's blood-shot eyes, dodging the acid words, the granite fists.

"What the hell are you staring at?" Sam wheeled around, and with an iron hand backed by carpenter's muscles, pounded Caleb in the face.

Caleb hadn't braced for it. Those reflexes had left him, too. His head popped back, the room swirled, and the floor turned to liquid, drinking him in.

He fell down on one knee. His next awareness was pain–excruciating pain–radiating from his nose to the back of his neck. He tried to focus through the fog that now made up his field of vision and thought he saw arms coming at him again. Heaving himself up, he grabbed Sam's right wrist and twisted it clockwise until he turned. He pressed the wrist into the small of his back, shoving him face-first into the wall. "We done with this?" Caleb yelled, immediately realizing the fruitlessness of it because this was Sam. This drunk idiot he had kissing the wall was still his deaf brother.

Sam dropped his head in what seemed like a conciliatory gesture. Caleb loosened his grip. A wave of dizziness passed through him and he felt like throwing up. He fell back against the wall, slowly sliding down until his rear hit the floor. He closed his eyes.

Several moments passed before a noise jolted him. He tried to stand again, but his muscles were stiff and unresponsive. He knew he had to get out of there, but his body wouldn't obey.

Okay, he said to himself, take things slow. He tried to lift himself onto his knees but the room tried to spin again, so he closed his eyes and mentally commanded it to be still. Queasiness rocked through his stomach, then passed. He reached for his face and found a throbbing, blood-soaked balloon where his eye used to be. He strained to pry it open, feeling immediate relief when his vision seemed okay.

Footsteps sounded from the bathroom. His assailant returned to the kitchen, towel in hand. He went to the freezer, piled ice in the towel, and brought it over to Caleb.

When Caleb put the ice pack to his eye it stung like a mother. He could feel the flesh tightening around his cheek and brow. Behind the socket, a construction crew cranked up jackhammers that drummed against his brain. After a few minutes, he instructed his body to stand and it managed to comply. He dropped the ice pack on the table. Sam started to go over to him, but must have changed his mind. Caleb shrugged at him. He had nothing else to say. He walked out the door.

It was close to midnight when he drove home. He sat in the truck and stared up at his bedroom window. The lights were out. Shannon was sound asleep. He could slip into bed without waking her and maybe avoid a hundred questions, at least for a while.

He fingered the eye. How could Sam hit him? He'd never seen anything close to violence in his brother before. And he'd never seen Sam drink like that. Was it the first time? Or had he lost control before? Had Sam ever hurt Anne? Could he have killed her?

Caleb's breath caught in his throat. He couldn't let himself believe it, not for a second. Not just because Sam loved Anne so completely, but because Sam–the real Sam, not the drunk–was his brother. Not that what he thought really mattered. He couldn't help Sam, not after tonight. Long ago, Caleb had learned to let go of people who were destructive to him. First his father. Later Mariel. And now Sam.

He climbed out of the truck, crept up the steps and unlocked the door. He eased into the bedroom, dropped his clothes on the floor, then slid into the tangle of sheets beside Shannon. She curled into him. He laid his face in her hair, breathing her in. She stirred, nestling into his neck. He slipped the sleeve of her gown off her ivory shoulder, one of his favorite parts of her, and kissed it.

Her hand reached up and guided his lips to hers. He saw her pale eyes, wide awake now, and turned his head so she couldn't see his eye. He kissed a trail up her long, supple neck, found her earlobe with his tongue, then continued the journey until he found her lips. Her fingers slipped around his ribs, then down, pulling off his jockeys.

Their lovemaking had its own rhythm, slow and easy, then the gentle crescendo. He loved to please her first. He knew the magic places, knew her cues. The subtle changes in her breath, the flicker of her eyelids.

He reveled in her body. Its soft contours, and inside, its steel strength. He let his fingers drink up her pale, velvety flesh. His mouth found her nipple, as his hand slipped between her legs. She arched up, giving herself to him completely–trusting, loving, welcoming. She grabbed him, holding tight, breath suspended, then emitting a soft, gentle gasp that aroused him like nothing else could.

And then she pulled him up to her mouth. She kissed him as her hands, below, stirred him to the familiar fever. His mind and soul reeled with love for her, with need for release. They clung to each other, breathless, their bodies one and more than one. When they finished, they collapsed together, tangled in each other's arms for a long while. "What happened, Caleb?" she asked.

He sighed, wanting to hide the truth, but knowing with her, he was exposed.

She reached over and switched on the lamp. "Jesus!" she shrieked, seeing his face.

He took her hand and kissed it. "It's okay. Just a shiner."

"People will think I'm abusing you. What the hell happened?"

He shrugged. A strand of her hair fell across his chest and he twisted it between his fingers. "Sam did it," he said, disgusted by the truth of those words.

"What?"

He took in a deep breath and let it all out. She listened, squeezing him at the tougher parts.

"I can't believe it. It just doesn't sound like Sam."

"No, it doesn't."

She leaned over and peered in his eyes. "Is this ... making you wonder about him? About if he killed Anne?"

He stroked the tears from her cheek. "I can't let myself think that. But what I think doesn't matter. Sam's going to have to fight that battle on his own."

CHAPTER EIGHT

Two days later, Matthew returned from a conference and appeared in the doorway to Caleb's office. "So what happened to your eye?" he asked, studying Caleb carefully over his bifocals.

Caleb fingered the bruise, which had turned a pale pewter gray with a crimson patch across the bridge of his nose. He'd explained it so many times that the lie should come easy. But somehow, it didn't. Caleb swallowed. "I ran into the closet door."

"Hmm. Did you get your schnoz X-rayed?"

"Nah. I figured any change in it would be an improvement. How's the day looking?"

Matthew flipped open the appointment book that lay balanced on top of his foot-high stack of medical records and turned to Wednesday. "I'm pretty well booked. I think Janice set you up with an intake, so your day's packed, too. Sure wish I could find some help." Matthew carried his work down the hall to his office.

Caleb started to head for the coffeepot when Janice caught him. "Percy Elias is on line one. He says it's urgent."

Caleb shrugged and wasn't hurried as he reached for his mug. Percy Elias considered a bad hair day an emergency. Janice took his arm. "I think it's different this time. You'd better take it."

Caleb nodded, hitting the lit button on the wall phone. "Percy? This is Caleb. What's up?"

"It's Melanie." His voice was panicked. "I can't wake her up. I shook her real hard. Then I splashed water on her face. Nothing works!"

"Whoa! Slow down. Where are you?"

"I'm at Melanie's. She didn't show up for work and didn't answer her phone, so I stopped over to check on her. The front door was unlocked and I found her–"

"Okay, okay. Take it easy. Tell me about Melanie."

"She's out cold on the sofa here, I can't wake her up. It looks like she threw up on herself. There're two empty pill bottles on the table."

Caleb felt his own heart pounding. "Did you call nine-one-one?"

"No ... I didn't know ..."

"It's okay. Just hold on a second. Don't hang up." Caleb pressed HOLD, used the other phone line to dial 911. Janice materialized, holding Melanie's file so he could give the operator Melanie's home address. Caleb took a deep breath, hoping to force calm into his voice. "Okay Percy, I'm back. The EMTs are on their way. Check her breathing for me."

"Oh God!" Percy's panic escalated. "She's barely breathing at all! She looks bad, Caleb. Real bad. I should have got here sooner–"

"We're lucky you got there at all. I'm putting you on hold again for just a second." He turned to Janice. "Get Matthew and tell him what happened. Percy? Pick up the empty bottles and read them to me."

"They're old. Her mother's name is on the prescription. One says Deseryl, the other's Parnate." He spelled them out.

"Okay, that's helpful. Now talk to Melanie. See if you get a response. I'll be with you in a second." Matthew appeared in the doorway and Caleb handed him the medicine names he had jotted down.

"This is bad," Matthew said. "Any way to know how much she took?"

"I doubt it."

"I'll call this in to the ER. Make sure the medicine bottles are sent with her."

Caleb pressed the phone line again. "Percy? Any response?"

"No. God! She's so still, like she's–I should have come sooner. I knew something was wrong, I just knew it!"

"Relax, Percy. You're doing great. Now, go open the front door and listen for the siren. You may need to flag them down so they don't miss the address. When the EMTs arrive, send those medicine bottles with her, okay?"

He stayed on the line, and Caleb could hear his rapid, frantic breathing. After what felt like an eternity, Percy said with obvious relief: "I hear sirens."

"Okay, I'll hold on while you get them."

A few minutes later, an emergency technician was on the line. Matthew took down the vital signs she read out and shook his head. The expression on his normally placid face fueled Caleb's anxiety. Matthew told them he'd meet the ambulance at Westville Memorial.

"Not good, huh?" Caleb asked.

"Depends on how much she took. Damn, I didn't expect this."

"Me either. She's been depressed, but I thought she was stable enough–" Caleb swallowed. "I want to go to the hospital with you."

"Let me finish up with my patient and I'll meet you up front."

They pulled in right behind the ambulance, and followed the gurney into the emergency room. Matthew seemed to know the attending physician, and the two of them rushed Melanie into an examining room. That left Caleb with a desperate, panic-ridden Percy in the hall.

"She looks dead, Caleb."

"But she's not, thanks to you."

"She had a seizure on the way over. They had to pull over and give her an injection."

That didn't sound good. It meant nervous system involvement. Which could mean–What? A stroke? Brain damage? He glanced anxiously toward the examining room.

"I should call someone," Percy was saying. "Her mother. And work, I guess."

Caleb nodded. Having something to do would be good for Percy. He watched as his client rushed over to the nurse's station and begged for a phone.

Caleb leaned against the wall and stared at the closed door. He wondered what they were doing to Melanie. Was it too late to pump her stomach? Was it too late to protect her brain or heart from the poison she'd ingested? Was it too late to save her life?

Percy found him again, and now looked downright ill. His vibrating hands came in and out of his pockets while his eyes roamed all over the room, unable to fix on anything. Caleb laid a hand on Percy's shoulder and guided him to a seat in the waiting area. "You look rough, Percy."

"She's been such a good friend, you know. Always there for me. Always smiling when things get tense."

"You get her mother?"

"No. I left a message at her house, but I don't know where she works. I called the office–they're checking Melanie's personnel file for her mother's work number."

"Good. Then you've done all you can do."

Percy wedged a shaky, pale knuckle between his lips. His

eyes never quit moving. He was clearly doing his very best to hold it together.

"Seriously, Percy. There isn't anything else you can do here. Go on home and relax."

"No. I should be here. I want to see her when she wakes up."

"You can–but not for a while. She'll be sedated. They'll only let family in, you know that. You go home, let me and Matthew see to Melanie."

Percy looked around again and said, "I don't have fond memories from this place."

Caleb nodded, knowing quite well Percy's history with this place. He had admitted Percy here twice for detox. Percy's roommate died of AIDS here a few months ago. Last year, when his mother had a massive coronary and nearly died, Percy's father threw Percy out of her hospital room upstairs here. That had been his last contact with his family. It was no wonder Percy looked so rough.

"You okay?" Caleb asked.

"I will be when she is." He stood up, shoving his hands in the back pockets of his black Levis. "I'll stop by work, see if they reached her mom. Then I'll be home. You call me, Caleb, when you have any news."

"Scout's honor." Caleb walked Percy out and watched as he headed toward his car. He wondered if Percy was too fragile to handle this stress. It would be a test of sorts, Caleb concluded. If it was too much for Percy to handle, Caleb would help put the pieces back together.

He returned to the examining room and tried to look through the small glass window, but a curtain around the bed blocked his view. He ambled back to the waiting area and sat on one of the hard plastic chairs facing a suspended TV set where Vanna

White flickered under lines of dark static. He tried to focus on Vanna as she twirled an "S" for a gleeful, overweight contestant, but his eyes soon shifted to the heavy door where nurses and technicians paraded in and out.

Twenty minutes later, Matthew appeared and motioned him over beside the reception desk. He looked grave. "Any family here?" he asked.

"Not yet. How is she?"

"We're moving her to intensive care. She's had one seizure already, so we need to keep a close eye on her. They did gastric lavage, but most of the drug had already been metabolized. Her liver panel wasn't good, so we may be looking at liver damage. Our worst problem is cardiac–she's developed an arrhythmia which could mean complications with the heart muscle itself. Unfortunately, this often happens with this kind of overdose. All in all, I don't think she could have picked a more lethal medicine."

"Jesus." Caleb searched Matthew's strained face and asked, "She gonna make it?"

"Truthfully? I don't know. She's young, but she ingested a huge amount. It's such a damn waste."

"I swear to God, I wasn't expecting this. She's been brittle, but I didn't think she was this desperate," Caleb said.

"Don't beat yourself up, Caleb. You and I both know this can't always be predicted. It keeps us humble."

A tall mass of a man approached them from the nurse's station, lumbering over like a bear in command. A definite presence. An expensive three-piece suit looked incongruous on his slumped posture. He looked to be about fifty, with thinning dyed black hair and dark, wide-set eyes. His face needed a good pressing; wrinkles and folds of flesh hung loose around a bulbous nose. He looked like someone who'd lost a lot of weight and needed cosmetic surgery to remove the excess skin. He asked for Dr. Rhyker. "I want to know about Melanie Carson."

Matthew studied him. "Are you a relative?"

"I'm her employer."

Matthew extended a hand and introduced himself, then asked, "Do you know if anyone got in touch with her mother?"

"I left my girl back at the office working on that. How is Melanie?"

"We're moving her to intensive care. We won't really know anything conclusive for twenty-four hours." He noticed Caleb's look at the man and added, "I didn't get your name ..."

"Edinger. Bill Edinger. Melanie's been with us a long time. The company's small, we're like family to each other."

Yep. One big, sick, incestuous family, Caleb thought, remembering his recent sessions with Melanie.

"Are you the treating physician?" Edinger asked.

"I'm a psychiatrist. The attending emergency physician is Dr. Holland; he's still with her. This is Caleb Knowles." Caleb nodded but made no effort to shake hands. Matthew continued, "It would be good to have family here, if you can help with that." He disappeared again behind the examining room door.

Edinger turned to Caleb and studied him for a long moment. "You a doctor, too?"

"Social worker."

"Caleb, right? You must be Melanie's counselor."

Caleb couldn't imagine Melanie telling this perpetrator she was in therapy. He didn't respond.

"Percy Elias told me about you. I've been very worried about our Melanie. I suppose it's good she's been seeing someone, but I had no idea how bad off she was."

Caleb thought he heard a sarcastic edge in the man's voice and wondered what it meant. He glanced at the door to the examining room with dread.

"This suicide attempt–is it her first time?" Edinger asked.

Caleb grit his teeth. "Look, *Bill*, my relationship with Melanie is confidential. I have no intention of telling you anything. And I think your presence here is inappropriate, given recent history." As soon as the words spilled out, he wished he could snatch them back. He'd violated his client's confidence. But his need to protect her from this man superseded the ethical issues.

"I just want to help Melanie," he said smiling. It seemed a strange expression, given the situation.

"Okay, here's something you can do. Call your personnel department. Find out why they canceled Melanie's insurance. Make sure she's covered for this visit to the ER, for the tests they're running on her, and for whatever else she's gonna need to get well. Do that, Mr. Edinger, since you care so much for Melanie."

Edinger launched a wide-eyed stare at him, but Caleb met the stare, unwavering.

"Caleb? Could I see you?" Matthew walked up, coaxing Caleb away from Edinger. "She had another seizure. They hooked her up to a respirator–she's breathing erratically on her own. They're trying diazepam to control the seizures."

It knocked the wind out of him. He fell back against the wall and uttered, "Jesus."

"I know. She may still pull through. It's hard to say." He tried to sound encouraging.

"I keep asking myself what I missed."

"Probably nothing. She was determined. And she was secretive. You know that's the most dangerous pattern when it comes to suicides."

Caleb nodded, but felt no comfort. "Can I see her?"

"Not now. Just family's allowed in. Of course, rules like that have never really affected you before." Matthew returned to their patient.

"Caleb?" Stewart Brearly, dressed in full clerical garb, approached him. He held a small wooden box and black leather Bible. "What on earth are you doing here? Everything okay?"

"One of my patients is here. She OD'd."

Stewart shook his head. "That's always such a tragic thing. How's she doing?"

"Touch and go. Matthew says I can't blame myself because these things happen and it keeps us humble. I feel pretty damn humble now."

"I'll bet."

"What are you doing here?" Caleb asked.

Stewart tapped the wooden box. "I'm bringing Communion for a couple of our congregants."

"No kidding? Sort of a Sacrament-to-go or something?"

"Hardly." Stewart winced. "It's actually one of the best things I get to do. Talking to people when they're very ill, when they're grappling with mortality issues–it can be a very spiritual thing." His gaze drifted up the hall, though it didn't seem to fix on anything. His lips pulled back in a serene, contented smile.

Caleb had always envied Stewart. He seemed to be a man at peace with himself, a man sure of his calling to "serve the Lord." While Caleb always tried to help his clients, to do the best he could for them, he always knew that deep down, his motives were selfish. It felt good to help people. And helping others sort through the tangles in their lives often helped Caleb tease out his own. There was nothing altruistic in Caleb's career choice.

"What happened to your eye, Caleb?"

He started to lie again, but thought better of it. "I ran into a fist. It was attached to my brother."

"Dear Lord," Stewart said. "Sam must be really suffering to do something like that."

"Yeah, he may be suffering, but I'm the one with the shiner."

Caleb touched the bruise, felt the sting that hadn't yet left it.

"I'm very worried about him, Caleb. We have to–"

Caleb lifted a hand, stopping him. "Don't go there, Stewie. I don't want to know what your concerns are. All I know is, Sam's on his own with this one."

Stewart stepped back as though he'd been struck himself. "Okay. But Sam's–"

"I can't talk about him right now." He cocked a thumb toward the room where Melanie was. "I have to get back to my patient."

"Okay Caleb. Okay. I'll say a prayer for her."

Caleb left him and approached the nurse's station, where he was informed that Melanie had been moved to the fourth floor. He felt a presence move up behind him.

"Any more news about Melanie?" Bill Edinger asked, his voice more demanding than inquisitive.

Caleb took a deep breath, realizing another altercation with him was pointless. "Like Matthew said, they moved her up to intensive care. She won't be allowed visitors for a long time. If you want to help, get her insurance straightened out. And get her family here."

Edinger nodded. "I want her to have the best of care, Knowles. You make sure she gets it. I'll check on her later."

"You do that," Caleb grumbled.

The trick to maneuvering around wherever you damn well please in a hospital is to act like you belong there. He'd mastered the technique years ago, when Sam spent long weeks in one hospital after the other. Caleb used the staff elevator to get to the fourth floor, eyed Melanie's name on the chart cart in the nurse's station, and found her room number.

She looked so small, like a child, the curves of her body

barely interrupting the flat surface of the bed. He wasn't sure he was in the right place until he moved in close enough to study her face. Several beeping machines surrounded her. IV tubes sprouted from both wrists, a hose running from her nose and her mouth connected to the machine that seemed to be breathing for her. She looked pale as death. She looked like Anne.

"What happened, Mel? Why didn't you call me?" He stroked her small hand, below where the IVs entered her arm. Her flesh was cool and rubbery. "Come on, Mel. You're a fighter. You've got to fight like hell right now." He felt like he'd failed her somehow, and he wanted another chance.

He knew the hospital staff couldn't leave her alone for more than a few minutes, and he was stretching it. Squeezing her fingers he said, "I'll see you soon."

CHAPTER NINE

"There's a Phillip Etheridge here to see you." Janice's voice had a berating edge to it that meant, "And he's not on the appointment book."

"He's Sam's lawyer, Janice. Send him back." Caleb had barely stood when Phillip hurried in, wearing gray linen trousers with suspenders over a darker gray linen shirt. Caleb concluded that he'd left the suit jacket in his new BMW. Phillip took a seat, loosened his silk tie, and pulled out a long cigarette. Apparently, the THANK YOU FOR NOT SMOKING sign on Caleb's desk didn't apply to him.

"How'd you get that shiner?" he asked.

"I ran into a door."

"Ahuh." Phillip raised a cynical brow.

"So what brings you by?" Caleb pulled a hidden ashtray from the bottom of his desk.

"Sam, of course. I'm working on his bail."

"Bail? Sam's in jail?"

"You didn't know? Sam was arrested yesterday. They charged him with murder." Phillip lifted his briefcase to his lap, flicked open the lock, and retrieved a long, manila file.

"Jesus."

"He didn't call you?"

Caleb shook his head.

"Not that the jail has a teletype. Detective Briscoe contacted me yesterday so I could be there for the questioning. There's a bond hearing today at one and I think I can get him out, playing up his handicap, his reputation in the community. And thanks to Stewart Brearly, the police have several advocacy groups demanding his release."

Caleb sighed. This was what Stewart had tried to tell him at the hospital, only he'd been too stubborn to listen to him.

"We can expect a very high bond," Phillip continued. "I'm thinking a hundred thousand, maybe even two. I'll have to pull together ten percent to get him out."

Ten thousand dollars was considerably more than Caleb had in his savings account, which had been emptied by the divorce. But maybe he could get a second mortgage. "I'll see what I can scrape together."

Phillip squinted over twirls of blue smoke. His eyes, almost the same color, were quick and perceptive. His blond hair had hints of gray that predicted a distinguished aging process, befitting an attorney. "Sam says he can cover it. I'm getting tax documents as an appraisal of his house, which we'll put up. And he's got a pretty fat savings account."

"How could they charge him, Phillip?"

"Well, all hell's broken loose. I haven't seen the autopsy report yet, but Bentille said it showed Anne was pregnant. Sam claims he didn't know. So now Bentille's theorizing maybe the baby wasn't Sam's–that may be what they fought about, etcetera, etcetera. They took tissue from the fetus for DNA testing, and they want a blood sample from Sam."

"Jesus. How's Sam doing?"

Phillip took a long drag off the cigarette. "He's a mess. I think he needs help. I mean professional help, like you get here."

"How'd Sam take the news about the baby?"

"Rough. The police have been real nasty with him. They

told him about the pregnancy on Monday morning, then lit into him for about three hours of questioning. Tuesday, they do the arrest, he spends the night in jail, then first thing this morning, three more hours of interrogation. And Bentille starts with this 'maybe it isn't your baby' crap. That nearly killed him."

"I would think so." Caleb felt something kick in his gut.

Phillip zeroed in on him. "You knew Anne was pregnant? Did she tell you?"

"No. I found out after the funeral; Anne's sister told me. She may be the only person Anne told."

"I wonder why she was being so secretive," Phillip said, eyeing Caleb as though he thought Caleb might know.

"Maybe you should talk to Elaine. I have her number at home if you want it."

Phillip gave a quick nod. He took a long drag on the cigarette, tapped ashes into the small ashtray, and puffed again. "You must not be a smoker," Phillip commented, crushing out the last ember from his cigarette.

"I gave it up seven years ago."

"Good move. It's a damn nuisance. You feel like a criminal every time you light up. It's illegal everywhere, like it's pot or crack or something." Talking about his addiction inspired him to light up again. "Let me tell you about Frank Bentille. He can be a problem. He gets his jaws around an idea and he's like a pit bull. He won't let go for anything. Can't stand it when the facts don't support his opinion, you know?

"Also, it doesn't help that this case is grabbing the headlines. I think Bentille has political fantasies, God help him, and that just tightens his grip on Sam as a suspect. He's getting some pressure, too. Apparently, Anne Farrell's father was a huge contributor to the campaign of my favorite pro-life senator, Cal Moultrie. Moultrie's keeping a close eye on this case, and Frank

Bentille loves the attention. He calls Moultrie's office regularly with updates. This is not what we need."

"Terrific."

"So we have to find holes in the case as quick as we can. The DNA tests usually take a few weeks, but Bentille put a rush on them. And they aren't likely to help Sam, unless the killer left some of his skin tissue or blood on the weapon, and I haven't heard they found any. You got any other ideas?"

Caleb shook his head. "What frustrates the hell out of me is the police haven't even checked into any other possibility. If Sam didn't kill her, someone else did. But they haven't done shit to investigate."

"Why'd you say 'if' just then?" Phillip interrupted.

Involuntarily, Caleb touched the bruised eye. "Sam isn't capable of killing anyone. We both know that."

"Agreed," Phillip said, without hesitation. "Look, the police know most murders like this are domestic. They think they got enough on Sam, so why bother looking anywhere else? Me, I think the case is weak, but we gotta get to work."

"How did he do in jail last night? They treat him okay?"

Phillip rubbed his eyes with the palms of his hands. "Jail's a disgusting place, Caleb. Sam's a big, strong guy. But he can't hear. So he doesn't know what's coming up behind him. Or what they might be saying about him in the shower room– Sorry. I'm just worried. He survived last night, but if he gets convicted–"

Caleb blinked back the image of Sam .. of other inmates ... of what might happen ... One thing he realized, though. Phillip was the right man to defend him. Clearly, he took this case very seriously.

Phillip stood to leave, but stopped at the door. "We gotta get to work on this, Caleb."

"I'll do what I can."

In the distance, fat storm clouds were rolling in. This was the season when nature had her tantrums. She'd replace sweltering, dead-still air with thunder rumbles, swirling winds, and blinding downpours, usually timed to hit when rush hour was at its peak. A storm might only last twenty minutes, but the destruction could be felt for days. Sometimes, there was a sacrificial trailer torn and splintered in its wake. Sometimes the city lost all power, plummeting Westville's techno-philliac humanoids into a hushed, fearful darkness. All in all, it was a hell of a way to break up the monotony of summer.

Phillip had called and left a message that Sam's bond had been posted and Sam had been released. Caleb just needed to see him, to make sure he was all right. He pulled into Sam's drive, spotting the green van in the garage. He climbed out and freed Cleo from the back of the truck; she followed him up the steps of the porch, where he hit the door signal.

He heard no movement inside. He pressed the signal four more times, still with no response. He decided to try the studio. Crossing over to the studio's side door, he pressed the door signal, but still heard no answer. At the far end of the porch, Caleb found the potted geranium that hid Sam's extra key. He unlocked the door and, instructing Cleo to wait on the porch, stepped inside.

He knew he shouldn't go into the studio, but he felt a morbid impulse to return to the room, to see where Anne had died.

Nothing had changed. Police tape webbed across the door frame. Fragments of plaster from the broken pedestals covered the wood floor. The closer he got to where Anne had died, the more brutal the destruction became. He stepped over the overturned pedestals that framed the spot where her body was found.

The blood was still there, dark stains of brown on the glimmering pine floor, crimson spatters against the ivory wall. Immediately, he remembered Anne's contorted, blood-drenched body. He remember her hands, her fingers digging into her thumbs, silently screaming "No."

"What happened, Anne?" he whispered. "Who did this to you?" He looked around the room again. Maybe he'd missed something. Maybe there was a clue or something that might point to who did this. Yeah, right. Five forensics experts had searched every millimeter of the studio and now Caleb Knowles, armed with a social work degree, was going to swoop in and solve the crime. Matthew had medicines that helped with delusions of grandeur, he thought.

The large bay window in the front of the studio looked out on Maple Street. From it, he could see three children playing jump rope in the street. He'd met them before; they lived next door to Sam. The oldest girl, about eleven, had become Sam's junior apprentice, sometimes helping him clean up the workshop, wash his van, or even help with staining cabinets. Sam said she was left in charge of her younger siblings every afternoon, a typical latch key kid. Sam kept an eye out for those children.

Caleb left the studio, closing the door carefully, then headed to the back door. He found a piece of scrap paper and left a note saying he'd stopped by. On the back porch, he found Cleo napping soundly in a huge snoring heap. He stepped over her and walked down the steps and around to the front of Sam's house.

The older child advised the others to swing the rope higher and faster. The proper rhythm established, she dashed in, twirled around, and started an indiscernible chant that sounded remotely like a rap song. Her siblings joined in her chorus. She seemed tireless, never missing a step, twirling to face one child, then the other, on one foot, then both ... an agile, strong girl.

Finally, the youngest gave out. Too tired or bored to go on, she dropped her end of the rope on the ground. Ignoring her sister's bark to continue, she picked up a stick and started hitting a pine cone down the street.

Caleb eased over to them. "Hi guys. How are you doing?"

"Do I look like a guy to you?" the jumper asked.

He grinned. "Not at all. Sorry."

She walked over to him and regarded him with wary eyes. "I know you. You Sam's brother."

"That's right. I'm Caleb." He extended a hand, and reluctantly, she took it. "I'm waiting on Sam."

"He left on his bike a while ago."

"I guess I'll keep waiting then."

"My name's Laquanda. That's Marcus," she said, pointing at the boy. "And over there acting up is Tashika. She's six. Marcus is eight. I'm almost twelve," she said with authority. She dug her hands into the deep pockets of her dirty pink sundress. She had on sneakers that had once been white, with pink socks. Her ample black hair, shoulder-length, was gathered in pigtails, two on the sides, one in back, each with a tiny braid at the end. Her black eyes locked on his, thirsting for attention. He liked her immediately, understanding Sam's attachment.

"You guys lived here long?"

"Since I was two. Mama moved us in with her ma, but then she died and Mama got the house."

Cleo must have heard their voices and awakened. She clambered over to Caleb and when she noticed the children, her rear end vibrated with excitement. The smallest child ran over to Laquanda and hid behind her. "That's a big dog, mister. Is it a wolf?"

"No. She's a big baby. She'd love for you to come over and pet her." Laquanda looked nervous, but seemed to want to impress her siblings. Hesitantly, she extended a hand that was immediately greeted by a huge wet tongue. Cleo then plopped down, rolled over, begging that her stomach get the proper attention.

"She wants you to scratch right here," Caleb instructed.

Laquanda touched the thick black and white fur and Cleo squirmed with glee. "She is a big baby." Soon Tashika felt brave and stroked her, and Cleo twitched and grumbled her delight at their attention. When the girls were done, Cleo romped up the front steps to resume her nap.

Laquanda looked up at the studio and her face turned into a frown. "Miss Anne died in there."

"I know."

"I'm gonna miss her. She was real nice."

"Did you see her often?"

"Yeah. We saw her the day she got killed. She come out on the porch, where your dog is, while we was playing ball."

"You remember anything else?"

Laquanda shrugged. Marcus, who had been on the other side of the street snapping the jump rope like it was a whip, came over. He was a plump kid, with cocoa-colored skin and big, wondering eyes. "I remember sumpin'," he exclaimed.

Caleb leaned over and smiled encouragingly.

"Ms. Anne come down to the sidewalk and look up the road a long time. Then she looked the other way, like this." He dramatically placed his hand on his forehead like he was shielding his eyes from the sun, and stared at the intersection of Saluda and Maple Street. "Then she went back to the porch and stood there some more."

"Marcus, is it?"

He nodded.

"Sounds like maybe she was looking for someone?"

Marcus smiled and said, "Yeah, she musta been."

"She wasn't waiting on Sam though. He was inside working. I could hear the sander going like crazy," Laquanda interjected.

"Did anyone ever show up?"

Laquanda shrugged. "Not while we was out here."

"Anything else happen? Did you hear anything?"

"Mama made us come back inside."

"Did you guys talk to the police that day?"

Marcus shook his head. "When all those police and ambulance people come, we stayed in the house. Mama said she smelled trouble and she was keepin' her nose out of it."

As if on cue, Mama stuck her head out the front door. She was a big, round woman, barely more than a kid herself. "You kids come on in. Can't you see a storm's comin'? Get on in here."

"Comin', Ma," Laquanda yelled. Apologetically, she turned to Caleb. "We gotta go."

He watched the three of them amble home, Tashika towed reluctantly by her domineering older sister.

Caleb started back to his truck when he heard a whirring and clicking sound and turned to see his brother coming up the drive. Sam had two sacks of groceries strapped to the back of his ten-speed, and a leather backpack held a third. He wheeled the bike to the bottom of the steps, dismounted, and as he lifted it onto the porch, noticed Caleb.

Sam studied him for a long moment. "How's the eye?"

"It hurts. It's been great fun explaining it to everyone."

Sam leaned the bike against the porch rail, removed his helmet, and came over for a closer look at the bruise. Caleb stepped back.

"I'm surprised you're here," Sam said. Up close, Sam looked even more haggard. His angular face had thinned and now wore an unhealthy, washed-out pallor. The dark eyes looked bone-weary and lost.

"Me, too," Caleb signed. "You sober?"

Sam flinched and turned away. He didn't seem to know what to say.

Caleb waited for his brother's eyes to come back to him. "You remember what happened? Or is it all a big drunken blur?"

"I remember. I know what I did," Sam said.

"Do you? You remember knocking the crap out of me? It was a great impression of dear ole Dad." Caleb's hands flew with anger. "Is this a new coping technique? Drinking yourself into oblivion?"

Sam blinked at the words coming at him, without answering.

"You, of all people, should know better," Caleb signed.

Sam started to speak but hesitated. His eyes–the old eyes–looked filled with pain. "I've never gotten drunk like that before. I never will again. Not that it matters."

"What the hell got into you?"

Sam sank back against the porch rail as if a strong wind had hit him dead on. "What the hell do you think got into me? First Anne is killed. Then I find out we were expecting a baby, only that baby is dead, too. Then I spend a night in jail, get a taste of my future." He passed a massive hand over his face. "I was numb for a while there. You didn't like it, but I thought it worked quite well." He tried a quick smile that just as quickly vanished. "But then it all crashed in on me–I didn't know what to do. So I got drunk. I guess I hoped drinking might make me numb again. I was so desperate not to feel–" His voice cracked and he sucked in a deep, staggered breath. "Pretty stupid."

Caleb watched him closely as his own rage evaporated. Sam looked like a broken man. It was no wonder. All the losses, piled on top of each other. He reached over and squeezed Sam's arm to get his attention. "You are your own worst enemy now, Sam. You have to let me help."

He shook his head and pointed at Caleb's eye. "After what I did, you'd better stay away."

Caleb waited while Sam's mournful eyes took in the yard, the sky, the street. Finally, they came back to Caleb. "Look, we're brothers," Caleb said. "You need to let me help you through this."

Sam wiped his eyes and cleared his throat. "They charged me with murder, Caleb. They think I killed Anne. And our baby, I guess." He seemed to be saying it to himself as much as to Caleb.

"Elaine told me Anne was pregnant," Caleb's hands came across his stomach, locking fingers. "I didn't think you knew."

"Elaine's the only one who knew. Not me. Not her parents. Not until yesterday."

"Have you heard from them?"

"Oh, yeah. I just got an e-mail from Monroe. He's having a hard time, I guess."

"Did he threaten you?"

Sam shrugged. "He thinks I killed her. He's just being a father."

"You need to be careful around him," Caleb cautioned.

Sam shook his head, tears brimming in his eyes again. "I can't let it sink in. Someone killed her, Caleb. And killed my child."

Caleb laid a hand on Sam's shoulder and squeezed it. "Okay," Caleb signed. "Here we go again. You're coming home with me. Staying here, by yourself, with that damn police tape draped everywhere is stupid. Just for a few weeks. Until this legal crap is cleared up. Let's pack up your things."

Caleb met Shannon at the door and explained about the situation with Sam.

"Oh yeah, that makes sense." Shannon's voice rang out hotly. Her turquoise eyes were wide with fire. She wore a T-shirt which read GIVE ME SOME CHOCOLATE AND NO ONE GETS HURT. Catch her during a certain time of the month, she meant it. "Sam's staying here, after what he did to you?"

Sam came in from the kitchen and immediately picked up on the tension in the room. He turned to Caleb, concerned.

"You should have talked to me first," she said behind Sam.

Caleb waited until Sam moved to the sofa and said, "We'll talk later."

"I'm deaf, not an idiot," Sam said. "Please don't talk like I'm not here."

Caleb shot her an angry look, but she didn't back down. Instead, she blurted out, "Okay, Caleb you sign this so he gets every word."

"Shannon–"

"Caleb says you're staying with us. I figure Caleb's gone wacko or something, considering the last time you were together you beat the shit out of him."

"He may be wacko," Sam agreed, stepping closer to her. "Maybe it's genetic, because I've been out of my mind lately. I'll understand if you don't want me to stay." He moved toward the door.

Shannon shook her head and stopped him, her hand on his arm. "There won't be any drinking here."

"No," Sam answered.

"You get mad, you need to hit something, you get out of here."

"Agreed."

"And you stop shutting us out, Sam. Let us help."

"I'm working on that one. That's why I'm here."

She slipped her arms around him and looked up into his face. "We love you, you know."

CHAPTER TEN

Caleb was scooping coffee into the filter basket for the second pot when the phone rang.

"Caleb? This is Elaine Halloway." She hesitated. "Anne's sister."

He wedged the phone between his chin and shoulder and hit the brew button. "Hey, Elaine. What's up?"

"Dad called me last night. He told me they've arrested Sam for Anne's murder."

"He's out on bond now. He's staying with me and Shannon."

"How is he?"

"He's terrible. He just found out about the baby."

"I was afraid of that. Who told him?"

"The police, unfortunately."

She let out a sigh. "Then ..." she paused, "she was still pregnant when she died, right?"

"Right," Caleb answered. "Why?"

"I wasn't sure."

Caleb wondered if she was being purposefully vague. "You're the one who told us, Elaine."

"I told you she had been pregnant. But I wasn't sure she still was. She was thinking about getting an abortion."

"An abortion? Why?"

"I don't know. I thought maybe Sam didn't want it, but apparently that wasn't the problem. I told her I thought she'd be a great mother. I told her I'd come and help however she needed me to. But she was determined."

"That's why she didn't tell Sam," Caleb said. "He would have wanted her to keep the baby."

"She wouldn't have listened. I did my best to talk her out of the abortion. I told her we'd adopt it. Trip and I have been trying to have a kid for eight years. We've been to fertility clinics, sperm banks, adoption agencies–we're on a dozen waiting lists for international adoption.

"She knew it, too. She knew how much we wanted to have a child. I'm almost forty-three now, so adoption's about the only hope I have left. So when she told me about the abortion, I wasn't exactly an objective ear. She got mad and said I didn't understand. And she was right, I didn't. I asked her if it was money. Our folks would help out if they needed it. But she said no, she and Sam were doing fine."

"Do you think she was scared of the responsibility?" Caleb asked.

"Of course she was. Two deaf parents. How could they manage a baby?"

"I don't know of much that my brother can't manage," he said.

"I knew she'd regret it if she had the abortion. I kept hoping she'd change her mind. Doesn't matter now, I guess."

"Why didn't you tell anyone this before?" Caleb asked.

"I guess I was afraid, too. I didn't want anyone to know. Not Sam. And especially not my dad."

"I'm not sure you can keep it under wraps now." He cradled the receiver.

Shannon drifted in with her empty mug. "Who was on the phone?"

Caleb poured her some coffee and told her about the call from Elaine. "So what do you think?" Caleb asked her.

"I think she must be in a very sad place. Coping with infertility. Now this loss."

"But don't you think it's a little presumptuous? That was Sam's baby, not theirs. Yet she seemed to feel entitled to it."

Shannon cocked her head a little to the side, the way she did when something puzzled her. "I think she was just that desperate. The drive to have a baby–to be someone's mother–it can be overwhelming. Not just because that's what society expects. Hormones kick in, too. They are powerful forces."

Caleb looked over at her, unsure if he should tread in this territory. "You feel it, too?" he asked.

"Sure I do. I have no idea if I have any fertility problems, because I've never tried to be get pregnant. I hope I will one day."

Now he knew he was walking through land mines. This had always been the sore spot in their relationship. Shannon wanted marriage, wanted babies, wanted PTAs and car pools. And she deserved all that and more. But Caleb, still reeling from the rollercoaster ride with Mariel, grew nauseous at the thought of marriage. He hoped Shannon couldn't read the terror on his face.

"Uh-oh," she said. "There you go. First the eyes glass over. The teeth clench in steely resolve. The face pales and–"

"Yeah, yeah," he said.

"Relax, Caleb," she laughed and reached over to squeeze his hand. "This isn't an ultimatum. Not yet, anyway."

Caleb brought some coffee, cream, no sugar, to Julia's room and opened the door, Cleo at his heels. He was met with a comical sight: a six-foot-four, two-hundred-pound man snoring in a canopied dwarf bed. At least the fifteen stuffed animals had been removed from the bed and neatly assembled along the chest of drawers.

Sunlight filtered through the lace-curtained windows and webbed the cream-yellow walls with delicate shadows. The room was as bright and alive as his daughter. In a way, it retained her essence when Julia was away from them. When Caleb missed her, he'd find himself standing here, at the foot of her bed, feeling her all around him. He wished that she lived here, that she could be with him all the time.

Caleb crossed to the bed and, setting the coffee down on the nightstand, stooped under the canopy. Sam was sleeping so soundly Caleb had to shake him several times before getting movement out of him. Sam shifted in the knotted sheets, rolled over, and drifted off again.

Cleo decided to help. She lunged for the bed, plopping two massive paws on Sam's chest. The bed shook like a boat about to capsize.

"Jesus!" Sam's groggy eyes opened to see the huge tongue dangling from Cleo's mouth. "Talk about your rude awakening."

Caleb placed his hand in front of his eyes, thumb touching forefinger, then popped them apart. "Wake up," the sign said.

"I'm trying," he responded.

Caleb handed him the coffee and Sam gulped it down. "I was really out cold."

"Guess you needed it."

"First good sleep I've had in ten days."

"I should have let you sleep in. But you said you needed to get up."

Sam nodded. "I have a lot to do today."

"Anything I can help with?"

Sam ran his fingers through the fur on Cleo's neck, looking

pensive. Caleb nudged him. "What?" he signed, brushing his right index finger across the palm of his left hand.

"I have to go to over to Anne's office and clean out her desk. I haven't been able to go through any of her things. Stewart wanted to clean out the closet and pack up her stuff—but I wouldn't let him. It's stupid, I know, but I just couldn't bring myself to do it."

"It's not stupid."

"Her supervisor sent me an e-mail message yesterday. They want me to come in today for her things."

How sensitive, Caleb thought. "I could go with you."

Sam looked relieved. "You sure? It's over in Carrolton, but not far."

"Absolutely."

"Maybe over your lunch hour?"

"Pick me up at one."

All Caleb knew about The Skolnick and Bagardis Accounting Firm was that it was on Main Street, a section of Carrolton he always avoided. Something about Main Street made him uneasy, made him fear for his safety. Main Street was the financial center of South Carolina.

His work often took Caleb through crime-infested neighborhoods and gang-ridden Projects. But it was this cold, corporate world of skyscrapers and stockbrokers and people in crisp suits that really scared him. It was the callous pursuit of the almighty dollar, without regard for human suffering. It was this grim predictor of what humanity might become that churned his stomach.

The Skolnick and Bagardis firm filled the seventh floor of a towering office monolith that was the color of an old penny. Sam parked the van at a meter and looked nervous as he stared at the building. He pointed at a copper sign that held the firm's logo in huge swirling letters.

"You sure you're up to this?" Caleb signed.

"Nope. But I gotta do it. Let's go." He climbed out of the van, retrieved four cardboard boxes from the back, handed two to Caleb. They passed through a small courtyard at the entrance of the building where cement benches and a patchwork of summer flowers surrounded a murky pool of water fed by a large metal fountain. A brick walkway led to another copper structure, an abstract monstrosity with cubes and triangles and a silver sphere that looked like a giant eyeball.

"That supposed to be art?"

Sam grinned at him. "I know the sculptor. The commission was thirty thousand."

"I'm in the wrong line of work."

The plush lobby was empty and hushed, except for the sterile peals from the elevator bell. When the doors opened, they stepped into the black elevator and pressed the button for seven. A Muzak version of "Synchronicity" trickled out from a small speaker. Caleb looked enviously at his deaf sibling.

The ride was quick and they emerged on the seventh floor. They couldn't miss the glossy lacquered doors, emblazoned with the swirly logo for Skolnick and Bagardis. A male secretary with slick black hair and a slicker silk suit greeted them at the reception desk. He was pale, like someone who didn't get out much, and his handshake was anemic. But he moved briskly, escorting them to Anne's office. Sam sucked in a deep breath before opening the door.

It looked spartan. There was a desk and chair, a computer on its stand, and a small window that looked out on the parking garage. There was a thirsty fern shedding brown leaves on the window sill. There was a banker's lamp and pencil holder on her desk. And on top of the file cabinet, there was a framed photo showing Anne nestled cozily under Sam's arm. They looked happy and in love and eager for their future together. Caleb could read it in Anne's big halogen smile and in Sam's winking eye.

He dropped the photo in a box, face down. No need for Sam to see it, not yet. Caleb took a seat at the desk to rummage through the drawers.

"This is odd," Sam said from behind him.

Caleb pivoted in the desk chair to face him. "What?"

Sam held up another photograph. "I found this stuck in the back of her file cabinet."

Caleb reached over and took it. It looked like an anniversary photo of Anne's parents: Monroe, looking stern and uncomfortable in his suit and Louise, smiling over the pink corsage on her Sunday dress.

"Anne loved this picture. It was always on her desk, right there." Sam pointed to an empty corner by the phone.

Caleb thought about Monroe Farrell, the devout, hyper-conservative Christian. And he imagined Anne, struggling with her decision about the abortion. It wasn't hard to understand why she moved the picture. Caleb shrugged at Sam, then continued loading his box.

"Are you Sam?" someone asked from behind him.

The woman came over to them and extended a hand. She was a heavyish woman, forty or so, with olive skin and a sad smile. She had salt-and-pepper curls with dangly silver earrings bobbing through them. She wore an airy blue skirt and long tunic–a style likely chosen to hide her weight. A silver cross with lapis in the center hung across her ample chest. "I'm Patrice Dutton. I worked with Anne."

Caleb signed what she said and Sam replied: "She told me about you."

"I'm sorry to be meeting you under these circumstances." Patrice talked slow, but with a loud voice. While the volume was unnecessary, slower speech made lipreading easier for Sam.

"All Anne's things are in here?" Caleb asked.

She shook her head. "I don't really even know. The police came yesterday. They may have taken some things. I know the second and third drawers of that file cabinet are our records–everything else you find was Anne's." Caleb signed the instructions to Sam, who returned to his packing.

"How's he doing?" Patrice asked.

"He's had better years."

"I read in the newspaper that they arrested him. From what she told me about him, that's ridiculous."

Caleb nodded.

"That's an insult to her memory," Patrice said.

"Sounds like you knew her pretty well."

She glanced over at Sam uncomfortably. "Can I buy you a cup of coffee?"

Caleb could see she wanted to talk and wondered if she knew something that could help Sam–anything she said about Anne would be useful. He was having an increasing realization that he hadn't known his future sister-in-law very well at all. He went over to his brother and signed that he'd be back soon.

Patrice took Caleb to a small conference room. The navy carpet felt as thick as a pillow. Eight leather chairs surrounded an oval mahogany table which filled the center of the room. The walls, papered in textured gray, held prints by O'Keefe and Monet–probably selected more for color than artistic content. Beside the door, a smaller table held a silver coffee urn and black mugs, each emblazoned with the firm's logo.

Patrice poured him some coffee and he helped himself to two sugars. He took a sip and hoped she didn't see him flinch–

the coffee wasn't warm enough and had no flavor to speak of. A ritzy place like this, he expected good coffee. He set it down politely and took a seat at the table.

"Patrice, is there something you wanted to tell me?"

She drummed fingers against her mug. "I wish I could help you."

"Maybe you can. I'm trying to learn everything I can about Anne, to help my brother. Maybe you can educate me about her work."

"Her work? Nothing much to say about it. She was in our auditing division. We handle about two hundred accounts for local businesses, in addition to some regional accounts. Anne handled a dozen accounts, but everything's been pretty standard, if that's what you mean."

"Did you notice anything different about her lately?"

She took a long sip of coffee and looked like she was mulling over what to say. "I don't know sign language. Anne showed me a few things, but no one here could really talk to her, not like you and your brother talk. She could lipread, of course, but I could tell that was a strain for her. And her voice was strange, her consonants were never very clear, so she was hard to understand. It's such a shame. She ended up by herself most of the time. I had lunch with her once or twice, but I don't think she was very comfortable with hearing people."

Caleb nodded. "Lots of deaf people feel that way."

"Not your brother?"

"Oh, sometimes he does. He's what they call a late-deafened adult–he lost his hearing when he was a teenager, when he was already comfortable with traditional English. That makes his situation different."

"You don't look much like him."

Caleb grinned. "He got the looks."

"He is a handsome devil. Anne used to show me that picture in her office. She was so proud of him." Patrice leaned toward Caleb and studied him. "Now, *you* have an unusual look. I've never seen eyes like yours, they're brown, but they have those flecks of gold. Almost like amber. Very unusual."

Ah, the new millennium, Caleb thought. Women were empowered to flirt boldly, only he hadn't a clue how to respond. He squirmed, eager to change the subject.

"Relax," she said laughing. "I'm not trying to pick you up. I just like to study people. You seem like a sensitive guy. Softhearted. I'll bet you work in human services somewhere."

"I'm a counselor," he said.

"Aha! That's a perfect fit."

"For someone who's so fascinated by people, you've chosen a strange career."

She twirled the cross with her finger. "I was a theater major in school. Starved three years as a waitress in Atlanta, hoping to get on with a professional company. Then decided I needed to find a profession where I could at least support myself. Dad was an accountant, so voila!" She opened her hands dramatically, the theater-major in her sneaking out.

"I guess Anne got into accounting at Gallaudet College."

"Anne was a whiz. I mean it, you have a problem, can't get something balanced, show it to Anne. Inside five minutes she's showing you the mistake. It was a gift."

Something else he hadn't known about her, he thought.

"Did Anne have many visitors here?"

"Not really. One guy from over in programming, Darrel Lindler. He seemed to have a strange fascination for Anne. He'd send her e-mail on the computer, and stop 'round now and then. He's an odd fellow, but I think Anne felt sorry for him."

"Odd how?"

"Odd as in socially inept. We nicknamed him 'Eeyore' because he kind of mopes around, all dreary most of the time. Most of us avoid him, but Anne actually sought him out. I think she knew he was lonely and wanted to help. But not surprisingly, he misinterpreted it. I think he even asked her out."

"What happened?"

"She brushed him off, in a nice way," Patrice said.

"How did he handle that?"

"You mean, did he feel all rejected and go postal? Nah. He's pretty accustomed to rejection, I'm afraid. I'm sure he's harmless."

"Darrel Lindler was his name?" Caleb mentally filed it away. Maybe he'd get the chance to meet this guy.

"Yes. I think he's out today, though."

"It might be useful to talk to him. Patrice, do you remember anything else about Anne that might help?"

"She seemed more withdrawn, I guess. Monday, the day before she died, something happened. She came in my office after lunch, very upset. She said she was taking her work home with her and wouldn't be in that next day. God, I wish she had come in."

"No idea what upset her?"

She shrugged. "Honestly? I thought she had a fight with Sam. In another life, I was married. Before my wedding I turned into a real banshee. I picked fights with my fiancé just for the hell of it. I guess I wanted him to break it off, because I knew I wasn't ready for marriage.

"Anyway, Anne was a high-strung woman. I could imagine her stirring up some turbulence as D-day got closer. I thought maybe she wanted to work at home to smooth things over with Sam."

A woman appeared in the doorway. "Patrice? I've been waiting on you."

Patrice leapt from her seat. "Sorry, Marie. This is Caleb Knowles. He came with Anne's fiancé to get her things."

Marie's hair was tinted pale blond and looked to have the texture of a brillo pad. Thick makeup didn't hide the wrinkles that fingered out from sharp, unwelcoming eyes. Her navy suit had full-back shoulder pads, exuding power, with a capital P. She strode over to him and took a firm grasp of his hand. "I'm Marie Bagardis."

"Bagardis like on my coffee mug? Jeepers."

She smiled indulgently.

"Marie started this firm," Patrice sputtered. Her boss's presence seemed to have fueled anxiety. "Her partner was Elizabeth Skolnick, but she retired last year." She turned to Marie. "Caleb was just asking me some questions about Anne."

"I'm sorry for your loss," she said with all the warmth of an ice pack. "Patrice, your one o'clock client is in my office. He needs to ask you some questions about the audit report."

Patrice nodded quickly and shoved her coffee mug on the table. "I'd better go, Caleb. I hope everything turns out okay."

Caleb glanced up at his other companion, who made no effort to move. Caleb smiled up at her, trying to muster all the charm he could. "So Marie. Is this an all-woman firm? Just the one male secretary?"

"Not exactly. But all our managers are women," she said, sounding quite proud of that. Caleb started feeling sorry for the anemic little man who had showed them in.

"I have a favor to ask," Marie said.

"Okay."

"Anne was working on a report for me. I understand that she took some files home, and we need them back. Could you get them for me?"

He shrugged. "I could try."

"They're in manila folders, with green tabs at the top. One has a computer disk attached to a side pocket."

"All right. I'll take a look. How many files are we talking about?"

"Two. One would be titled 'Aud 'ninety-eight.'" She spelled it out for him, as if he was intellectually challenged. "The other would be marked 'CarolinaCorp, first quarter, 'ninety-nine.'"

Well, well, well. That was certainly interesting. He remembered Percy Elias saying he had met Anne at the office. But he hadn't made the connection that Anne may have known Bill Edinger.

"The files are confidential. It's important that we recover them as soon as possible. It wasn't really appropriate for Anne to take them home, but, well ..."

"If I find them, I'll give you a call," he told her. She smiled, all teeth, no cordiality. He was glad to leave her, glad to leave that sterile conference room.

He almost got lost trying to navigate his way back to Anne's office. The male secretary waved him down by the elevator and motioned him in the right direction. Pushing the door open, Caleb shook his head at Sam.

"Where you been?" Sam asked. He was leaning against the desk, pawing about in the boxes stacked in front of him. He looked relieved to be done with his task.

"Getting a foul taste of corporate America. Even the coffee here sucks," Caleb signed in quick, aggravated gestures. "I got to meet Anne's boss, by the way. What a bitch."

"Don't mince your words, Caleb. Tell me what you really think."

"Why was Anne home from work the day she died?" Caleb asked it impulsively, regretting it when he saw Sam flinch.

"She sometimes brought her work home. I think something had upset her at the office."

"You know what it was?"

"You met Marie. Anne had argued with her about an audit she was doing, but I don't know the particulars. I was up in Charlotte all day Monday, to meet with the owners of the Farrow Gallery about an exhibit. I got home late, she was already in bed. The next morning–that morning–she told me she was staying home. I was happy about it. I was in my workshop, sanding that new piece, thinking how great it would be if she worked at home all the time. I'm thinking that, while someone came in and killed her." He shuddered, trying to shake it off.

Caleb squeezed his shoulder and wished he hadn't brought it up. Sam grabbed a couple of boxes and handed them to him, then reached for two himself.

After Sam dropped him off at the counseling center, Caleb found Janice and asked if there was any word on Melanie Carson. She said no, but Matthew planned to check on her during rounds that day. She handed him a large stack of messages, so he took them back to his office and started to lift the phone receiver when Janice buzzed him from her desk.

"You have a visitor. I'll send her on back," she said.

Saved by the bell, he thought, dropping the notes back on his desk.

"What the hell happened to your face?" Claudia Briscoe asked from the doorway.

"I caught a flyball with my eyebrow. What brings you by?"

She sat, clicking long dark nails against the arm of the chair impatiently. "I was in the neighborhood. Hope this isn't inconvenient."

"I'm between clients." He tried to size her up. He used to trust Claudia, as a friend, as a cop. But since Sam's arrest, he wasn't sure what to think about her.

"I expected you'd be coming to see me," she said.

"You mean when you arrested my brother?"

"Well, yes."

"That sure was an impressive move by our men and women in blue, let me tell you. Arrest a deaf guy, charge him. Hell, go on and execute him. No need to investigate further, or like, find the real murderer."

She compressed her lips. "You just don't get it, do you?"

"Well, no, Claudia. I've been operating under the belief that it was your job to find Anne's killer. Guess I got that all wrong."

A chilly silence fell between them.

Claudia's face was a tough read. Her pursed lips emoted resolve, but the eyes seemed to seek peace between them. Caleb waited, letting the ball sit in her court.

"I can imagine if it was my brother, I wouldn't want to believe something so heinous," she said finally.

"No. You wouldn't. And if your brother had been falsely accused, I bet you'd fight like a grizzly to help him out."

"We've done our job, Caleb. You may not believe it, but it's true. I can't give you any specifics, but we have the evidence we need. The reality is, your brother committed this crime."

Those words felt like ice water in his face. "Dear God, Claudia–this is wrong. Real wrong."

"I'm sure that's how you see it. Let's say I'm not here as a police officer, I'm here as a friend. I want you to be prepared for what's coming," Her expression softened, like she was feeling genuinely sympathetic. Somehow, that really pissed him off.

"Maybe I don't need you as a friend right now. I need you to be a detective. I need you to do your damn job."

She smoothed down her linen skirt as she stood. "I can see this was a mistake."

"No, wait–" He held his hand up to stop her. "I'm sorry.

But please, hear me out. I've learned some things about Anne that you should know."

She hugged her purse as she stared down at him. But at least she didn't bolt.

"Look, two things you may not know. One, right before she died, Anne expected a visitor. Someone other than Sam. Three kids in the neighborhood noticed her on the porch, looking up and down the street as if expecting someone. And Sam was definitely inside at the time."

"Did anyone show?"

"The kids didn't know because they had to go home. But it might be useful to question them."

"And the second?" Claudia asked.

"The day before she died. Something happened that upset her. Bad enough that she left work early. Sam was working in Charlotte that day."

"Okay."

"Okay what? Have the police checked into any of that?" Caleb asked.

She wavered. Then she sat back down, opened her purse, and pulled out a notepad. "You know the names of the children who saw her that day?"

He gave her their names and descriptions, then told her about his conversation with Patrice Dutton. She scribbled down a few notes, then closed the pad and replaced it in her purse.

"So you'll look into it?"

"I'll ask a few questions. It pays to be thorough. But honestly, I'm not expecting any great revelations here."

He resisted the impulse to argue with her. "I'd appreciate any help you can give."

CHAPTER ELEVEN

He needed to check on Melanie, so as soon as Caleb finished with his last client, he headed to the hospital. During the ride, his mind sorted out Sam's situation, which never really left his consciousness. Claudia had agreed to check on his leads, but her attitude hadn't changed, she still acted as though the police had some kind of trump card that would seal the case against Sam. He wished he knew what the hell it was.

His head started to throb behind his eyes. If felt like his brain was in overdrive, sorting through all the disasters surrounding him. Anne, Sam, now Melanie. And he couldn't fix any of them.

He parked the truck in the visitor's lot and headed for the main entrance. A nurse thwarted his attempt to enter Melanie's room and shuffled him into the ICU waiting area. She pointed to an older woman, saying she was Mrs. Carson, Melanie's mother.

On a TV suspended from the ceiling, Montel questioned a lesbian woman about her marriage to a transsexual. Mrs. Carson seemed mildly interested. She was a short, round woman, with Melanie's fair skin but less comely features. Her eyes, nose, and mouth were scrunched in the middle of a pillowy face. She wore a sleeveless green blouse tucked into greener polyester pants. Chewed nails fingered an unlit cigarette.

"You her counselor?" she asked, when Caleb introduced himself.

He nodded.

"Damn. I thought she'd been spared this, Mr. Knowles. We got bad nerves in my family, but I thought my Mellie would be spared."

He smiled, relieved that there was no blame in her voice. "How is she?"

"The doctor don't know if she'll make it. He ain't sayin' that, but I can read between the lines."

"She's young, and strong. That's in her favor."

"It was my pills she took. I see Dr. Foster up at Baptist Hospital, been going to him for years. He tried me on that Parnate stuff last year, but it screwed with my blood pressure, so he took me off. I left the damn pills in my medicine cabinet, which was damn stupid. I should have flushed them. If I had, maybe my Melanie would be okay right now. 'Stead of in that room, fighting to stay alive."

"You had no way of knowing."

Her eyes were tired and mournful, like someone who had known loss, had been beaten up by life. Caleb knew about her abusive marriage, her own struggles with mental illness, yet there was no anger in her, no rage at God for being unfair–instead, she seemed resigned that this was what life gave her. She'd handle it the best she could.

"She come over that night. Melanie called me from work and seemed down or somethin'. So I said, 'Mellie, why don't you come by for supper?' I fried a chicken, which is her favorite. When she come by, I saw that she'd lost weight. Skin and bones, Harold said. He's my husband. He said, 'We gotta fatten you up girl.' But Mellie hardly ate a bite."

"Did she talk to you?"

Mrs. Carson shook her head. She twirled the unlit Salem and stared at it longingly. "Naw. She always kept things to herself when she was upset. Even when she were a little thing, I knew when something was bothering her because that's the only time she'd be quiet. Rest of the time, she was a little chatterbox, always cuttin' the fool with me and her big sister."

He could imagine it. Melanie teased the humor out of life, that was how she survived. She'd once described her mother's hometown in Arkansas as "the land of the singlewides and the double names" and a place where "the gene pool was missing some chlorine." Her ability to laugh had always served as the buoy that kept her afloat. Until now.

He wondered what had happened to push her this far. What had he missed? "She didn't say anything to you that might have hinted at suicide, did she?"

She shook her head. "I wish she had. I'd have been on her like white on rice, I tell you. I tried to kill myself once. Me and Harold were going through a real bad time, so I took some pills and downed a fifth of bourbon. It was a damn crazy thing to do. But sometimes you just can't think right. Guess that's what happened to Mellie."

Caleb nodded. Despite his efforts to pull it out of her, Melanie had always been vague about the details of her parents' marital problems, probably out of loyalty. "When Melanie was younger, do you ever remember her getting depressed?"

"Sometimes, I guess. She was a moody child. Like me."

"Did she get moody when you and Harold were having problems?"

She returned her attention back to the unlit cigarette, staring at it for what felt like a long time. "I reckon. Once when things got so bad, and I had to go to the hospital for a few months, and Harold had to take care of her and her little sister. I guess it was hard on Mellie. When I got out, she was all quiet like, and she wouldn't let me out of her sight. I think she was scared I was gone for good."

Caleb felt his breath catch in his throat. Early in therapy

with her, he had suspected that Melanie had been sexually abused, though she'd always denied it. She had some of the classic symptoms: gaps in her memory from childhood; denial of her own sexuality; a fear of men. If her mother–the closest thing to a protector in her life–had been away from home for several months, who knew what could have happened?

He asked,"How was Melanie's relationship with your husband?"

Her eyes shifted sideways to study him. Her lips parted, then closed, then opened to receive the cigarette, now bent at the filter. "She's always been his favorite."

The nurse returned and told Mrs. Carson she could see Melanie. She labored to stand, as though her joints had stiffened. "They let me in every half hour. Sorry you can't go. Just family. I hoped Harold would be here by now–he's late gettin' off work."

She walked Caleb to the elevator and thanked him for talking to her. She clutched his hand with a strong, powerful grasp. "You keep her in your prayers. She needs that. We all gotta pray for my girl."

When the elevator door opened, a short, wiry-looking man came out and approached them. He smelled of sweat and housepaint and wore stained, ill-fitting trousers. He peered up at Caleb and scowled.

"Harold, this is Mr. Knowles. He's been Melanie's counselor."

Harold's nose twitched like a rabbit's. He didn't take Caleb's hand. "Her counselor? The girl's almost dead. Don't look like counseling did her much good."

Caleb didn't respond. He stepped in the elevator, pushed the button to the lobby. The doors didn't hurry to close, and Harold Carson's eyes stayed on him until they did. Caleb waved weakly at Mrs. Carson, and the elevator finally took him down.

***

That next morning, the headache was back. Caleb had gone to bed early after a late supper, leaving Sam and Shannon to deal with the dishes. Morning guilt drove him to cook breakfast, but he had little appetite for the pancakes and sausage. Shannon had managed to scarf down her meal and then help herself to Caleb's uneaten links. Her hearty appetite wouldn't be effected by less than a nuclear war, Caleb often commented. After draining the last of her coffee, she kissed Caleb, grabbed her riding boots, and headed for work. She said she'd go to the stable later, if weather permitted.

Sam said he planned to spend the morning on his billing, which used to be Anne's job. Once a month, she'd send out statements for him, and though Sam said it was an unpleasant but necessary task, it helped to be busy. He still hadn't been able to return to the studio, and he was worried about a backlog of work there. Still, Caleb was glad that Sam was taking his time. No need to go back there before he was ready. Whenever that might be.

Caleb showered, dressed, popped a few aspirin, then headed for the office. He knew he had a nightmarish day ahead–Matthew hadn't hired anyone, so he was managing a hellacious caseload. He remembered eight appointments on his book for the day, and at some point, he needed to check in on Melanie. He wished the aspirin would do its job.

Janice greeted him with an enthusiastic "good morning" and he grumbled back at her on his way to the coffee. Undaunted, she followed him to relay four messages that had already come in that morning. She also told him that Melanie's condition was unchanged.

He took the coffee back to his office where chaos reigned. Stacks of papers, charts, and unfinished progress notes topped his desk and filing cabinet. No matter how hard he tried, which truthfully wasn't very hard, he could not get himself organized. God just hadn't provided him with those kind of genes. He perused the mounds before him and wondered just how far behind he'd gotten. The recent distractions in his life sure hadn't helped.

Janice buzzed him on the phone. "Mariel's on line two."

Oh great, he thought. A talk with his ex-wife was just what his headache needed.

"Caleb? We've got a problem with Julia." Her voice was cool.

"She sick?"

"No. But someone at her daycare told her about Sam. She's devastated. I thought you would have explained it all to her."

"I meant to. But I couldn't quite figure out how to explain murder to a four-year-old child."

"You're the therapist."

He took a deep breath to quell the familiar urge to choke her. "What does she know?"

"Oh, everything. She told me how Anne was murdered. She knows Sam was arrested. She thinks he's in prison right now and she won't ever see him again. She's heart-broken."

"Where is she now?"

"I took her on to daycare. The teacher said she'd call if Julia doesn't settle down."

"I'll stop by there and check on her. Soon as I have a break."

"Please do. Call me after."

He hung up the phone, feeling worse than ever.

After four clients back to back, he signed out for lunch and headed for the daycare center. Julia's teacher intercepted him in the hall. She was an attractive woman, in her twenties, with bright eyes and a ready, dimpled smile. But she wasn't smiling now.

"Poor Julia," she said, shaking her head. "She didn't touch

her lunch. She's not playing with the other kids. She's usually such a fireball, I can't stand to see her so miserable."

"Mind if I take her off for a bit?"

"Not at all. I hope she'll be okay. I hope you all will."

"Daddy!" Julia ran over to him, threw her arms around his neck and squeezed with all her might. He could feel her fear.

"Hey Monkey-face. How about a lunch date?"

She nodded, her limp hand reaching for his. He led her out of the building and they climbed in his truck. Caleb wasn't sure where to take her, and decided to try home. Maybe Cleo would help, he thought. And maybe Sam would be there and could help explain this new reality to her.

During the ride, Julia wrapped both hands around the door handle, holding on as though worried the door would fly open. Caleb played her favorite Beatles tape, but she didn't seem to notice. Her pained eyes stared out the window. When they pulled into his drive, he reached for her and she scooted over to climb out his side of the truck but her movements were stiff and mechanical.

Cleo heard the door and came running, her paws scrambling on the floor as she fought for the traction she needed to tackle them. She stood almost eye to eye with her favorite humanoid and exuberantly licked Julia's face. Julia patted her head and turned away. Confused, Cleo nuzzled into her for more.

"Wait here, Sweetie. I'll be right back." He found Sam mulling over bills and invoices in the dining room.

"Home for lunch?" he asked.

"Home on a mission. And I need your help." He quickly filled him in on the problem with Julia.

"God, I'm sorry. Maybe I should talk to her."

"That's what I was hoping."

Sam sneaked up on her in the living room. Julia squealed as he scooped her up and kissed her neck.

"I thought you were in jail," she exclaimed.

"Can you sign it, honey?"

Instead, tears came to her eyes. "Is Anne here?"

Caleb sighed. He guessed she thought that since her friend was wrong about Sam, maybe she was wrong about Anne's death. He noticed a cloud passing over Sam's face.

"Come sit with me, honey. I need to talk to you."

Sam sat her down on the sofa, positioning her so that he could watch her reactions, and keeping his arms around her. Caleb watched as Julia's uncle explained about death, about heaven, about grief. She listened intently, absorbing, questioning, and trusting his answers. Caleb signed for Sam when he needed to, but mostly they managed on their own.

"So we get to see Anne when we go to heaven?" Julia summarized.

"That's right."

"And you aren't going to jail?"

He stumbled over that one. Caleb interjected, "No, he's not, Sweetie. We're gonna find the person who killed Anne and send him to jail."

Sam shot him a skeptical look but didn't say anything.

Julia reached up and touched Sam's face. "Are you sad?"

"Yes. I'm sad because I miss her."

"Me, too." She slipped her tiny arms around his neck and squeezed hard. Sam held on, too, comforted by the easy love of a four-year-old.

Caleb glanced at his watch and remembered the long list of clients he had yet to see. Sam looked up at him. "You need to go?"

"Afraid so."

"Why not let Julia stay with me? I'll get her back to daycare."

"You sure?"

"I'm sure, Daddy!" His daughter piped up. Her eyes had some of the old sparkle.

Sam added, "I think we both need it."

"Okay. I'll call her teacher and let her know." He made the call, then left the two of them in the kitchen where grilled cheese sandwiches were in the works.

Back in the office, he had good news. Melanie was conscious, though groggy. The respirator had been removed. A series of tests were scheduled to check cardiac and neurological functions, but all in all, Matthew was optimistic and told Caleb he could see her the next day. Caleb finished his appointments with more energy, relieved about Melanie and about his daughter. Maybe life was starting to sort itself out now.

Shannon beat him home that evening. She'd fired up the grill and had burgers ready for him to cook. Caleb sprinted up the stairs, threw on some jeans and a T-shirt, and returned to the kitchen. Grabbing the needed implements and ground beef, he headed out to the backyard with Shannon following.

"You've gotten a couple of strange calls, Mr. Knowles." She wagged a pickle at him, then popped it in her mouth.

"Uh-oh. Was it my mistress?"

"Could be. If you've changed your sexual orientation since we last talked. No, it was some weird guy. He asked for Mr. Knowles, I said you weren't home yet, he asked who I was, I wouldn't tell him, he got huffy then hung up. Fifteen minutes later, he called again. Then again just before you got home. You piss off a patient today?"

He shrugged. Calls at home were an annoying but sometimes unavoidable part of the job. He mashed down on the burgers and fingers of fire erupted through the grill. "I'll be wanting cheese on mine," he said to Shannon.

She trudged back up the steps into the kitchen. A moment

later, Sam appeared, a plate of cheese slices in his hand. "Shannon sent me out. She said she was going to make some slaw, which scared me just a little. I remember the last time you left her alone in the kitchen."

Caleb set down the spatula and signed: "It was just a minor fire. More smoke damage than anything. Besides, her culinary skills are much improved now, thanks to me."

Sam scowled. "That's even more frightening. At least she won't be using the stove. She can manage a knife?"

Caleb thought that over. It was a risk, but the nearest Doc-in-a-box was only eight blocks away. Sam scrutinized Caleb's finesse with the burgers for a moment, then took the spatula from his hand. "You'll burn them to a crisp," he grumbled.

Caleb grinned, glad to be freed of cooking responsibility. He took a seat on a lounge chair, leaned back, and enjoyed letting his family do all the work. He'd only relaxed for a moment though, when Shannon stuck her head out the door and announced, "Your anonymous friend's back on the phone. You want to take it?"

He growled, signed at Sam that he had a phone call, and went inside.

"Knowles? This you?" The voice was gruff and vaguely familiar.

"This is Caleb Knowles. Who's speaking, please?"

"Don't remember me, huh? You met me yesterday. At the hospital." It was coming back. Harold Carson, Melanie's father. He remembered their exchange in front of the hospital elevator.

"I understand Melanie's doing better," Caleb said, trying to sound casual.

"She's holdin' her own. We're a tough breed, Knowles. We may not be rich or nothin', but we hold our own."

"I know you're relieved for her."

"Don't you start your crap with me, Knowles. You know what you did. You can't cover it up."

Confused, Caleb asked, "Could you tell me what you mean by that, Mr. Carson?"

"Don't play therapist with me," he rasped. "I know all about you. I called to tell you one thing. You stay away from my girl. I don't want you visiting her in the hospital or anywhere else. You done enough already. Understand?"

"I'm sorry for Melanie's condition, but I don't think now's a good time for her to quit therapy."

"That's just it. You ain't her therapist no more. I'm firing you. If you don't stay away from her ..." He let silence suspend between them for a moment.

"Look, Mr. Carson. I'll be glad to meet with you and Mrs. Carson and Melanie, and if together we decide she needs another therapist, I'll arrange it for you. But let's make that decision when Melanie's well enough to speak for herself."

"*No!*" he boomed, then he took it down a few decibels. "Stay away from her. I mean it." There was a long pause followed by a dial tone.

Caleb cradled the receiver, then glanced at Shannon. She was up to her elbows in cabbage and mayonnaise, and had apparently made enough slaw to feed most of western civilization. She looked over at him and grinned.

He smiled back. Whatever his concerns were, Caleb concluded, he didn't need to worry Shannon. Besides, Carson was probably harmless. Melanie was doing better. Carson just needed to let off a little steam.

Shannon dug out a forkful of slaw and slipped it into his mouth. The mayonnaise made a thick film on his tongue, disguising any hint of other flavors. He smiled, shaking his head. "Don't quit your day job, sweetheart."

CHAPTER TWELVE

"Dr. Knowles?" Caleb had heard the voice before, but couldn't quite place it. "This is Patrice Dutton. We met yesterday at my office, remember?"

"Sure, Patrice. But I'm not a doctor. I'm a social worker."

"Sorry. I got your phone number from Anne's old Rolodex." She spoke in a rush, as if she was very nervous. "I hope this isn't inconvenient."

"What's up?"

"You remember we talked about a guy who works here who had sort of a thing for Anne? Well, Darrel Lindler's here today. I didn't know if you'd want to talk with him or not."

He grabbed the Slinky off his desk as he thought about it. It certainly wasn't his place to question anyone about Anne's murder. He wasn't a detective, and Claudia had told him more than once to mind his own business. But hell, no one else was investigating Anne's death. He groped through the mound of paper on his desk until he uncovered his appointment book. He found today's agenda–it looked hellish. "The best I can do is around lunchtime. Will he be there?"

"I'll make sure of it."

Caleb sauntered through the chrome corridors of Skolnick and Bagardis, hands wedged in the pockets of his chinos. He decided this was an undeniably masculine-looking place, despite the fact that all its managers were women. Of course, Marie Bagardis seemed more than a little comfortable with her masculine side, and probably felt right at home in this steely atmosphere. It exuded a subliminal message, something along the lines of: "We can break your balls if we need to." He wondered if his sperm count diminished by a few hundred for every minute he spent there. He couldn't imagine how Anne survived such a place. Or why.

The thin male secretary smiled and paged Patrice, who promptly appeared. "Darrel's in my office," she said. "He's pretty nervous–be gentle with him."

Caleb shrugged, wondering what she expected. Then again, he didn't know how he should approach this man. Caleb wasn't here in his usual role of therapist, he was here to investigate. He realized just how much he was out of his element. He followed Patrice into the conference room.

Darrel Lindler looked like a scared little man. About five-four, he probably weighed one-thirty soaking wet. His skin had the pallor of someone allergic to sunlight. His eyes were far apart and undefended, and registered sheer terror when Caleb approached him. Chalky, thin hands clung to a book called *The Zen of Computers.*

Caleb sat beside him, introduced himself, and extended his hand, but Mr. Lindler couldn't seem to peel his fingers from the book. "Did Patrice explain why I'm here?" Caleb asked.

"About Anne," he answered, in an unusually high voice.

"Yes. She was a friend of mine. I'm trying to learn what I can about her death."

"I don't know why you wanted to talk to me." He tried to sound indignant, but the squeak in his voice betrayed him. Caleb remembered Patrice called him "Eeyore" and understood why.

"Anne was deaf," Caleb went on. "Deaf people sometimes

have a struggle getting by in the hearing world. She only made a few friends here at work, and I understand you were one of them."

"I liked her. She was always nice to me." This seemed to surprise him. Caleb supposed that Mr. Lindler lived an isolated life.

"In what ways was she nice to you?"

"She'd sit with me on breaks. A couple of times, she ate lunch with me." His index finger scribbled on the cover of the book. "I don't make friends easily. I'm shy, I guess. She never seemed to mind."

"Did you know her well?"

"I didn't know the details of her life. But I understood her. She was kind. And delicate. And very sensitive. I don't know why anyone would hurt her."

"But someone did. Any ideas about that?"

Lindler shot him a look of alarm. "No, I don't know who could kill her," Lindler stammered. "I know she'd been upset the last few weeks before her death. I wanted to help, you know? So I tried to take her out, maybe get her mind off things. She turned me down."

"How did you feel about that?"

"I think she thought I wanted a date, but I didn't. I knew she was getting married. I just wanted to make her feel better." He relaxed his grip on the book and wiped the sweat from his forehead.

"Darrel, do you have any idea what she was upset about?"

"I think somebody hurt her feelings. I came in her office once, she was on the teletext talking to someone. Her fingers moved on that keyboard furiously. Then the call ended abruptly, and she looked over at me. She was crying. I asked what was wrong, she said it was personal. She looked as frail as a wounded bird. She was trembling, which made me think she was scared. I hated to see her like that."

"Any idea who was on the other line?"

"No. I guess I thought it was her fiancé, but later on she talked about him and she didn't seem angry at all. A couple of days later she met someone for lunch, when she came back, she was upset again."

"Darrel," Patrice interjected, lifting a finger. "Your office is in the opposite end of the building. But it sounds like you spent a great deal of time with Anne."

His mouth popped open, as if he'd been exposed. "She and I were working together on a project, Patrice."

"What project?"

"She inherited an audit account and came to me for all the historical data we had on file. Some of the old audits had been coded wrong–it was a nightmare finding the right records." He squirmed again, clutching the book to his chest. "That data was entered before I came here, I would never make that kind of mistake," he said defensively.

"What do you mean?" Caleb asked.

"I mean, the files were entered under inaccurate accounts. All of them. We use a system of coding numbers that includes the date the file was opened, the account number, and the auditor's employee number. These files were stuck all over the place, under completely random digits. It was weird. Anne and I probably worked twenty hours to find them."

"You checked all the indexes?" Patrice asked, looking puzzled.

"Of course. That was the first thing we tried. Then we pulled old hard copies, to see if the file numbers had changed. Nothing worked. It made no sense."

Patrice shook her head. Caleb could see the wheels turning behind her eyes.

"What was the name of the account?" Caleb asked.

Darrel started to answer, but Patrice raised her hand to silence him. "That's confidential information, Caleb. And it has no relevance to Anne's death."

"But this is real unusual, right? For files to be lost like that? Did the police ask you questions about her work?"

Patrice shot him a look that said she wasn't about to answer him. Darrel squirmed again in his seat and said, "Can I go now? I need to get back downstairs."

Patrice glanced at Caleb, who nodded. "Okay, Darrel. Thanks for your help."

After Darrel scurried out Patrice stood to leave, but Caleb remained in his seat. "Was there something else?" she asked.

"I'm just a little confused. This accounting talk gets over my head. The files that disappeared ... that means something to you, doesn't it?"

She took her time about sitting back down. She ran a fingernail under her bracelet so that the charms dangled and clinked against each other. She looked like she wasn't sure what to say. "We don't make that kind of mistake here. You met Marie. She's a very detail-oriented person. She runs a tight shop."

Caleb shrugged. "So someone went to a lot of effort to hide something, right?"

"Honestly, I don't know what to think. But I'll be looking into this more."

Caleb reached for his wallet and pulled out a business card. He wrote his home phone number on the back. "If you find anything, I hope you'll let me know."

Reluctantly, she took the card. "Look, Caleb. That data is confidential. In your business, you know what that means. If I have some reason to believe it bears directly on Anne's death, then you may hear from me. But otherwise, I can't discuss it."

She hurried out.

CHAPTER THIRTEEN

Later that afternoon, Matthew had stopped by Caleb's office to say he was on his way to the hospital and invited Caleb along. They passed through the crowded hospital lobby and hit the button on Elevator C. The elevator took a slow journey up, smelling like old tuna fish. Just the thought of hospital food made Caleb's stomach revolt. When they arrived at the fourth floor, Matthew stopped by the nurse's station for a look at Melanie's chart and latest lab results while Caleb headed straight for her room.

Melanie, curled on her side, slept peacefully. A wide window poured blanching white sunlight into the antiseptic room, and Caleb wondered how she could sleep in all that glare. Despite the assaulting sunbeams, the temperature was about 65 degrees. He'd noticed before that the hospital kept its AC running at a temperature conducive to rigor mortis. Not a cheery thought.

Melanie stirred a little and gradually opened her eyes. The sunlight made her blink uncomfortably. Caleb went to the window and adjusted the blinds into a more humane angle.

"Well hello, Mel," he said.

Languid eyes slowly found their way to him. Her face was puffy, the pallor tinged in yellow. Creases around her eyes and mouth looked crusty. Her brown hair splayed across the pillow in greasy tendrils. She looked like someone close to death, which of course, she had been. Caleb eased over to her and sat beside the bed.

"Nice to see you awake."

"What time is it?"

"Eleven-forty a.m. Friday morning."

"Friday ..." She seemed to be trying to get her bearings, which Caleb took as a good sign.

"Yep. Friday. A few more hours and the weekend is upon us. You got plans? Going out dancing?"

She tried to smile, at least it looked like she did. "No. I think I'll be hanging around here a while longer." Her voice was raspy and low.

"Probably a good idea. Everybody loves hospital food. How are you feeling, Mel?"

"My insides feel raw. My throat hurts."

"And you sound like Lauren Bacall. It's from the tube, it went from your nose down to your stomach. They must have taken it out this morning."

"This morning ..." She struggled to sort it out.

"Yep, that's the good news. The other good news is you're doing very well. There was no permanent damage, from what I've heard. Matthew'll be in soon to give you more details."

Her eyes left him and took an aimless journey around the room. He wondered how she was processing all that had happened. "I wasn't expecting to still be around."

"You almost weren't. Are you disappointed?"

She closed her eyes. "I made the decision to die. That was hard enough. And now I know I failed."

Caleb reached for her hand–it felt ice cold. "I can't see you as a failure, Mel. You fought courageously to come back. Something inside you wanted to stick around."

A tear leaked out of her closed eyelid. "It's hard, you know?"

"What is?"

She winced, like suddenly feeling a wave of pain. "Sometimes just living is."

He studied her closely, wondering if she was still suicidal. If she was, he'd need to warn Matthew and initiate the hospital suicide precautions, which meant they'd move her to the locked ward and maybe put her in restraints. He didn't want that for her unless absolutely necessary. "Talk to me. What's hard about being alive right now, Mel?"

"My mom. Everyone. So worried about me. I didn't mean to make them worry," she whispered, her voice choking on the words. "I wanted to end my own pain. But instead, I hurt them."

"Tell me about your pain."

"I can't ..." She began to cry again.

Handing her a tissue, he said, "You can talk about it. Your pain lies to you and tells you that no one can understand, that it must never be spoken. But I'm telling you that you have to talk about it, that's the way you're going to get better."

She ground the tissue into her eyes. "It's never been this bad."

"When did it get worse?"

"After Mr. Edinger ..."

"I asked you before if anything like that had happened before. Have you remembered something?"

She started tearing the tissue into tiny flecks which she piled on top of the blanket draped over her. "Flashes," she whispered. "I remember things in flashes. A hand holding my arm. Hot breath on my neck. A dark blue shirt brushing across my face."

"How old were you?"

A shoulder heaved up in a half shrug. "Eight or nine."

"Do you know who it was?"

"I can't see a face, but there's something familiar about it." Tears welled again and streamed down.

Maybe it was too soon, Caleb thought, or maybe her defenses wouldn't let her look at the face. If the perpetrator was someone close, someone like her father, it might be more than she could deal with right now. "What else do you remember?"

"It's blurry around the edges. I smelled something sickeningly sweet, like bad cologne. And there was a fan, whirring and clicking. That's all."

"The flashes are coming more often now?"

She nodded. "I can't make them stop!"

"When you took the pills, were you having them then?"

"They came so fast that day. I thought I was losing my mind. I thought I'd end up in some institution or something, and I'd be terrified like that forever." She scooped some errant tissue flecks back into the pile. "That's why I wanted to die."

"I know this is terrifying you. What happened with Bill Edinger is triggering memories that you've kept buried for a long time. But now that they're coming to the surface, you can start dealing with them. That's how you heal, Melanie."

She flicked away the shreds of tissue so that they fell like snow onto the floor. "Well, if I had a choice, I'd keep them buried. This is really hard, Caleb."

He reached over and squeezed her hand. "If it gets overwhelming, you need to let me and Matthew know. Anytime, day or night, call the emergency number. You don't have to go through this alone. And I'd like to hook you up with a survivor's support group. It helps to know you aren't the only one who's been through this."

Her gaze shifted from Caleb's face to the door behind him. "Is my dad here?" she asked suddenly.

"I haven't seen him today. Does he know what happened?"

"No. I don't want him to know–he worships Mr. Edinger. He's worked for the family for years, you know. He's the one who talked Mr. Edinger into hiring me."

Caleb tried not to let the surprise register on his face. If Harold Carson had molested her fifteen years ago, and it was Harold Carson's idol who had continued where he left off years later ... Those questions would have to wait.

"My dad doesn't understand what happened. And he hates counselors and social workers–especially since he and Mom had to fight social workers to get custody of me and my sister."

Caleb nodded. "I met your dad the other day."

She made a feeble gesture with her hand. "Please avoid him, if you can. He blames you for this, you know. It's completely stupid, but he does. And he's not one to change his mind very easily. Stay out of his way, Caleb." She eyed him with unexpected intensity. He gave her a vague nod in response.

Matthew slipped into the room and came to the foot of the bed. "Hi, Dr. Rhyker," she said to him.

Caleb knew Matthew wanted to examine her, so he excused himself and decided to wait for Matthew in the small waiting area near the elevator. It had probably been a smoking area before the world got smoke free. He himself was about ready to restart the habit.

The elevator door chimed and opened, letting two men out. The shorter man spoke in an animated, loud voice that rang out along the hushed hospital corridor. As they passed the sitting area, he froze, recognizing Caleb. His jowly face oozed sweat as he spat out, "What the hell are you doing here?"

"Nice to see you, Mr. Carson." Caleb rose, but didn't bother extending a hand.

Harold Carson's nostrils flared out wide; his breath felt hot in Caleb's face. The taller man laid a restraining hand on Carson's shoulder.

"Easy now, Harold," Bill Edinger said. He looked at Caleb and added, "Harold here is having a hard time with Melanie's situation. It's understandable. That's his little girl."

Caleb eyed the unlikely duo. Bill Edinger was a South Carolina blue-blood, son of a retired senator. His prominent family had rooted in Westville many generations ago–Memorial Park had a statue of a General Wentworth Edinger. In contrast, Harold Carson's lineage may have included a grandparent married to a sibling.

Edinger removed his paw from Harold when it looked like he'd regained control. "Why don't you go check on her, Harold?" Carson grumbled what sounded like an assent and headed down the hall, but Edinger remained.

"You planning to see her?" Caleb asked.

"I'd like to. God knows, I've been worried about her. But her doctor's restricted her visitors to just family."

Thank you, Matthew, Caleb thought. Melanie needed time and space to heal. She did not need to see this man.

"I know who you are, Knowles," Edinger mumbled. He walked up close, crossing his arms over his barrel chest. His plum silk jacket emitted the stench of stale cigar smoke.

"Seems like we already covered that."

"No. I mean I know about your brother. You see, I worked with Anne Farrell."

Hearing him say her name made Caleb catch his breath. He couldn't think of what to say.

"I explained it all to Harold," Edinger went on. "How you've been distracted by your brother's troubles. Especially after his arrest for Anne's murder. I told Harold that was why you weren't able to help Melanie."

This was a conversation that needed to end. Caleb could wait for Matthew down in the main lobby. He reached over and hit the elevator button.

"Anne Farrell didn't deserve that kind of death, Knowles. I was very fond of that girl. Whatever drove your brother to kill her–"

"Enough. Don't take that thought any further, Edinger." Caleb's eyes held steady, but Edinger didn't exactly flinch. He passed a hand down over the jowls of his face and looked like he might yawn.

"Like I said," Edinger continued. "Anne's company was auditing us. She was in and out of the office, so I saw a great deal of her. Fact was, I was going to offer her a job. I thought we could use a full-time accountant, rather than contracting out with Skolnick and Bagardis. I never really liked that firm. A bit glitzy for my taste.

"Anne was different. Down-to-earth, no nonsense about her. And damn, she knew her business. Sure, she was hard to talk to. But what she could do with numbers, she was amazing." Edinger looked like he could continue their chat indefinitely, and Caleb was grateful when the elevator door finally opened and let him inside. Bill Edinger watched him closely until the doors slid shut.

CHAPTER FOURTEEN

Percy Elias looked shaky. He arrived on time for his four o'clock appointment, which for Percy was a bad sign. He took his usual seat across from Caleb, but his body stayed in constant motion. His hands vibrated with such force that he had to lace them together to hold them still. He crossed his legs in a gesture of self-restraint, but a foot bobbed up and down, kicking a side table. Each sentence spoken had little to do with what preceded it, and the words came out like machine-gun fire. Clearly, Percy had decompensated.

Caleb had suspected this was coming. The stress of Melanie's overdose, at a time when Percy's recovery was still precarious ... The issue was, how bad was he?

Caleb leaned forward and said, "I'm a little worried about you, Percy."

"Me? I'm okay. I mean, work sucks, and my personal life has no stimulation. I go to movies a lot. Did you see the new Antonio Banderas film? That guy is gorgeous! I love the accent. Where's he from? Spain? Where could I pick up a Spanish man?"

Caleb wrote "tangential" on his yellow notepad. "Let's get back on track, here," he said, hoping the timbre of his voice might reel Percy in. "You seem a bit jumpy."

"I'm energized!"

"Okay. How long have you been this 'energized'?"

"All my life!" Percy's eyes widened as if he'd revealed a profound revelation. He tilted his head and winked at Caleb. "You know, you're a good-looking man, too. I love that hair. You can't get that dark red out of a bottle. I know, because I've tried! And your eyes, that unique shade of brown ... they've been looking through me for years, haven't they, Caleb? You ever think of me like a man?"

Caleb didn't take the bait. "How are you sleeping?"

"Alone! No thanks to you. Really, I don't need much sleep. My batteries are charged, man."

Caleb nodded. His "batteries" seemed on overload. "Anything extra helping your batteries? What are you taking?"

Percy slammed his fist against the arm of the chair with such force that Caleb worried that he'd hurt himself. "Shit!"

"Easy, Percy. You know the drill here. I have to ask you that."

"*No*. I'm not on drugs. This high is *au naturel*."

"Okay then. Tell me how you're experiencing this 'high.' You aren't sleeping." He noted that on the pad. "How about your appetite?"

"Excellent! I could eat a horse. I wouldn't really though. I don't think you should eat animals. Maybe I'll be a vegetarian. Or a veterinarian." He nodded as though this was the wisest plan he'd ever heard.

Caleb scribbled down: "Loose associations." Then he asked, "How about concentration? Any problems there?"

Percy leapt from his seat and paced over to the window. It looked like the walls of Caleb's office could barely contain him. "That's a game show, isn't it?" He thought he was quite funny, and giggled impishly to himself.

"How's the job?"

Percy wheeled around and came back to his chair, then stood behind it. Leaning into its back, he made it rock back and forth, clomping the legs against the floor. He looked like someone strung out on crack, or someone in the apex of a manic episode. For Percy, it could be both.

Caleb repeated: "Everything okay at work?"

"Work sucks! That prick, Mr. Edinger, he's been down on me. He thinks I'm a little fag. Like he's some macho stud himself. I hate that bastard. I hate the way he treated Melanie. And me. And everybody. He owns the place, thinks he's God! We're his little puppets!"

"Did something happen?"

"Sticking his nose in my business! He asked about my coming here, what kind of 'mental problems' I had. As if it was any of his fuckin' business. I'm great at my job! Hell, I could run that whole place. Edinger's lucky to have me."

"What's he been saying to you?" Caleb knew his question was only partly due to Percy's condition and felt a tinge of guilt about his self-interest.

"He said that I'm not well. That I need to go somewhere else for help. Not come here anymore."

"He said what?" Caleb asked, not wanting to believe it.

Percy spun around again. He paced back and forth, like a trapped animal, from the window to the door. Caleb kept a close eye on him, half expecting him to bolt. "He said this is a small town. He said if I keep coming here, people will know my business. He said you had records of all my problems, my 'breakdowns,' he called it. He said you shrinks are the most screwed-up people in the world. Get your rocks off, listening to other people expose themselves.

"I told him you were the most normal person I knew." He punched a finger at Caleb. "He said you were as fucked-up as the rest of the shrinks and that was why Melanie tried to kill herself. Then he talked about your brother being a murderer—"

Caleb picked up his pen again and wrote down "Speech pressured." He was assembling a long list of reasons that Bill Edinger should be knocked senseless. He sucked in a deep, steadying breath, forcing his mind to focus on the issue at hand, which was Percy's decompensation.

"Percy, could you sit back down?"

He obliged, but it was hard on him. Manic energy surged through him like the tide. Untreated, he'd burn himself out after a week or so, a week of dangerous potential. Then he'd crash like a hard drive, landing in a pit of extreme depression. Suicide could happen anytime along the way. Caleb tapped his hand gently. "Percy, are you taking your medicine?"

"I stopped." He offered a wide, crooked grin.

"Why?"

"It was what Edinger said. And not just him, you know. Snake, too. He said I acted like I was crazy. He called me a fucked-up crazy little fag. I'm not crazy, I told him that. And I got mad, flushed my medicine down the toilet."

"All your medicine? Even the lithium?" Caleb asked, dreading the answer.

"All of it. I'll show them!"

"When did you see Snake again?" That was a dismal development. Snake's history of drug dealing, shooting up, criminal connections, sexual violence ... A big part of Percy's recovery was tied to leaving his old lover and that lifestyle far behind.

"He came to see me at work, you know? And, get *this*! Edinger gives him a job! So Snake's been around nearly every goddamn day. Helping on one of the construction sites. He's strong, and he can be a good worker until he gets a fix."

"Terrific," Caleb muttered.

"Not to worry. He gets paid today, so he'll spend the weekend shooting up. He won't be back." Percy started rocking the chair and banging his head audibly against the wall.

"How long have you been off the lithium?"

Percy's fingers started drumming against the arm of the chair. "Four days."

"I see."

"I tried to go see Melanie. At the hospital. They wouldn't let me in her room. I keep thinking about her, you know? I keep remembering her lying on that sofa, with the vomit on her sweater. I just couldn't get her to wake up." He shook his head, like he was trying to shake out the image. "And I think about Anne. All the time. I see her eyes wide open, dead. I see her in the coffin, deep in the ground, all alone. I can't do anything for her, you know. She was so nice. And she's dead now." His speech slowed a little; his eyes widened with sorrow. But a second later, he started rocking the chair forcefully against the wall. "Melanie isn't dead!" he said enthusiastically. "She's going to be fine! That's what that fuckhead Edinger told me!"

Caleb nodded. "Percy, I think I know what's going on here. Does this feel like a manic episode to you?"

Percy's green eyes flared at him. He rocked the chair back, then jumped out, nearly knocking it over. "You just don't get it! I've never felt so good. I can do anything, man, anything. And it ain't got nothin' to do with drugs."

In slow, careful movements, Caleb stood, slipped his hands in his pockets, doing his best to look unthreatening. "This has everything to do with drugs. I'm glad you aren't on the cocaine. But you're also off the drugs that you need."

Percy scowled at him for a long moment.

"Think about it, Percy. When was the last time you felt like this? Maybe April, a year ago? Right before we put you back in the hospital?"

Percy looked all around the room then back at Caleb. "Shit. Shit!"

"Can I get you to see Dr. Rhyker? He could probably see you this afternoon."

"You want me back on the medication. You think I'm crazy, too!"

"I don't want you back in the hospital. If we can get you straightened out now, maybe we can prevent that. What do you think?"

"I think you're pissing me off." He glanced at the door and looked like escape was imminent.

Caleb crossed over to him and laid an easy hand on his shoulder. "You need to let us help you with this. The fact that you showed up today tells me some part of you knows that."

Percy's eyes avoided him for a moment, then sought him out. He grinned feebly, actually looking relieved.

Caleb got him in to see Matthew right away. Matthew gave him an injection of Haldol and scrips for Lithobid. Caleb wrote down the "on-call" number for Percy and made sure the number found its way into Percy's wallet. This was Caleb's weekend to cover for emergencies, so he assured Percy he'd be available if Percy needed him. His client left the counseling center with considerably less exuberance than when he arrived.

CHAPTER FIFTEEN

Saturday morning sneaked into the bedroom. Bright sunbeams crept through the Venetian blinds to slash the walls and covers of the bed. Shannon stirred awake and nudged Caleb, who burrowed deeper beneath the jumble of sheets.

"I need coffee. Wake up," she said.

"Coffee's a good idea," Caleb answered in a groggy voice.

"Well, it isn't going to make itself. Get up." She batted pitiful eyes at him and he growled back at her, fumbling out of bed. At the top of the stairs, he could smell it. Sam was up, the coffee was made, life was beginning to look good.

He brought up a huge mug for Shannon and a smaller one for himself. He showered while she sipped coffee and perused the newspaper. When he finished shaving, Shannon slipped into the tub, saying she expected pancakes when she came downstairs.

Caleb let Cleo herd him to her empty food bowl and followed her instructions to remedy the situation. He refilled his coffee cup and had fired up the griddle for the pancakes he'd been ordered to prepare. When the phone rang, his ex-wife, Mariel, sounded irritated that he answered the phone. She knew it was his day to have Julia, she began. But their daughter had a birthday party at noon, and given all the confusion–caused by his family problems–surely Julia needed the diversion. Her tone irked him, but he had to agree. She said she'd bring Julia to his house from the skating rink at two-thirty.

Six pancakes later, the phone rang again.

"Caleb? This is Patrice Dutton. Sorry to bother you."

"No problem, Patrice. How's it going?" He flipped three more pancakes onto a plate which he put in the oven to stay warm.

"Okay, I guess. My boss, Marie Bagardis, you met her, remember?"

"Oh yeah. The power dresser."

She laughed nervously. "Right. Well, Marie asked me to give you a call. I tried your office several times yesterday, but your secretary said you were in session. I hope it's okay to call you at home."

"Sure. What's up?"

"Marie talked to you about some files Anne had. She needs them right away."

His conversation with the ice queen came back to him. He remembered being curious about the file on Bill Edinger's company. He couldn't help but wonder if it was the same report that Darrel Lindler had mentioned to them. "I'm sorry, Patrice. I forgot all about it. My life's gotten so crazed it's a wonder I remember to dress."

"It's just that those files are highly confidential. I mean, if one of your medical records was missing–"

"My boss would have my hide," Caleb answered. "I'll go by Sam's today and look for the files. Give me your number, and I'll get back to you." He wrote it down and she apologized, repeatedly, for the inconvenience.

Sam made his way to the coffeepot. He looked like he needed the caffeine. "I forgot to tell you. Phillip sends his regards."

"You met with him? How'd it go?" Caleb signed.

"You don't want to know." His brother sounded exhausted.

"Yes I do."

Sam took a seat at the table. "There's no news, really. Phillip questioned me long and hard about Anne's death–I guess he wanted me to practice defending myself. I didn't do too well."

Caleb nodded and signed: "How could you? You didn't see anything."

"No. The fact is, I can't begin to imagine why someone would hurt Anne. I just know I wasn't there to save her." Sam sighed, lowered his coffee, and studied his hands for a long moment. "We lived a simple life, you know? Anne went to work, she came home. Sometimes, we'd go out to eat. Sometimes we'd play bridge. Or visit a gallery. That was about it, really. Except one afternoon, out of nowhere, someone comes into my studio and kills her." Sam's voice had an unfamiliar edge to it.

"Do you get mad, thinking about it?"

"Are you being my therapist?" Sam asked with a hint of sarcasm.

Caleb shook his head. "I'm off the clock. This is more my 'concerned sibling' role."

Sam's eyes narrowed. "Do I get mad? Yeah. I've discovered a place in myself that seethes with rage. I feel pulled to that place, feel myself dancing around the edge of it. That scares the hell out of me. So I pull myself back, and sometimes even that's a battle." He winced at his brother. "Are you sorry you asked?"

Caleb shook his head, relieved that Sam was talking. "Maybe you need to feel it."

"I think it's too dangerous." Sam thumped his fingers against the mug.

Caleb asked: "What's getting to you, Sam? Is it the legal problems? Or is it Anne?"

"I miss her. I feel her absence more–in almost every moment I'm awake. I can't figure out how God let this happen."

There it was. Like their friend Stewart, Sam was a religious man whose faith had always been unshakable. But that was before the brutal murder of his new family. "Hell, Sam. I can't help you with that. I'm no good on that spirituality crap."

Sam raised his brows. "Spirituality 'crap,' Caleb?"

"You know what I mean. I'm barely this side of agnosticism. You need to talk to Stewart."

"I suppose. But Stewie's having a hard time himself. Even before all this, he was on the edge of burn out. The demands of his profession are even worse than yours, I think. The church is filled with needy people, and each one of them holds Stewart personally responsible for the void they feel inside. It drains him. Partly because he believes it himself. He feels guilty if one of his flock goes untended, but the more popular he gets, the larger the flock grows. It's become unmanageable."

"Can't he get help? Hire an assistant or something?"

"That would be up to the bishop. And Stewart doesn't like the idea of asking for help. He sees it as a weakness. Can you imagine that?" Sam smirked at the joke on himself.

"Not at all. Shannon calls it a 'Y-chromosome' defect." Caleb pondered his coffee and Sam's assessment of their friend. "You and Stewart have talked about this."

"Sure. Plenty of times. We went camping a while back and I hashed it out with him. But he's stubborn. Stubborn and burned-out."

"Too burned-out to help a friend? I doubt it. You should talk to him. It would do you both good."

Shannon came downstairs just as Caleb piled the pancakes onto three plates. She attacked her food with a fervor that inspired awe in the Knowles brothers, finishing her four and one of Caleb's. Sam poked at his stack and then offered the remains to a grateful Cleo. Caleb mentioned that he needed to run an errand so Sam volunteered to clean up. Caleb felt a little guilty for not telling Sam about his plans to scavenge Sam's house for the files. But Sam would want to help, and he didn't need that reminder of Anne's death.

A half hour later, Caleb pulled his truck in back of Sam's mill house. Retrieving the hidden key from under a planter, he let himself in through the back door. He made his way to the front of the house and opened the French doors leading to the studio. Everything there was as it had been before–the scars of violence seen in the wood fragments, broken glass, overturned pedestals, and, finally, the dried blood. The stains were darker now, the hue of chocolate, and seemed a permanent blemish on the once beautiful pale oak floors.

He turned to enter the small office where Anne had been working. He rarely went in this room, the space was so small that the desk, computer, and two chairs made it claustrophobic. Sam only used it for mailings, paying bills and keeping up with orders and supplies. Caleb dropped into a chair and started sorting through the drawers.

He found the files in the bottom drawer–two ledger-size manila folders, each about an inch thick. He opened one marked "CarolinaCorp, 1 quarter 99." Inside, attached ledger sheets held long lists of figures under headings like debits, credits, expenses, and recapitulation–Caleb would have been about as comfortable reading a manual on nuclear fusion. In the margins, comments and notes had been scrawled in red, most with question marks. Again, these made no sense to him.

He closed the file, and opened the other, marked Edinger, Aud 98. He found more of the same, except for a long, narrative portion on the back flap of the folder. This looked like a summary of last year's audit, with more hand-scrawled notations in the margins. The language of the text was beyond his comprehension. He wondered if it was Anne's writing, and he wondered what it meant. Somehow, he had to find out.

He remembered Marie Bagardis had also mentioned a computer disk that should have been attached to one of the files. He noticed a small pocket on the front of the first folder, but found it empty. He searched the desk drawers but didn't find the missing disk. He pivoted the desk chair to face the computer stand–a small plastic flip file beside the monitor held about a dozen disks, but each was in his brother's handwriting.

He eyed the computer itself. He found the disk slot and pushed the button; a beige disk popped out that read Aud98. Bingo. He slid the disk in the pocket of the folder.

Ten minutes later, he pulled into the parking lot of Westville Counseling Center. Though he'd promised to check on Percy, he'd forgotten to take Percy's number home with him. Inside, the clinic was eerily quiet; he found himself making more noise than usual, just trying to fill the silent space. He jogged up the stairs and opened the door to his office. After securing Anne's disk and files in a drawer in his filing cabinet, he retrieved his Rolodex from under a mound on his desk, found Percy Elias's number and dialed it.

Percy answered the phone after about a dozen rings. He sounded sleep-drunk, but gradually, he grew coherent. He was feeling better, he said, although yesterday's shot had made him sleep about fourteen hours. He planned on going to work that afternoon. Yes, he was taking his medicine. Snake had called wanting a favor and Percy had the good sense to hang up on him. And he appreciated that Caleb cared enough to call.

Caleb's next call was to Patrice Dutton's office. After navigating the voice-mail labyrinth, he left a message for her saying that the files were safe at his office and gave the clinic's address. He hoped she wouldn't come for them for a few days. Confidential or not, he'd need to figure out what the hell they meant.

***

Julia McElroy Knowles arrived at the house promptly at 3:00 PM with a full agenda for their afternoon. Despite the three-digit temperature and what felt like four hundred percent humidity, she dragged Caleb and a hesitant Cleo to the park for a half hour of swings, tetherball, and catch. An easy breeze only stirred the hot, moist air, but Julia was tireless and had to be coaxed home. They barely made it in the door when the phone rang.

"Caleb? It's Elaine Halloway."

"Hi, Elaine. How are you doing?"

"Okay, I guess." She wasn't very convincing.

"I know. It takes a while for it all to sink in," Caleb said.

"I'd like to come to Westville, Caleb. I was hoping to talk to you."

"Sure. When?"

"Now, if it's okay."

"I'll be here." Caleb gave her directions to his house and hung up, then leaned back on the sofa. In the kitchen, he could hear Julia coaxing Shannon into a Crazy Eights marathon. He closed his eyes, soon succumbing to a delicious summer nap.

Something crawled onto his chest. Startled, he jerked up to find his daughter peering down at him, demanding that he pour her a glass of juice. He wrapped his arms around her and glanced up at the clock—he'd slept for almost two hours. Shannon was surely tired of babysitting by now.

He rolled off the sofa so Julia could mount his back and ride him into the kitchen. Cleo assisted with the dismount, and the two of them wrestled on the floor while Caleb poured a tumbler of apple juice. Julia downed it quickly, wiped her mouth with the bottom of her T-shirt, and held up the glass for more. "You need to take your nap now, Monkey," Caleb said.

She promptly dropped to the floor and pulled Cleo down to

her lap, in an effort to delay naptime. Shannon reached down and scooped her up. "I think I'll sleep, too. Come on, Julia."

Caleb leaned over to kiss each of them and watched as they headed toward the stairs.

He piled hazelnut-flavored coffee grounds into the filter basket and had just started the coffee brewing when he saw the dark blue Mazda pull into his drive. Elaine must have left Charlotte as soon as she got off the phone with him. He opened the door for her and led her into the kitchen.

She looked rough. Her dark hair had been sloppily gathered into a knot on her head, a wrinkled cotton blouse was half-tucked in khaki shorts so narrow they might have been two-dimensional. She wasn't wearing any makeup, or if she was, it had been worn away by sweat and maybe tears. Her red-rimmed eyes were evasive. When she took the coffee, Caleb noticed her hand was shaking.

"How's it been, Elaine?" he asked in his therapist's voice. Sometimes those reflexes kicked in before he could contain them.

"We've had a tough time. My whole family, I mean. Some days, you think you're pulling it together. You think 'Okay, I'm getting better now.' But then something happens, like you run into her favorite Sunday school teacher or put on the blouse she gave you for Christmas, and it all starts again."

"It hasn't been very long, Elaine. You have to give yourself time."

"Yeah, well, I wish I had a dollar for every time I heard that! And those crappy greeting cards ... 'In your time of sorrow ...' 'Time heals all wounds ...' 'So sorry for your loss ...' They make me ill. They are so trite, so meaningless. And then I feel guilty, because I know the people who send them mean well, it's just I ..." her words trailed off, her eyes fell to the table.

"Is there something I can do for you?"

She shook her head. "Is Sam here?"

"No. I think he's at Stewart's. Did you want to see him?"

"I don't know. I guess I need to talk to him, but I'm not sure I'm ready. Hell, I don't know what I want." Her hands made their way up to her face and she rubbed her eyes with her palms. She looked like someone used to being in control, now grappling with a storm of emotions. "I just feel so guilty, you know? Like I should have done something."

"What could you have done?"

She sighed, and resumed her study of the table. "There's something you don't know. No one knows, really, except me and Trip. And Anne."

He leaned forward, curious. "What is it?"

"I told you about when Anne came to see me and told me about the baby. I said that was the last time I saw her, which was a lie. I saw her again. I saw her the day before she died."

Caleb waited as she took a long swallow of coffee, clutching the mug with both hands.

"Trip and I came down that Monday afternoon. We were at her house when she got home from work that day. Sam wasn't home; I think he was out of town."

Caleb nodded. "Why did you come down?"

"It was Trip's idea. He was so excited about Anne's baby, about the possibility that we could adopt it. She'd had a few weeks to think it over, maybe she'd changed her mind. Or maybe we could help her change her mind." She tapped the rim of the mug in rhythm with her words.

"You tried to talk her out of the abortion?"

"Oh, yeah. We were a formidable team. We donned our best holier-than-thou attitudes, we talked about how the baby was a little life inside her who deserved a chance. About how happy we would be, how happy the child would be in our home."

"How did Anne react?"

"She cried. She said we didn't understand, that she didn't have a choice." Elaine cleared her throat and averted her eyes again. Her voice dropped down to a whisper. "That's when she told us we were too late–she'd already had the abortion. There wasn't a baby anymore, she'd already taken care of it."

"She lied to you," Caleb said.

She nodded. "I let her have it. I talked about Dad. About how she had killed his only grandchild. About how Dad would be devastated, if he knew–"

"Did you threaten to tell him?"

"Not with my words. But she saw the threat in my eyes. It was emotional blackmail." She sipped at the coffee again but her trembling hand couldn't get the cup down before spilling tiny lakes of coffee on the table. "Pretty screwed up, huh? So you see, I have good reason to feel guilty. What I did to my sister was horrible. And that was the last time I saw her."

Caleb just sat there, absorbing it. He wasn't sure what to say.

"It's hard, not being able to have a baby. It's a primal drive, one I can't really describe to you. We've tried everything, and it's not going to happen. It's a lousy excuse, but we were desperate. So desperate I destroyed my relationship with my sister."

"Maybe you're being a little hard on yourself."

She shook her head. "You don't get it. My father is a rabid Fundamentalist. If I told him Anne ended the pregnancy, he'd never forgive her. Her name would have never been spoken in that house again.

"Anne was always dependent on our folks. When she moved down here, Dad threatened to disown her because he thinks it's a mortal sin to live with someone out of wedlock. It devastated her. You see, she needed to know her parents were there for her, that she always had a safety net. So if I told Dad about the abortion, it would be like cutting her lifeline. She knew it, and I knew it. Do you understand what I'm saying?"

He nodded, now fully comprehending her guilt.

She ran both hands over her face, then looked at him through the web of fingers. "So you're the shrink. How do I live with myself?"

He was silent for a moment. Then he offered, "You can set things right. Maybe start by talking to Sam. It may help."

"I want to, I'm just not brave enough. Should I go to the police?"

"Yes. They need to know you saw her that afternoon. I doubt it will help Sam's case, though."

"I wish it would. I love your brother, Caleb. I wanted him to be a part of my family." She finished the coffee and set her mug in the sink. Caleb noticed the tremor in her hand had calmed. He walked her to the front door. "I'm sorry to dump all this on you," she said.

"It's okay."

"The ironic thing is, I wouldn't really have told Dad. But now, he'll have to know. It will come out in the trial, and that's no way for him to hear it."

Caleb tried to imagine how Monroe Farrell would take that bit of news. It could make him even more dangerous.

"Stay in touch, Elaine." He watched her drive off, mulling over what she had said. Why hadn't Elaine admitted to visiting Anne before? Surely Sam needed to know, but it was up to Elaine to tell him. And knowing the dark truth about Anne's last days would make it even harder on his brother.

CHAPTER SIXTEEN

Sunday night became the boys' night out. It was Shannon's idea, and she practically shoved them out the door as soon as Mariel had come for Julia. Shannon needed the house, she said, and some peace and quiet. She had chocolate and wine and a girlfriend coming over–no men were allowed on the premises.

"Pizza." Caleb signed as best he could, maneuvering around the steering wheel.

"Chinese," he answered. The cab of Caleb's Toyota wasn't quite big enough for Sam's six-four frame; his knees knocked uncomfortably against the dash. He once commented that if he stretched out his legs, he'd poke out the headlights.

"Sicilian Pizza. At Montovia's."

"Korean. The Orient Express," Sam said.

Caleb stopped at a red light and pivoted. "Too expensive. Too quiet. Too red."

Sam scowled at him. "McDonald's, then."

"I'd rather fast."

Sam didn't answer, but pointed at the light, which had just blinked green.

"Mexican, then? Sancho's?" Caleb asked.

"You win. Pizza."

At the next intersection, Caleb added: "I want to stop by my office. I forgot something." He didn't tell Sam he wanted to get Anne's files, to spend some time with them before Patrice took them back. He hated being so damn secretive, but there was no point in telling Sam who'd just get mad at Caleb for meddling. Besides, it might unfairly raise his hopes.

Caleb eased his truck onto Lake Drive, where traffic was light. Sam stared out his window, the silence thickening in the cab of the truck. Caleb wheeled into his usual parking spot at the clinic, turned off the ignition, and faced Sam.

"What?" Sam asked.

"That's what I want to know. You suddenly got quiet," he signed, crossing hands at chin level, then pulling them down and apart.

Sam shrugged, but his eyes looked melancholic, avoiding Caleb's.

Caleb tapped his shoulder. "What?"

Sam rubbed both hands through his hair and bumped his elbows on the roof of the truck. "Shit," he muttered.

"Okay. That's a start."

"You mentioned Sancho's Restaurant. Anne loved that place. She dragged me there all the time. That woman ate like a horse, you know–as small as she was, she could really eat."

"I remember. We both fall for women with big appetites."

Sam sighed and commented, "I look forward to the day I can remember things like that and not want to slam my fist into a wall." He opened and closed his fist a few times, then asked, "You need help getting whatever we're here for?"

"Nope. It's a couple of files. Be back in a second."

Caleb opened the clinic's back door and stepped into darkness. His hand fumbled along the wall until it found the light switch. As he flipped it, he heard a muffled noise that sounded like something hitting the floor.

He froze. He didn't remember any cars in the parking lot. Matthew sometimes worked on weekends, but he would have turned on the lights.

Caleb heard another thud, then a voice, muted and indiscernible. Quickly, he flipped off the light and fumbled his way to the bottom of the stairs. He looked up. No lights, no sign of movement. Cautiously, he eased behind Janice's desk and peered into the breakroom. It looked empty. But beyond it, in the records room, he could see a thin, darting beam of light.

Why would someone break in there? There was nothing of value in that room. Matthew kept all meds and the petty cash in his office safe.

Breathless, Caleb flattened himself against the wall like he'd seen TV detectives do. Obviously, he needed to get help. There was a phone on Janice's desk–but it was so close to the intruders that he'd be heard. He needed to get upstairs, maybe to his office, and call from there.

A creaking noise startled him, then the door opened slightly. "Don't see anything," a voice said, sounding gruff and edgy.

Caleb remained frozen, but tried to peer in the room. He saw two figures moving around the room. One looked huge, like the front of a Mack truck, and the other was smaller and quicker. Two small shafts of light swirled around the room, then focused on something in the center of the floor. Caleb craned to see what it was, and barely made out a pile of cloth–they looked to be towels or rags or something. And there was a smell. Strong. Out of place. Gasoline.

What the hell? Why bring gasoline inside? Shit. These men were going to start a fire.

Think ... think! There were no weapons here unless, of course, the intruders had guns, but they didn't feel like sharing. Caleb needed to get to a phone and call the police. Or just get Sam and the two of them could chase these creeps out of here. Suddenly, the front door looked light years away.

Carefully, he slid down the wall to its end and advanced

toward the door. He tiptoed on the old wooden floor, and cringed when he heard it creak.

"There's someone ... hold it!" The man's voice boomed out. Caleb started running, but both intruders bounded after him. The smaller one caught up, threw himself against Caleb, hurling him downward. Caleb struggled to free himself but his assailant was quick and strong for his size. The other man grabbed Caleb's arm and jerked him up, hoisting him against the wall.

"Who the fuck is this?" he growled.

The smaller one came up so close that Caleb could feel his breath.

"Knowles. That's Knowles."

Caleb peered down at the smaller man shining the flashlight in his eyes. Immediately, he recognized Harold Carson.

"Look, I don't know why you guys are here, but if you leave now, we'll forget this whole thing." Panic rippled through him. He could hear it in his own voice.

The larger, unknown man tightened his hold, his forearm pressing hard into Caleb's chest. "Gutless prick," he rasped.

Carson looked nervous, his eyes ping-ponging between Caleb and his partner. "What are we going to do with him?"

The stranger stepped back, without relinquishing his hold. His eyes bored into Caleb, dark, cold eyes, like black glass. Eyes without fear. Caleb planted his heels against the wall for balance, then quickly jerked his knee up, hoping for direct contact with the man's balls.

"Fuck!" the man groaned, cupping his hand over the injury. Caleb pulled free and tried to bolt to the door. But Carson grabbed his arm, pinning him back against the wall. Caleb pushed up on his toes, hoping to use the shift in his weight to knock Carson off balance, but it didn't work. The other man moved toward him, looking huge and furious. He shoved his arm against

Caleb's chest, positioning his elbow on Caleb's ribs. Suddenly, he dug in. An intense, knife-like pain shot through Caleb's chest. He tried to move, but couldn't.

The man moved his hand up to Caleb's throat and knocked Caleb's head against the wall. "You die, Knowles. You die for that." He held up his right fist, clenched it, then opened it, then clenched it again. It looked like he was pumping air into it, making it swell. Caleb tried to pull free again, but the stranger held tight. Caleb stared at the fist, poised, ready. He saw a patch of blue on the wrist that blurred as it crashed toward him, pounding into his chest. His head bounced off the paneling as if made of rubber. The faces faded, his muscles left him. Like a broken marionette, he crumpled to the floor.

He heard a voice echoing in his head. He wished it would go away so that he could drift, at peace, along the murky waters of oblivion. But the voice kept screaming, louder and louder, calling him. He wondered what it wanted, and why it wouldn't just leave him the hell alone. Annoyed, he tried to pull himself into consciousness, but quickly reversed course. His head hurt there; his breathing burned his lungs. It was better to be asleep. If only that damn voice would shut up.

He worked hard to pry open his eyes. He couldn't see the source of the voice. He couldn't see anything, because of all the smoke. Just as well. He closed his eyes again, hoping to return to blessed unconsciousness. Hard to get there. Hard to breathe, with all that smoke coating his nostrils and mouth. His lungs felt scorched now.

"Caleb!" the voice screamed.

His heavy eyes blinked open, momentarily stunned by the bright yellow glow of flames lapping at the table across the room. Fire. The room was on fire!

Calm, he told himself. Be calm. He heard crackling sounds from the flames as they ate up the oxygen around him. He heard himself trying to breathe, to fill lungs hungry for air. But all he inhaled was smoke, thick and hot. He quickly succumbed to labored coughs that didn't dislodge the hot coals in his chest.

He needed to get out of that room. Slow easy breaths, he told himself. Stay low, crawl to the door. It seemed miles away. He could barely see it. The fire looked to be only a few feet from the door frame.

He pulled himself up on his elbows, head and heart pounding, and tried to slide forward. His body wanted to obey, but the smoke, thick as mud, made it impossible to see. There was no air left to breathe. The heat drenched him in sweat as he managed to crawl a few feet, then buckled. There was no point, really. He couldn't get to the door. It was too far away. And the fire was so close, it would take him soon. The darkness crowded in.

"Caleb! Caleb!" Sam bounded through the door.

Caleb raised his hand to wave away smoke so that Sam would see him, but only collapsed again. Too late, he thought. Just as well. He wasn't frightened, really. In fact, he felt no emotions at all. It was as though he'd detached himself from the experience and was watching it all from somewhere else. He would die. There was no reason to be afraid. There was no point, really. He shut his eyes and let the comforting darkness close around him.

He felt a wet rag slapped across his face. "Breathe, damn you!" He opened his eyes on Sam's blackened face. He tried to speak, but couldn't. He felt himself being lifted, Sam's arms carrying him like a sack of potatoes. Hot air and smoke swirled around them as Sam carried him out the flame-licked door.

Sam rushed into the waiting area and laid Caleb on the sofa. Immediately, Caleb pointed to a fire extinguisher. Sam watched him but didn't seem to know what Caleb wanted, so Caleb pointed again.

Sam got it. Caleb could hear the hissing spray, coughs and sputters from Sam, and finally, blessedly, sirens.

His brother returned to him, soot-covered and teary. "Fire's out," he gasped, grabbing a chair and bending over it to cough and pant for air. When his coughs finally subsided, he turned to Caleb. "You okay?"

Caleb tried to talk again, then remembered his hands. He shook his head and touched his right temple: "Don't know."

Sam took the wet handkerchief, now completely black, and wiped Caleb's face. "You're bleeding."

Caleb touched his lip, felt moisture where the blood trickled out. He felt the back of his head. The lump was soft and sore, but didn't seem to be bleeding . He forced a grin at Sam. "Thanks for getting me out of there," he signed.

"I was getting hungry," Sam said.

Caleb laughed, but it turned into violent, spasmodic coughs. Sam laid his arm around Caleb's back, supporting him until his hacking subsided. Soon the front door burst open and they watched the firefighters and EMTs pour in.

A half hour later, Sam and Caleb found themselves in the emergency room of Westville General, sucking on oxygen. Dr. Bryant Wheeler, a long-time friend and poker buddy, studied them carefully over his bifocals. Matthew Rhyker stood beside him, watching with obvious concern.

"Caleb was unconscious," Sam said, removing his mask.

"That happened before the fire." It hurt to talk. He must have been thoroughly scalded, from his teeth to the depths of his innards. Bryant had his penlight out and shot irritating beams of light into and away from his eyes. Then he felt Caleb's head around the lump.

"Jesus," Caleb exclaimed.

"Wouldn't hurt to get that X-rayed," Bryant said. "Let me take a look at your chest." He ran his hand along Caleb's ribs, and Caleb flinched again.

"Christ, Bryant! See if I ever let you do a proctological on me."

"Rib fracture?" Matthew asked Bryant.

He nodded. "All we can do is tape that. At least I don't see any burns. You're lucky you didn't breathe in any flames, my friend." Bryant turned to Sam. "How about you?"

"I'll live," he said.

Caleb pointed to the gauze the EMT had wrapped around his arm. "He's got a bit of a burn there."

Carefully, Bryant removed the gauze and studied the inflamed patch of skin. "Burns are nothing to play around with," he said, with Caleb signing for him. "I'll put some antibiotic ointment on it now, but come into my office tomorrow and let me take another look at it."

Caleb nodded, he'd make sure Sam kept the appointment. After listening to Bryant's instructions to rest and avoid exertion, Caleb and Sam rode with Matthew back to the clinic. The waiting area and upstairs offices had mimimal smoke damage, thanks to the steel door on the records room, but the files and the supply area were a drenched, ashen mess.

Caleb led Sam to the conference room. They sure as hell were lucky, he thought. The fire had been so close; he remembered thinking–no, *knowing*–that he would die. A curious experience, one to hang on to. One to remember until ripe old age, thanks to Sam. "You're mighty quiet," he signed at his brother.

"What the hell happened here?"

"That's what I want to know." From the doorway, Claudia Briscoe shook her head at the two soot-covered men as Matthew came up behind her. "You two sure are complicating my life these days," Claudia added.

"Sorry for the inconvenience. Next time I almost get killed, I'll try to keep it during your normal work hours."

"That would be nice. So what the hell did happen here?"

Speaking and signing, Caleb recounted his evening.

"You recognize them?" she asked.

He nodded. "One of them." He looked at Matthew and said, "I don't know what to do here, related to confidentiality."

"It was a patient?" Matthew asked, raising his voice.

"A family member of a patient. A patient in the hospital. You can probably guess who."

"Oh hell," Matthew said, crinkling his nose like he'd tasted something sour, "no rules of confidentiality apply here. You tell her everything you know. Just leave out specifics about our client."

Caleb nodded and told her about Harold Carson, including the threatening call he'd received from Carson at his house. She asked more details about Carson's description, and Matthew gave her his address from Melanie's record.

"What about the other man?"

"Didn't know him." Caleb gave as accurate a description as he could, but the light had been poor and his own terror veiled his perceptions about the attacker. It seemed like the man was nine feet tall and about as wide, but that couldn't be right. The one detail he did recall was the odd blue patch on his wrist.

"Could it have been a scar?"

"I guess. It was curved, but symmetrical."

"Maybe a tatoo, then," Claudia commented.

He nodded.

"What's your take on this, Dr. Rhyker? Why do you think Carson torched the office?"

He shrugged. "He's clearly angry with Caleb. And he's primitive. This may be some misguided protectiveness of his daughter. Maybe he started the fire in our medical records room to eliminate any proof his daughter came here."

"That makes sense," Caleb replied. "He seemed to view it as a shameful thing. How bad's the damage?"

Matthew shook his head. "Most of the records are okay because the file cabinets were fireproof. The room itself is a loss, but the fire didn't spread. Looks like they ransacked your office, Caleb. Though the way you keep it, it's hard to say for sure."

"Funny, boss. I wonder why they went in there?"

"You'll need to check and see if anything's missing." Claudia turned to Sam. "Back to the fire, Sam, how did you know something was wrong?"

Caleb signed her question and Sam answered: "I was waiting in the truck. Two men came running out the back door, jumped in a car parked across the street and left." No, he hadn't seen them up close, and he didn't think to get a tag number. The car was a beige four-door, and looked new; maybe a Ford, maybe a Chevy. Sam had seen smoke, and gotten in the building through the door Caleb had unlocked.

"How did you call it in?"

"I dialed nine-one-one, put the phone down, and went looking for Caleb."

"Thank God you found him," Matthew said.

Reluctantly, Caleb decided to take a look at his office. Opening the door, he gasped at what he found. The office looked like it had been lifted, turned upside down, and shaken. Books and files lay in disheveled heaps on the floor. Drawers gaped open like hungry mouths. A broken lamp rested precariously on an overturned file cabinet.

"Shit," Caleb mumbled. It would take hours of cleaning and sorting before he could tell Claudia if anything was missing.

Matthew joined him in the doorway. "This will keep 'til tomorrow. You should go home."

A while later, two blackened and worn-out men clambered into the truck. Caleb gladly handed over the keys to Sam, who asked: "You ready to head home?"

Caleb shook his head. The last thing he wanted to do was walk in his house looking like they did. "We'd scare Shannon shitless. Let's go to your place and get cleaned up."

Sam thought it over and said, "I've got a better idea. Stewart's place is only two blocks from here."

As they drove through the moonless night, Caleb leaned back, opened the window, and let the cool wind blow on his face. He tried sucking the air in, letting it soothe his scalded lungs, but that just fed the flame that still smoldered like hot coals in his chest. He closed the window and leaned his throbbing head against it. At least he was alive, he thought. That was good enough for now.

Sam pulled the truck into the tree-lined drive of the rectory behind St. John's Lutheran Church. They could see lights on upstairs in the narrow, two-story stone cottage. Sam rang the bell a few times and the door finally opened.

"Dear Lord, what happened?" Stewart Brearly, dressed in an open bathrobe and shorts, hurriedly ushered them in. His bleary eyes looked them over carefully as Sam explained about the fire and asked if they could shower and change there before going home.

"Of course. You both could have been killed!" He shook his head in disbelief, then signed to Sam: "Is there anything else I can do?"

"Lend us clothes?" Sam asked.

Stewart grinned and signed, "I think I can manage that. You've got about four inches on me, but I have some sweats that might work. Caleb, you'll be easier."

Caleb, still feeling scorched, winded, and exhausted, signed that Sam should shower first. Stewart guided Caleb to the kitchen and poured him some juice.

"You're lucky to be here, my friend," he said.

"Don't I know it."

"I can't imagine the effect of all this random violence in your lives–it's truly unthinkable." Stewart's breath smelled faintly of alcohol and Caleb noticed a perspiring tumbler on the table. Stewart smiled and lifted the glass. "I was having a night-cap. Care for one?"

"I better not. I need to keep my head clear." The throbbing between his temples felt like a bass drum banged by a manic percussionist.

"Would aspirin help?" Stewart queried.

"Nah. I think I just need to ride this out." He looked into the juice, wondering what to do. He needed to talk to someone objective, someone he could trust. He looked up at the minister. "You mentioned random violence ... I'm not so sure this was random. Anne's death ... this fire ... in a very strange way, they may be connected."

It seemed to surprise him. He stroked his silver beard with obvious interest. "Tell me more."

"I'd like to discuss this with you, off the record. My professional role here is overlapping with my personal life and it's damned awkward. I want to be careful where I go with this." Caleb put the juice on the table and leaned back. "What I say needs to stay in here, okay?"

Stewart nodded and commented, "I'm a minister, remember?"

"Yeah, I remember." Without using names, he described the situation with his client, the history of sexual abuse, and her father's involvement with the fire.

"He must be a pretty marginal guy, going to such lengths to

protect his secret." Stewart shook his head. "How does this connect to Anne?"

"The guy is good friends with Bill Edinger. Know him?"

"Know of him. Who doesn't?"

"My client worked for him at CarolinaCorp. And Anne had been doing an audit there over the past several months."

"Are you thinking Bill Edinger had something to do with the fire?"

"No. Maybe. I don't know. But he has a secret to protect, too." Caleb told Stewart about Edinger's harassment and intimidation of his client.

Stewart stroked his beard again. "I think it's a stretch, Caleb. Bill Edinger wouldn't be as impulsive as your client's father. He'd realize that burning her records wouldn't erase what he'd done. What would he have to gain?"

Caleb closed his eyes, his mind flashing back to the clinic. The record room was nearly destroyed. And his office looked like a tornado had hit it. What the hell did they want in his office? Suddenly, it hit him. "The files," he said aloud.

"Files? You mean medical records?"

"No. I mean audit files." He explained that he'd stored Anne's work in a drawer in his office. "Shit! I didn't check to see if that stuff was still there!"

"What can you tell me about Anne's files? Did she uncover something suspicious in the audit?" Stewart asked.

"Damned if I know. Something didn't look right. She had all kinds of notations and question marks in the margins, but it was all a foreign language to me. If they took them–" The realization winded him, and a spasm of coughs returned.

"Easy, Caleb. Take another swallow of juice. Where'd you leave the files?"

"In my file cabinet. The office was a disaster. They tossed

everything from the desk on the floor, they even dumped my trash."

"You keep the file cabinet locked?"

Caleb nodded.

"So they may not have gotten into it. You can check tomorrow. Did they trash all the offices?"

"No. Just mine."

"Any way Edinger would know you had the report?" Stewart asked.

Caleb thought about it. Patrice Dutton knew. Had she told Edinger? And if so, did she have an inkling of what he might do? "Maybe. Someone at Anne's office called about it yesterday." He leaned back, taking it in. Maybe the fire was related to Anne's files. Maybe Anne had uncovered something Edinger wanted to hide. If Edinger was desperate enough to have the building torched, maybe he was desperate enough to commit murder.

He felt a curious mixture of elation and disgust. This might help Sam—but how could something so horrible happen? What would drive Edinger to this extreme—money? Greed? Guilt?

"This could be good news for your brother, Caleb. Lord knows, he needs some." Stewart was smiling. For two weeks, he'd been a stressed, worried friend and now, for the first time, relief was evident on his face.

"But for now, keep it under wraps, okay? Until I know more," Caleb cautioned.

"Of course. So what do you do next?"

"Pray those files are still there. Then find someone to translate them into a language that mathematically-impaired people like me can understand. There's a computer disk, too. I have no idea what's on that thing. If something fishy turns up, I'll give it to the police."

CHAPTER SEVENTEEN

It was a long night. The coals searing the inside of Caleb's chest made it impossible for him to get comfortable. Every time he tried to lie flat, coughing spasms erupted, producing some grim-looking sooty phlegm. And when he did doze off, Stephen King nightmares invaded his sleep.

They came in a collage of technicolor images. He saw the flames surrounding him, inching closer, then lapping his flesh—he remembered holding up his hand, watching it melt like soft wax into the blaze. And again, there was the curious detachment. It wasn't until the flames slithered up his legs and around his torso that the pain came, and he opened his mouth to scream, but more fire came out where words should be. Gratefully, he'd awaken, where all the fire was gone, except the flame scorching his chest. Each time, Shannon shot up, peered down at him, asking if he was okay, wanting to take him to the hospital. He assured her that he was all right, hoping also to convince himself.

When morning came, he crawled out of bed and stumbled to the mirror. He didn't look as bad as he thought he would. A singed place on his right eyebrow looked a bit odd, but nothing else was immediately noticeable. He lifted his T-shirt to survey his chest. A huge, teal-colored bruise radiated from below his diaphragm to the bottom of his rib cage. He touched it, and wished he hadn't.

"Good morning." Shannon came up behind him and looked at his reflection in the mirror. "Mighty pretty bruise you got there."

"It is, isn't it?" He didn't recognize the deep, raspy voice that came out of his mouth, sounding like some cartoon villain. He lowered the shirt and turned to face her.

While giving him a kiss, she slipped under his arm. "I'm glad you're okay. You are okay, aren't you?"

He nodded. "How about Sam? He up yet?"

"Yes. I'm glad he's seeing Bryant. That burn on his arm looks bad to me."

"I hope it won't get infected."

"He says it doesn't hurt. But that may just be macho crap. You men and your Y-chromosomes. You going to work today?"

He nodded. "For a while, anyway. I want to check out the damage, and maybe call Claudia to see if they've arrested Carson."

She kissed him again and then busied herself getting ready for work.

Downstairs, Caleb found Sam at the table and saw why Shannon had been concerned. He looked gray and tired; his eyes were bright red and a bit swollen. Caleb noticed how the gauze on his arm looked wet, as if the wound beneath had oozed during the night. "Let me see it," Caleb signed, pointing to the burn.

"No. My doctor gets to see it. You aren't touching it."

Caleb growled and felt Sam's forehead, which was warm. He touched the arm below the gauze and it, too, felt hot to him. "You may be getting infected. What time's your appointment?"

"In one hour. I'll survive until then. How about you? How's your head? I mean, physically."

"I'm okay. I sound like Darth Vader when I talk, though."

He letter-signed the "Darth Vader" part slowly, and Sam squinted like comprehending him was a struggle.

Sam took a sip of coffee and flinched when the liquid hit his raw throat. All in all, he looked as miserable as Caleb felt. "You know, that was a close call last night."

"Did I thank you for saving my butt?"

"I almost didn't. That fire was pretty damn close to that butt of yours." This had clearly been a trauma for him, so soon after Anne.

"I never had any doubt you'd get me," Caleb lied. "But I tell you what, we need to live less stimulating lives."

He shrugged. "Mine will be less stimulating, once I go to prison."

Caleb stared at him. "Aren't we morose."

"We're realistic. When you get right down to it, nothing's changed. I'm facing charges for Anne's death, and we're not going to find her real killer. I think it's time I accept the inevitable. You should, too."

"Great." Caleb felt frustration surging inside him. "Let's review here. I have a client's father who wants to kill me. My office was nearly burned to the ground. Now my masochistic brother thinks he'd look good in prison stripes."

"Funny. Look, I need to get to the doctor." He stood, crossing to the door.

"Come by my office after your appointment and tell me how it went."

Caleb found Matthew in his office, surrounded by large stacks of records and disorganized papers. "How bad's the damage?"

"Could be worse," Matthew said. "Our over-zealous fire department made as much of a mess as the fire did. The records room smells like a chimney. But most of the files are salvageable. We weren't expecting you in today."

"I want to check out the remains of my office. Make sure nothing's missing. Then I'm all yours."

When he opened the window blinds, the destruction to his office looked worse than he remembered. The clinical notes, productivity forms, and reports that used to be piled high on his desk lay scattered everywhere. The Slinky and stapler from his bottom drawer made a tangled mass in the middle of the floor. "Damn," he grumbled. It had been a good Slinky.

He heard the phone buzz and, following the cord from the wall, located it under a chair. He lifted the receiver and punched the lit button.

"Caleb? This is Stewart. How are you feeling?"

"Like a chimney." He couldn't get used to the grating voice coming from his own mouth.

"Sam okay?"

Caleb glanced at his watch. "He's getting the arm looked at right now."

"Good. Look, I was wondering if I could stop by later. Maybe some time this afternoon." He sounded a bit tense, as though this was a strange request or something.

"Sure, Stewart. Come by the house later." He hung up the phone and returned it to its usual spot on his desk.

The file cabinet was overturned, but the lock had held. He used his key to open it, but the second drawer was jammed shut. Bracing his legs against the wall, he tried to heave it over so that the drawers faced up, but that bit of exertion made him crumple down in a fit of coughing.

"You need a hand?" Matthew came up behind him, and without waiting for an answer, crouched down and braced his shoulder into the cabinet, swaying it until it toppled over. With the drawers facing upward, Caleb wrapped his hand around the handle and pulled with as much thrust as he could muster. Finally, it gave and popped open; the two audit files and disk lay where he had left them. He lifted them out of the drawer and dropped them on his desk before Matthew noticed.

His boss lifted an overturned chair and sat. Caleb found his desk chair on the wrong side of the room and took a seat himself. "Janice convinced me to hire a few temps to come help restore our files. Looks like you'll need help, too."

Caleb looked at the dismal ruin around him. "I might have been better off if they'd burned me out. Then I could just start over from scratch."

Matthew grimaced. "The insurance companies would love that. They'd never pay us. You planning to stick around for a while today?"

He shrugged. "Hadn't really thought about it. Why?"

"You do what you need to. It's fine with me if you take a few days off. It's your call."

"I appreciate that. What's going on?"

"Two things that might interest you. Melanie Carson was discharged last night. She wants to come in today."

"Does she know what happened?"

"Probably. Claudia Briscoe called, she had some more questions for us. They already arrested Harold Carson."

"I guess that's good. We'll all be safer, with him locked up."

Matthew retrieved a small leather pouch from his pocket. The sweet smell of tobacco wafted through the air as he packed the pipe and lit it. "Maybe I should see Melanie today."

"I'm up to it," Caleb answered. "She's just beginning to deal with the abuse issues. I don't think a change is what she needs right now."

Matthew squinted over the fingers of blue smoke. His gaze on Caleb probed past their words. "You need to think this through. Say you do see Melanie. She knows her Dad was arrested. Maybe she's upset. Or angry. What if she defends him? Given what he did to you–how would that feel?"

He hadn't thought of that. In his mind, Harold Carson was an animal, plain and simple. But Melanie would feel differently–she may even be deeply hurt about the arrest. "Truthfully, I can't be too empathetic when it comes to Mr. Carson."

"I'll see Melanie, then. I'll let you know how it goes." He took a long, deliberate drag on the pipe and continued to study Caleb pensively. "Why don't you take the day off?"

"Seems like you're mighty anxious to get rid of me."

Matthew leaned forward, his elbows resting on his knees. "Well, my friend, I'm a bit worried about you. Think of the past three weeks. You've had more trauma than most people have in ten years. You're holding it together very well, considering."

"I hear a 'but' coming."

"But you're a lot like me. You suck in your feelings in some sort of misguided attempt at stoicism," Matthew said with unusual candor.

"Quit that high-falutin' doctor talk."

"Somehow, I don't think you're taking me serious. I'm genuinely concerned about you." His dark eyes said he meant it.

Caleb took in a deep breath that aggravated his seared insides, and erupted into another series of hacks. It was as if the soot had deposited itself so deep in his lungs that no matter how hard he coughed, it wouldn't come out.

"Sorry–this sure isn't helping." Matthew quickly dumped his pipe into the ashtray Caleb had gotten out and crushed out the smoldering tobacco.

"I don't know if you're trying to do a mental status exam on me," Caleb said, "but, if you are, I'll cut to the chase. No significant signs of depression, except for nightmares that might have been written by Wes Craven. Other than that, I'm okay–sort of on automatic pilot."

Matthew nodded, taking his time about replacing his pipe in its pouch. "Automatic pilot can be a good idea, at times."

"So I want to work. If I have problems with it, I'll let you know. If you see I'm having problems that I'm unaware of, you have my permission to knock the sense into me. Deal?"

"Deal. How's the rest of your household holding up?"

"Shannon's great. Sam's another story."

"He's had a devastating few weeks."

"Yes. And he thinks he's going to prison, which is more depressing than I can say. Nothing looks good to him—he looks back, he remembers Anne and feels that loss. He looks forward, he sees prison bars. And if he goes to prison, Matthew—I mean, Sam's a big guy and all, but he's deaf, and I imagine him locked up in a nest of primitive, antisocial personality disorders. He'd be vulnerable to—" saying it made it seem more real than ever before. He became aware of a lump working its way up his throat.

"That's the worst case, Caleb. He may not go to prison."

"I know, I know. I want to think we'll find the real killer. Because Sam won't survive it, Matthew. He won't survive prison."

"I don't know about that." Matthew stood, stretched, and approached the door. "Seems to me we often surprise ourselves by what we can survive."

Caleb watched him leave and reached for the audit files. He opened one folder and glanced through the long column of numbers. They meant nothing to him. His mother had smoked during pregnancy, which probably accounted for his mathematical deficits.

He flipped to the middle of the file and found a sheet that looked like a budget summary. Personnel expenses, contractual payments, and supply costs made long columns of numbers, some highlighted in red. At the far right of the sheet was the heading "Miscellaneous Expenses" and Caleb scowled down at the figures listed below it. Each amount was significantly larger than any other recorded sum. He noticed Anne's writing in the margin where she seemed to be questioning the validity of the charges–the miscellaneous expenditures totaled 1.4 million, nearly four times the supply and personnel costs combined. Something didn't seem right about it, but he couldn't tell from Anne's comments exactly what it meant. He needed help.

The phone book had been tossed under a chair. He lifted it, found the number for Skolnick and Bagardis, and dialed. "Patrice Dutton, please," he said to the receptionist.

A second later, a buoyant voice answered, "Patrice Dutton here."

"Hey, Patrice. This is Caleb Knowles. Remember me?"

"I was going to call you today. Can I come for Anne's files?"

"Sure. Come on by now, if you want." He gave her the address and hung up the phone. He felt a little guilty about misleading her, but concluded it was best to see her face to face and decide if he could trust her.

Janice stuck her head in Caleb's door and grimaced. "I didn't think your office could look any worse. I'd be glad to tackle that desk and get you straightened out."

It had been an ongoing debate between them. Janice saw it as her job to keep him organized. Caleb saw his office as a private inner sanctum. He thrived in the chaos that drove her to near madness–she handled it the way a parent copes with an adolescent's bedroom: She kept the door closed and pretended the mess wasn't there.

"There is method to my madness, you know," Caleb said.

"Ahuh." She raised her drawn-on eyebrows at him.

"Do me a favor?" Caleb asked, holding up the audit files. "Make copies of all this for me."

"Sure," she said, taking them. "And you have a visitor. Matthew said you weren't seeing clients today, so I'll have her wait to see him if you want. It's Ellen Campbell."

"She isn't due in until next week," he said, perplexed. They were lucky if Ellen made it to half of her scheduled appointments. He remembered her last visit–the job application with a threatening reference to a squirt gun. He was with Ellen when the police called about Anne's murder. "I'll see her. Bring her to the conference room."

Janice escorted Ellen to Caleb and winked as she handed him the copied files. Caleb tried not to grin back. Ellen had on a leather hat with yellow and orange ribbons tied around its brim. She wore a red blouse over a black blouse and a vinyl raincoat over both. A chartreuse polyester miniskirt was not too flattering to her pear-shaped figure, and the red stockings clashed with shiny pink heels that didn't look very comfortable. She balanced precariously as she found her way to a chair by the conference table.

"This is a nice surprise," Caleb said. "How are you, Ellen?"

She grinned. "You sound funny."

"I know I do." The rasp in his voice seemed to worsen as the day wore on.

"I don't get my shot today, do I?"

"Nope. You aren't scheduled until next week. So you just get to see me. What brings you here?"

"My mom's new Continental," she answered.

Again, he tried not to show his amusement. Ellen's concrete mind was doing its best.

"So why did she bring you here? You having a problem?"

She swung her legs back and forth with uncharacteristic zeal. He noticed an inch-wide run in the pantyhose. "Mom and I ate out last night. We had Chinese food at The Mandarin."

Okay, they'd take the long route to finding out why she was here. "Up on Calhoun Street?"

"Yep. I had shrimp fried rice. And an egg roll."

"You and your mom?"

"No, Mom had soup and beef lo mein." She nodded her head, the ribbons that dangled from the hat tossed about. "We took a shortcut home. We drove down this street."

Now it was starting to make sense. "What time, Ellen?"

"About eight-fifteen. It was dark and smoky. And very loud."

"You came by here and saw smoke? Did you see fire trucks?"

She nodded and the ribbons bobbed back and forth. "Oh yeah. And the police car. And the ambulance." She marked off each vehicle with a finger.

"Well, then you got to see all the excitement. We had a fire here last night."

"Mama wouldn't let me out of the car," she said, her voice rising to a higher pitch. "I saw your truck, Caleb. In the parking lot." She looked at him with an unexpected clarity that touched him. Ellen had seen his truck and knew he was there, in the fire.

"Yeah, I was here. That's why I talk funny–I got smoke in my chest. Did you think something had happened to me?"

Her eyes closed tightly like they always did when things got uncomfortable.

He leaned over and said, "Well, I'm fine. And the clinic's going to be okay. I hope it didn't scare you."

"I don't like the food in the hospital. Sometimes it tastes like poison. And the bugs ..."

Perplexed again, Caleb tried to imagine what bounced around behind her eyes. She mentioned the hospital ... because she saw the ambulance? "It's been almost a year since you went to the hospital."

"You said if I come here, I don't have to go. You said if I

take my pills and see Dr. Rhyker and come see you–" She stopped, studying him.

He smiled at her, understanding now. She relied on him, on this place, to keep her stable. If something happened to Caleb–or if the clinic burned–then she feared she'd be returned to an institution. Some were better than others, but Ellen had spent five years in a horrendous ward of a state facility.

"You're right. As long as you stay on your medicine and see the doctor regularly, you may keep yourself out of the hospital. If for any reason you can't see me, Ellen, there's always Dr. Rhyker. No matter what, we'll make sure you get your medicine so that you can stay out of the hospital."

She popped her eyes open and grinned again, shedding her anxiety.

"So Ellen. You and I talked last time about you getting a job. You still thinking about that?"

She nodded eagerly. "My brother drives a truck. My mama sells insurance."

And she wanted to be like them. She wanted to feel productive, to bring home a paycheck, to have a taste of normalcy in her otherwise off-center life. "You and I have talked about a rehabilitation center. Have you given that more thought?"

She pursed her lips. "Sometimes I don't do real well around other people."

"You do great with me. I think you should try it. They might train you to do a part-time job. Lots of people with mental illness work, and I don't see why you couldn't be one of them."

Suddenly, she relaxed and her expression became more "normal" than ever before. "Really?"

"Yes. I'll make some calls. We can talk more about it next week."

Ellen stood up, straightened her skirt, and coyly cocked her head to one side. "You be good, now," she said.

"You too, Ellen." He smiled as she hobbled out of the office.

Caleb returned to his office and began the difficult task of reassembling. He gathered the papers from the floor and stacked them in piles. The clinical notes went in a desk organizer for filing when the medical records were reassembled. The statistical reports, already two months overdue, were shoved in a drawer for continued neglect.

"What happened here?"

He pivoted his desk chair and found Patrice Dutton at his door. She wore dark knit pants and an olive floral top that nicely complemented her eyes. A heavy gold coin dangled from a thick chain around her neck, gold hoop earrings sparkled inside her thick gray curls. "Did you have a fire?" she asked.

He motioned her inside and freed a chair for her. "Yep. Last night."

She looked around at the chaos and shook her head. "Was anyone hurt?"

"Just me and my brother. But we survived." Caleb relayed the story of the arson and being rescued by Sam.

"You're lucky to be alive. Do they know who did it?"

"They have a pretty good idea. Which brings me to why I wanted to see you." He handed her the files. "They may have been after this."

"What? Anne's report? Why?"

"You tell me."

She opened a folder and her eyes darted back and forth between the columns of numbers. She turned a page, nimble fingers tracing a long line of figures. She hesitated, then asked, "Can I see the other file?"

Caleb nodded and handed it to her. She perused the ledger

sheets, her eyes bouncing back and forth between columns of numbers. After a moment, she shook her head. "I need to take these to the office. I'd like to run the figures on my computer and see what turns up."

Caleb held up his hand. "I'm not ready for you to take them yet, Patrice. From what I can tell, Anne may have uncovered something wrong with the CarolinaCorp account."

Again, she looked down at the reports. Her face was a tough read.

"Who knew I had her reports here?" Caleb asked. " Who did you tell?"

She shook her head. "No one except Marie. She called Sunday morning about them."

"I'll bet she did. CarolinaCorp is owned by Bill Edinger and I know a little bit about him. He's one sick son of a bitch. He may be responsible for the fire because he wanted these records burned. Do you see what I'm getting at?"

Her eyes widened at him. "You think he was embezzling? And if Anne found out about it ..."

He lifted a finger to stop her. "Look, I don't know anything for sure. But if he was embezzling and the proof's right there in your hands, then I need to take it to the police."

She stared down at the ledgers, a frightened look on her face. Her hands squeezed them so hard that her knuckles whitened. "Anne may have been killed because of these," she said, as if trying to make it sink in.

"Maybe. But I won't know until I find out what's in there. Which is why I need your help."

She uncurled her fingers from their death grip on the files. "Marie wants these returned as soon as possible. They are our property, Caleb. You can't keep them."

"I understand that. But can you at least take a look at them? Before you give them to Marie?"

She looked wary. "I don't know–"

Caleb reached over and squeezed her hand. "I know I'm asking a lot. But my brother's future is at stake. You could say I'm desperate. Can't you take the books home for a few hours, then give me a call? If you don't find anything, you can turn them over to Marie like nothing happened. But if you do find something–and I think you will–you may be saving Sam's life."

She gave him a tentative nod. "I like your brother. I'd like to help if I can."

Caleb opened a drawer and pulled out the computer disk. "You'll need this, too. Can you get back to me soon?"

"You'll hear from me later today."

"If I'm not here, try me at home," he said, tapping his cracked ribs. "I plan on making this a short day."

CHAPTER EIGHTEEN

Later that afternoon, Caleb turned off the tape player that had blared Bonnie Raitt at him during the two hours he spent re-assembling his office. He felt limp with fatigue, and the pain in his chest seemed to worsen with exertion. He'd never been one to nap, but he could hear his bed summoning him from across town. Maybe a stiff drink, followed by an hour of uninterrupted sleep, then maybe a good meal, then more sleep.

He also needed to check on his wayward brother. Sam hadn't come by after the doctor visit, and that arm had Caleb worried. Not to mention Sam's emotional state, and the precariousness of his sobriety ... Stop it. No need to assume the worst.

Caleb arched his cramped back and surveyed his progress. The furniture was back in place, the drawers had been restored in his desk and file cabinets. Overall, the office was as presentable as it ever was. He hit the light switch on his way out the door.

Three hours later, the doorbell woke him. Not that the nap had been all that refreshing. Each time he closed his eyes, the nightmares overpowered him. He didn't remember the details, but he vividly remembered his terror, grabbing at his chest like a claw. Waking up brought relief.

The sleep had deadened his nerves. He stared at the clock, confused that it said 5:00 PM when it felt like morning. The doorbell clanged again. Stiff limbs flailed to free him from the covers until finally his feet found the floor and carried the reluctant rest of him downstairs. It was when he opened the door and greeted the pastor on his porch that he remembered inviting Stewart to stop by. "Come on in."

Stewart looked rough. He forced a weak smile and followed Caleb inside. "Your brother here?"

Caleb shook his head. "Haven't seen him. Why?"

"I got another call from Monroe Farrell this morning. He thought Sam was still staying with me. He knows Anne was pregnant. He says Sam killed his grandchild, too."

"Shit."

"Monroe says he's coming down. He wants to see Sam."

Caleb let out a deflating sigh. "We probably need to frisk him at the door."

Stewart arched his brows and said, "Don't kid about it. I do think he's capable of violence. You didn't hear him on the phone."

Caleb shook his head. He thought about Harold Carson's primitive instinct to protect his daughter, and the violence and destruction that resulted. Monroe's daughter was gone, and Caleb had seen, first hand, the same primitive rage on Monroe's face. "What do you think we should do?"

"I convinced him to wait a few days then to come by the church, so I can try to talk some sense into him. But Sam needs to keep a low profile until he's gone."

Caleb nodded, glancing at his watch: 5:15. Sam had gone to the doctor that morning, and hadn't come home since. "I wish I knew where the hell he was."

The phone rang. "Caleb? Patrice Dutton here." She spoke loudly over bursts of static.

"Hey Patrice," Caleb practically yelled.

"I'm in the car. Can I come by? I have something to show you."

"Sure. I live over in Westville." He gave her directions and she said she'd be there in ten minutes. He hung up the phone and turned to Stewart. "Can I get you something to drink?"

He nodded, following Caleb to the kitchen. Caleb handed him a beer and grabbed a soda for himself.

Stewart took a few quick gulps from the Coors bottle like someone close to dehydration.

"You okay?"

"I can't stop thinking about Anne. She was such a beautiful woman. And a beautiful spirit. This is just so tragic."

"Yes, it is. This is hard for all of us. Especially Sam."

Stewart nodded, tears glistening in his dark blue eyes. "She would have been such a wonderful mother. Despite her disability, she would have made a fine mother and a great home for her child. I'm sure of it." He took another swallow. When the doorbell rang, it seemed to startle him and he wiped his eyes.

"Stick around, Stewart. This may be good news for us." They returned to the living room and Caleb answered the door.

Patrice Dutton held a fat briefcase and laptop computer. She wasn't smiling.

"Come on in, Patrice." He led her into the living room and Stewart stood to greet her.

Awkwardly, Patrice shook his hand as Caleb made introductions. "If this is a bad time–"

"No, it's fine. Come on in and have a seat."

She entered, surveying the surroundings. She moved to the sofa and sat, pulling one leg up under her with surprising agility. After an awkward moment, she turned to Stewart and said, "Have we met before?"

"Perhaps. Where might we have met?"

She shook her head, looking puzzled. "You look familiar, but I can't figure out how I know you."

Caleb couldn't tell if she was flirting, or if she really did remember Stewart. "The Rev here is a pretty visible fellow," he said. "He's the pastor at St. John's Lutheran Church and sits on a thousand charitable boards and committees. He's in the paper a lot. Personally, I think he needs an agent."

"Of course, that must be it." She looked like she didn't believe it, but let it drop.

"So what did you find out?" Caleb pointed at the briefcase beside her.

Her gaze shifted from Caleb to Stewart. "Maybe now isn't a good time."

"Now's great. Look, Stewart is Sam's best friend. Anything you tell us will help."

Patrice opened her briefcase. "I probably shouldn't show you all this, but I'm going to anyway." She pulled out a thick file and slapped it on the coffee table. "This is a disaster," she said grimacing. "I have never in my life seen books like these. And apparently, Anne agreed with me."

"What's wrong?" Caleb asked.

"CarolinaCorp has received a number of state and federal housing grants. I mean, we're talking about twelve million dollars worth. And these grants bring with them highly specific accountability requirements. One is that they submit an annual independent audit of their books."

Stewart leaned forward. "I served on the board for the state chapter of the United Housing Assistance Fund. I remember when a local non-profit over in Georgia got in trouble with them. They foreclosed on all the property they'd funded and pressed criminal charges on the agency director."

Patrice nodded. "Exactly. You don't mess around with federal dollars. Unless you're Bill Edinger." She opened the other vinyl case and pulled out her laptop, setting it beside the file. She switched it on, and soon the screen came up. She slid a disk from the small pocket on the side of the case and eased it into the tiny computer. A few maneuvers later, the screen paraded a long series of numbers. Patrice forwarded through the list until she found a line marked by an asterisk. "Edinger's been playing fast and dirty with the funding sources and with the IRS. He didn't pay Social Security taxes for two years, and when the IRS fined him, he used real estate trust funds to pay the IRS fines, which came to over a hundred thousand. He got federal housing money to finance construction on a low-income apartment development, only that's not where the two million went. He used most of it to cover old debts, then he wrote one check to himself and put it into his personal account. He wrote another one to some guy named Dargon Lyles. He isn't listed with personnel. I have no idea who he is."

"Did Anne catch all this?" Stewart asked.

She nodded. "And she was looking deeper, too. She couldn't figure out how Edinger got away with this stuff for so long."

"Good point," Stewart said. "Why wasn't this caught in an earlier audit?"

"That's what Anne wanted to know. Our company's handled this account for over ten years. And the same auditor managed it until last year."

"Who was it?" Caleb asked.

Her gaze shifted from the computer screen to Caleb's face and fixed on it for a long moment. "I'd rather not say. Not yet, anyway."

Caleb started to protest but Stewart beat him to it: "Your company's covered up for Edinger. Probably for years. This could be real bad for you."

She glared at Stewart. "Maybe. I don't know all the facts yet. I'm picking up where Anne left off in researching this."

"Anne knew who had the account?"

She nodded. "Caleb, you remember Darrel Lindler. He was the one who found the old files for her. She saved her e-mail correspondence with the previous auditor where she tried to get an explanation. She didn't get very far."

Caleb raised a hand. "Look, I'm pretty much clueless when it comes to bookkeeping, so try to give me a simple answer. How much money did Edinger take? And where did the money go?"

"I think Edinger has taken about three million over the past six years. Some went straight to his personal bank account, but I don't know what happened to the rest."

"That's a shitload of money," Caleb said.

Stewart smiled. "Which is exactly how any bookkeeper would phrase it." He turned back to Patrice. "What was Anne planning to do with this information?"

She clicked at the computer again. "Anne has a lot of stuff stored on this disk. This file contains Anne's personal notes on the work she was doing. Sort of like a diary. I don't think she planned on anyone else reading it, she just used it to sort out her thoughts.

"It's pretty long. She describes meeting with Bill Edinger to ask him about how he used the trust money. Apparently, he's quite a piece of work. He dodged her questions by coming on to her, even pressuring her to go out with him."

"What?" Caleb exclaimed.

Patrice lifted her hand. " Relax. Anne turned him down. In fact, she seemed repulsed by him. She tried to get the information from someone else at Edinger's, but no one would talk to her. She got frustrated and couldn't decide if she should tell anyone at the firm."

"Why not? Surely they'd want to know," Stewart said.

She scrolled through more of the text until she found the last paragraph, and read it aloud: "Edinger's not a stupid man. I need to find out why he thinks nothing will happen to him. Why hasn't anything happened before now? S and B could be in some serious trouble here."

"What's S and B?" Stewart asked.

"Skolnick and Bagardis. Our agency." Patrice sat back but her eyes stayed fixed on the amber screen. "It really is unbelievable. If what she says is true, and we've been covering the embezzlement, we can lose our brokerage license."

"Jesus," Caleb muttered.

"Anne usually played things by the book. She should have gone to Marie immediately when she noticed the problem."

"Who's Marie?" Stewart asked.

"She's the president of our firm," Patrice said. "Maybe she wanted to be sure of what the problem was before she went to Marie."

"Because Marie's a bit of a hard ass?"

Her laugh was boisterous and unexpected. "Well, you just come out and say what you think, don't you? I guess she is. It's hard to know which way Marie would go with this. She's a real stickler for the rules, but then, she has a long history with Bill Edinger. He was one of the firm's first clients, and I think he was an old family friend."

Caleb shook his head. Bill Edinger was turning up all over the place with connections to people in Caleb's life.

Caleb glanced at the long list of numbers flickering on the computer screen. "So what do we do now?"

"I honestly don't know," Patrice said, shaking her head. "I need to dig a little deeper. Then I guess I take all this to Marie."

Stewart eyed Caleb nervously. "And what if Marie decides to bury it? Like you said, your license is at stake."

"It's worse than that. We might be looking at criminal charges. I decided to go into accounting because it's a safe, disciplined field and my family thinks I need the structure. Now it looks like I'm working for a company that covers for an embezzler. And the one person who knows the truth gets murdered."

"Patrice, we may need these files to help Sam," Stewart said.

"I already thought of that." She opened the briefcase again and pulled out a folder. "I printed up all of Anne's notes. There's a copy of the disk in there, too. I know I'll get in big trouble for it, but it might help Sam. Besides, I'm not so wild about working at S and B right now. Let them fire me."

Caleb took the file. She turned off the computer and loaded it into the case. As she looked at each of them she said, "This really sucks, you know?"

"I know. I'm sorry, Patrice. And I can't thank you enough for your help."

"Sam's a good man. No need for him to be the victim here. Anne's death was bad enough."

Caleb couldn't have put it better himself. He walked her to the door.

When he returned to the living room, Stewart was grinning, for the first time in weeks, it seemed. "You going to tell Sam our news?"

"Maybe we should wait until we have something more conclusive."

Stewart headed toward the door. "I was really scared for Sam. I know he didn't kill Anne. But the way things were looking, I wasn't sure Sam would get cleared. I've prayed long and hard about this. And I'm finally feeling optimistic, my friend. You should, too."

Caleb watched as Stewart's Bronco pulled out of the drive. He wanted to be optimistic, to believe Sam would be cleared.

Then maybe this–all this–would go away. And maybe they'd have their lives back again. He wanted to believe it. But somehow, he couldn't.

A half hour later, keys rattled against the door as Shannon opened it, holding up Chinese take-out. "I cooked!"

"One of your best recipes," he said, following her into the kitchen.

"Should we wait on Sam?" she asked, as she spread out the cartons on the table.

He glanced at his watch: 6:30. Still no word from him. He wondered where the hell his brother was. "I guess we should go ahead. He can eat his whenever he shows up."

Caleb set the table and they sat down to the meal. Between forced bites of lo mein, Caleb did his best to recount the afternoon, while Shannon dove into her food with her usual zest, inserting questions about Edinger between large mouthfuls of noodles. Caleb couldn't drum up much interest in his dinner, but ate out of obligation to his recovering body and to Shannon, who had bought the meal.

"So let's piece this all together," she said, waving her fork at him. "Anne was auditing Edinger's company and discovered that he was embezzling. Anne doesn't report it because she wants to know if someone in her firm was involved–like in a cover-up or something. That might be a motive to kill her, to keep her quiet. But Anne's death was so violent. And messy. If someone deliberately planned to murder her, wouldn't they have chosen a neater way?"

"Neater, Shannon?"

"You know what I mean. In that studio, in the middle of the afternoon. And there was a nasty struggle there, Caleb. Don't you see what I'm getting at?" She plopped in another mouthful and slurped up a renegade lo mein noodle. "If this was deliberate and premeditated, the killer would have used a less risky method. Like maybe a drive-by shooting, or hit-and-run, right?"

He mulled it over, not liking it that she made sense.

"If I was going to kill someone, I'd want to be as anonymous as I could," she added.

"I'll try to remember that. In case I ever get a letter bomb or something." He trailed his fork across his plate. "What if it wasn't premeditated? What if Edinger showed up to talk with her and didn't like her answers? Maybe they got into a fight or something and he lost his temper. Maybe he picked up the Gabriel and hit her with it before he realized what he was doing."

"Those kids who were playing in the street ... they said she looked like she was waiting for someone. You think that was Edinger? Would she have invited him over to Sam's? I think she'd want to meet him on neutral territory. Like the office."

"Maybe she didn't want anyone to know." Caleb squinted, as if trying to see it.

"It would be nice if someone saw him there. When are you going to tell Claudia about your theory?"

"When it makes more sense. I won't be able to convince her until I'm completely sure myself. Maybe I should talk to Bill Edinger."

Her turquoise eyes sparked and she brought the fork closer to him. "Over my dead body. I mean it, Caleb—we know he's dangerous and he might be a murderer. Don't even think about talking to him. You leave that to the police, understand?"

He reached for her hand and disarmed her of the flatware. He stroked her fingers, brought them to his lips, and kissed them. "Yes ma'am. I understand."

At around 10:30, Shannon coaxed Caleb into bed, but he stayed awake, listening, hoping for the familiar rumbling of his brother's van. It was after midnight before he drifted off into a stormy slumber. Once again, the nightmares swooped in on his sleep. He saw Julia, sitting cross-legged on the floor of his office, her tiny hands squeezed around what looked like a headless doll. He tried to walk to her, but each step erupted a ring of fire that encircled her, inching closer and closer. She screamed for him. He tried to reach for her, but the fire lapped at his hands and melted his flesh. The fingers went first, then the hands, and gradually, the arms. He watched impotently as his daughter disappeared in a consuming mass of orange fire.

He lurched forward in the bed and popped his eyes open. No fire. No Julia. He was safe. He glanced over at Shannon, who was curled up on her side, her lips parted slightly, snoring delicately. He eased out of the bed so as not to wake her.

Quietly, he tiptoed out of the room and down the stairs. In the kitchen he turned on the fluorescent light, grateful for its blanching, sterile whiteness. He often thought it a cruel illuminator–he'd never have fluorescents in his office–but here, it seemed reassuring. It chased off the shadowy nightmare images and exposed all. Nothing could hide in darkness where there was no darkness. He sat at the table until the staccato rhythm of his heart settled to a calmer beat.

He noticed a sheet of paper propped against the salt shaker and lifted it. The note read:

Thanks for putting up with me, guys. You've been great. But I think it's time I sort things out on my own. I'll be in touch. Sam.

P.S. Caleb—I promise not to do anything that would cause you to worry but I know you will anyway.

He stared at it for a long time. It sure as hell wasn't good news. He'd gotten used to Sam being here, where he could keep an eye on him.

He reread the letter's last sentence. Yeah, Sam, he thought, you're right about that.

CHAPTER NINETEEN

Caleb leaned back in his desk chair, grateful for the two o'clock cancellation. He couldn't get focused on his work today. His body was in a precarious state of recovery, and his mind was light years away.

He started through a stack of clinical service notes that were two weeks overdue. Matthew and Janice had surely noticed by now and were only indulging him because of his injuries. But he wouldn't be able to milk that for long.

"I know you can't be my counselor right now," a voice said from behind him. He turned to find Melanie Carson standing in the doorway to his office. Her chestnut eyes were wide and beseeching. She looked wan–her clothes hung loose on her, sack-like; a sleeveless sweater was gathered at her tiny waist by a sash that probably kept her skirt from sliding off. "But I really need to talk to you. Please, Caleb. It's about my dad."

How she got by gate-keeping Janice, he couldn't figure. But there she stood, and he couldn't exactly turn her away. He motioned her in and she took her usual seat by the window. He came from behind his desk to sit across from her. "Excuse me a sec, Melanie." He lifted the phone and buzzed Janice's extension. "When Matthew gets out of his session, have him call me. I've got Melanie Carson here with me." He hung up before Janice asked the predictable questions and turned to his client. "How are you feeling, Mel?"

"Good. Okay, I mean. I need to put on some weight, though." She looked down at herself, embarrassed.

"I'm glad you haven't had any complications from the hospital. Matthew tells me you're healing up quite well."

"He's changed my meds. He only gives me three days' worth at a time," she said apologetically. "I think I scared him."

"You scared the daylights out of both of us. And your family."

She chewed at her bottom lip and seemed at a loss for words. Caleb hoped that his comment hadn't made her feel guilty. That wasn't his point. At least, he hoped it wasn't.

"It was a stupid thing to do. It won't happen again. But we don't need to go into that now. I need to talk to you about my dad. I need to explain things."

Caleb sucked in a deep breath, surprised at his own tension. "Okay. I'm listening, Mel."

"He's not a bad man. I don't say that as an excuse or apology. It's a fact. But he's a weak man. He has addictive habits, and a bad temper. And he hasn't an ounce of self-love. I now know how important that is, thanks to you and Dr. Rhyker and my therapy. But Dad hasn't a clue. It's a miserable way to live, Caleb.

"You have to know him in the context of his upbringing. His father, my grandfather, was a coal miner. Dirt poor, drunk most of the time. They lived in a three-room house, all eight of them. My grandfather died when my dad was thirteen. He had to quit school so he could get a job."

"We've discussed your father's family before. I do understand that he's a product of a pretty bad past."

"But you don't know it all, Caleb. I guess what's relevant here is that Dad never really grew up. He never had a chance. Barely past puberty, he was working on an uncle's farm to help support his family. He knew what hunger felt like, and cold. It was a desperate way to live."

Caleb tried to muster some sympathy for the man, because Melanie needed him to. But there was none there. The wounds were just too fresh, and Caleb wasn't ready to get past his own resentment. He looked at his client and knew he was doing her a tremendous disservice, letting her go on about this. "Melanie, maybe this isn't such a good idea."

She raised her hand to interrupt him. "I haven't explained myself very well. I'm not here to defend him. I want you to understand how it is with my dad when it comes to Bill Edinger."

That got his attention. "Go on."

"When Dad was thirteen, he ran away. You couldn't blame him. The family had fallen apart, his mom was chronically depressed. His younger brothers and sisters had been parceled out to relatives. So Dad hopped a coal train that brought him down here. He was homeless for a time. Then he got a job with Howard Edinger, Bill's father. Howard took him on as a yard boy, even took him home to live in a room over his garage. Dad was one year younger than Bill Edinger."

"So that's how they met?"

"Yeah. Like I said, Dad lived on the property. But he couldn't have been more different from Bill Edinger. While Dad grew up hungry and dirt poor, Bill grew up indulged and spoiled. He was the only son of the chosen family. And Dad, I guess you could say, was in awe of him."

"They became friends?"

"Strangely enough, they did. Howard Edinger bought Bill a car, some old Ford. Bill and Dad would spend hours working on the thing. Then on the weekends, they'd get some beer and ride through the countryside. I guess alcohol's the great equalizer, huh?"

"I suppose it can be."

"When Dad was eighteen, Howard had an addition put on the house, and the contractor hired Dad to help with the interior. Dad's been in that business ever–" She was interrupted by a gentle rap on the door.

Matthew stuck his head in and said, "Caleb? What's going on?"

"Melanie here managed to sneak by our eagle-eye secretary. She's filling me in on some details about her family. Thought you'd want to sit in, if you have the time." He knew Matthew didn't. He'd seen the schedule, a dozen or so appointments back to back. Matthew glanced down at his watch, then took a seat.

"Look, Dr. Rhyker. I'm not here for counseling. Right now, I'm here because Caleb deserves to know the truth, especially about the fire that almost killed him." She was direct, almost forceful.

"Seems like we're treading in muddy waters here," Matthew cautioned.

"I agree," Caleb said. "Melanie, you're used to this room as a place for confidences. What you say behind these walls stays behind these walls. But remember, I'm in the middle of a police investigation. It's hard for me to be objective, much less therapeutic. I think you should schedule a time to see Matthew about all this."

A shaky hand found its way up to her face, and she wiped her cheek where a tear had trickled down. "I said I'm not here for therapy and I meant it. But please, listen to me, Caleb–"

Caleb looked at his boss, who offered no advice. "Okay, Mel. I'm listening."

"I can't really tell you much about the fire. I know Dad was there, but it wasn't his idea. I know, deep in my heart, I know that Bill Edinger ordered him to do it."

What the hell was he supposed to do with that? He wanted to ask, "How do you know? What proof do you have?" But it wasn't ethical to use her to collect evidence, no matter how badly he wanted to. He looked uneasily at his boss.

"Bill Edinger's invaded your life lately, hasn't he?" Matthew asked.

She looked over at him, her eyes wide and clear now, seeing the truth in his statement. "Of course he has. Did you tell Caleb what he did to me?"

"I haven't discussed our sessions with Caleb. Maybe you should fill him in."

"Bill Edinger is a sick man," she said, her voice low and angry. "He manipulated me, Caleb, in a way that I can hardly describe. My suicide attempt was my doing, I have to take responsibility for it. But I wouldn't have gotten that–desperate–if not for him.

"The night before I tried to kill myself, he came over to my house. He was acting nice, but there was this edge to him. He spoke softly, but there was this subtle pressure in his voice, in the way he touched me. He stroked my hair, saying I looked nice ... my arm, saying how much he depended on me ... on my loyalty." Her voice shook, but her eyes held strong.

"Slow down, Mel," Caleb said, "you're saying that Edinger harassed you again?"

She nodded. "He said he needed me. That it would be disloyal to tell anyone about what he did. 'Sins of the past' he said." Her voice quaked again.

"Take your time, Melanie," Matthew said.

"He said we all have secrets, and we have friends to keep them safe. He said he knew I came here, and that I shouldn't pay someone to keep my secrets. He was so smooth, Caleb, so manipulative! He said he'd keep my secrets if I kept his. He took my hand and held it tight, but then smiled this weird, sick-looking smile. He leaned into me. His groin pressed up against my gut and I felt his–thing–get taller, you know? Getting hard. Pushing into me. It was so disgusting. His hands slid up my arms–then over–he touched my breasts. I couldn't move." Her arms folded across her chest protectively.

"He told me that he cared for me. That we're like a family at the company and we have to look out for each other. I wanted to die. Right then. It seemed the only way to escape him. I was so confused."

The bastard, Caleb thought. He could imagine it. The calculated moves, the double-edged messages. These were the maneuvers of a sexual abuser ... the "protect me while I molest you" mind-screw. No wonder Melanie was desperate for a way out. Even if it meant suicide.

"I felt so trapped by it all," she went on. "Like there was nothing–absolutely nothing I could do that felt right. And not doing anything felt worst of all. I couldn't stand to let him go on. I couldn't stand for him to touch me ever again. But for some reason, I couldn't think of a single way to stop it.

"Now, thinking back, there were dozens of things that I could have done. But then, there was nothing. Like I told you before, I was paralyzed. That got worse." She seemed to be reliving those feelings. Her taut lips hardly moved as she spoke.

"But you aren't paralyzed now, Melanie. You have choices," Matthew prompted.

"Choices–I only had one that night. I remember being at my mom's and going to the bathroom. The medicine cabinet was open. I saw all her pill bottles. Suddenly, I knew the answer. It was crystal clear, like a light shining in some terrifying darkness. And I knew which pills would work the best, because I always read up on Mom's medication. All I had to do was take the right thing, and it would all be over. It seemed quite simple, actually, just a matter of timing. And privacy."

"How does it seem to you now?" Caleb asked.

"Now? It seems stupid. I won't ever be trapped like that again."

"That's great, Melanie. You don't deserve to feel trapped."

"Bill Edinger came to see me in the hospital. He started the same old crap. Stroking my hand, saying how worried he'd been, and how disappointed my parents were in me–that same, distorted, manipulative crap! I remember looking at him and seeing, for the first time, how sick he was. It was there, behind his eyes." She looked over at Matthew, who nodded in encouragement.

"That's when I remembered what happened back when I was twelve. It's been coming back in flashes, but I can put it together now." She closed her eyes and took in a deep breath, as if bracing for something difficult. "Mom was in the hospital for a long time. Dad was working on Mr. Edinger's first housing project. One night, Mr. Edinger came over to the trailer. He brought a bottle of some expensive whiskey and he and Dad got real drunk. I think Dad passed out. That's when Mr. Edinger came into my room."

"You mean he–"

She nodded. "He was the one who molested me. I couldn't ever remember his face, you know, not until that moment in the hospital. But it was him. It was his mouth that panted against me that night. His legs that shoved ..." she paused, looking away.

"What did you do?" Caleb asked.

"I laid in that hospital bed with Mr. Edinger smiling down at me like he could do anything he wanted. So I told him to leave. He didn't go at first, so I yelled at him. Finally, he left."

"That's good, Melanie. Have you seen him since then?"

"No, but my dad has. Mama said that Mr. Edinger had been a big help to Dad, talking to his boss so he could get time off to be at the hospital. Later, I realized what was happening. Mr. Edinger was working on Dad, like he did with me. Dad was his new puppet."

"That's how he got your father to burn the clinic?"

"Yes. I don't know what he said, but Dad sees Bill Edinger as a powerful man, and he's very proud to call him a friend. I know it sounds pathetic. It is pathetic. Mr. Edinger convinced Dad you were the enemy, Caleb, and that somehow, my overdose was your fault."

"Does your dad know what Edinger did to you?" Caleb asked.

"Not yet. But he will. I plan to tell him everything." Her voice was stronger now, her tone, reflective. There was no fear in her eyes, just sad acceptance of the truth. This was an important step for her.

"Melanie, I appreciate your telling me all this," Caleb said.

"I had to. I owed you the truth, and I wanted you to know how sorry I am for all that's happened. But now, we have to move forward, right?"

"Absolutely," Matthew said.

She stood to leave, but hesitated. "There is one thing I can't figure out. Why did Mr. Edinger target me again after so long? And why try to burn up this place?"

Matthew started to respond, but Caleb raised a hand to stop him. "Let me ask you something. That first night, when you were in the office and he came in ... what were you doing?"

"Working on the books. The auditor had asked about some expense figures and I was having a tough time finding them."

"Did you ever find them?"

She shook her head. "Come to think of it, I didn't. I wound

up taking the books home, you know, to get away from him. I tried working on them those days I took off, but I couldn't concentrate. I still have them piled up in my living room."

"Does he know that?"

"He asked about them when I was in the hospital. Dad tried to get my keys from me, so Edinger could go in my house and collect them, but I didn't want that man anywhere near my home. His secretary left a few messages on my machine. I guess I should drop them off at the office."

Caleb shook his head, amazed at how everything was coming together. "How would you feel about turning them over to the police?"

"The police? Why?" It didn't take long for her to figure it out. "You mean, all this has something to do with the audit?" she asked.

"I don't know for sure. I have reason to believe that there's something wrong in those books. And Edinger went to great lengths to cover it up."

He glanced over at Matthew, who didn't look happy. Caleb had clearly crossed the line here, and Matthew had definitely noticed. "Look, Mel, the important thing is that you stay away from Edinger. I know, real well, how dangerous he can be. I want you safe."

"I am, finally. And I'll give those books to the police if it will help."

Caleb looked at her, then at his unhappy boss. "They may want to question you."

"It's okay, I guess. Maybe if they learn the truth about Bill Edinger, it will help my dad." She crossed over to Matthew and shook his hand. "I know you aren't happy about this little meeting. Caleb didn't want to talk to me, but I wouldn't take no for an answer. I'd have tied him to his chair and unplugged the phone if that's what it took. It might surprise you, but I can be tough to reckon with." She had some of the sparkle that Caleb had missed in recent weeks. He winked at her.

When she left them, Matthew remained in his seat. He retrieved his pipe from his coat pocket and stuck it in his mouth, not bothering to light it. His lips tightened around the mouthpiece as he stared at Caleb.

"Well, I know you're busy today. Thanks for stopping in."

"You and I need to talk."

"Okay." Caleb could see that his boss was feeling testy, and he wasn't one to let those feelings out easily. The pipe wedged tightly between Matthew's teeth probably served as a pacifier, holding back the anger that sparked his eyes. Caleb waited while Matthew chewed on the pipe and collected himself.

Finally, he said, "I didn't realize how that fire has affected you. I suppose it was a terrifying experience."

"Yes. But why do you bring it up?"

"I'm trying to understand this fixation you have on Bill Edinger." Matthew looked like he was doing his best to be therapeutic when he probably felt like choking Caleb.

"I'm sorry, Boss. I owe you an explanation. I guess I am fixated on Edinger. But not because of the fire. I believe that he killed Anne Farrell."

Matthew looked at Caleb as though he'd finally gone clear over the edge. Caleb held up a hand and started explaining. He told Matthew about Anne's work for Edinger, and the suspicions that she recorded on the computer disk. Matthew listened intently, absorbing the information both as a clinician and a friend.

"So you questioned Melanie because you thought it would help Sam," he said.

"Well, yes. It all fits, doesn't it?"

"I guess it does look that way. But nothing's been proven."

Matthew finally pulled out his tobacco pouch, loaded the pipe and lit it. Despite the fact that he probably had three clients waiting to see him, he wasn't in a hurry to leave. "So if you give the police this information, Sam may be cleared."

"Well, yeah."

"How's he handling all this?"

Caleb swallowed. "Not great. His whole life has been turned upside down."

"He still staying with you?"

"He moved out three days ago. Actually, I haven't heard from him since then." He was surprised by the tension in his own voice.

Matthew nodded the way he did when he was doing a therapy session. "I have a brother, you know. But we're not close. He lives out west, in another world, really. He's a stockbroker. Married, three kids, the whole bit. I wish we had something other than genes in common. I can tell it's different with you and Sam. I don't imagine there's anything you wouldn't do to help each other."

"That's pretty much true. I know I can't let him go to prison."

"I understand where you're coming from. But this situation with Melanie–she's still brittle, Caleb. Don't forget that you are a therapist, and with her, that role has to be your priority. Liability is one issue, but the important thing is to keep her stable. What happened today just gave her more stress. We can't do that to her, my friend, no matter how well-intended our motives."

Caleb sighed. The last thing he wanted was for Melanie to regress. "Shit, Matthew. I don't want to jeopardize her recovery. I promise to tread lightly from now on."

Matthew stood, approached the door, but didn't leave. He seemed to have something else weighing heavily on his mind.

"Caleb, stay away from Bill Edinger. This needs to be handled by the police. Believe me, there is nothing else for you to do. Understand?" His tone was strange and guarded. Caleb nodded in assent. "Good."

Matthew's words lingered behind when he left Caleb. They tumbled around in his brain, churning up confusion and guilt. Had he misused Melanie? No matter how desperate he was, he had no right to hurt a client, especially one as fragile as Melanie.

"Someone wants you on line one," Janice said hurriedly. "He wouldn't give me his name, but I think it's Percy Elias."

Caleb punched the extension and heard breathing, loud and fast, on the other end. "Hello?"

"Something's wrong. Inside my head. There's this buzzing, like white noise, and I can't make it stop!" Percy's voice was shrill and desperate, like he was poised on some perilous edge.

"Take it easy, Percy."

"Who is this?" Percy blurted out. "I asked to talk with Caleb! Where is he?"

"This is me, Percy. I just sound funny."

"I don't believe you," he said, crisply punctuating each word. "You are an imposter! You are trying to trick me!"

Caleb sighed, dismayed by the paranoia he heard in Percy's voice. "Listen, Percy. We had a fire here at the clinic. I breathed in a little smoke, that's why my voice sounds funny. Now please–tell me where you are."

Percy sucked in air, then exhaled in a loud puff. "The truth is revealed in the fire," he whispered. "That's what he told me. The truth is revealed in the fire."

"Percy, where are you?"

He heard a sniffling sound, like Percy was crying. "I'm nowhere. Sinking fast. Down, going down. In the ground. Like Anne. There's just too much static in my head."

"Okay," Caleb said. "You're going to be all right, Percy. Just tell me where you are."

"He told me. The truth is revealed in the fire. He knows all, doesn't he? He won't stay out of my head ..." His voice trailed off, to be replaced by sobs.

His delusional ramblings were thick; Percy was buried deep below. Somehow, Caleb needed to reach him. "I've got a cancellation now. Tell me where you are and I'll send a cab to bring you here."

"No!" The desperation rang out. "No. No one can know where I am. He'll *find* me."

"Percy! You need to let me help you. Tell me where you are."

"I am where ... I ... am, where I am, where I am ..." he said slowly, then he hung up.

"Shit," Caleb muttered, cradling the receiver and grabbing the Rolodex. He sifted through the cards for Percy's number and tried his home, but there was no answer. He dialed the number to CarolinaCorp, and was told that Percy hadn't shown up for work that day. Maybe he should go out looking for Percy, but he'd probably gone into Carrolton. Percy had lived on the streets there and knew the back alleys and corridors of the city's underbelly. Caleb wouldn't know where to begin. He stared down at the chart as the phone buzzed again.

"Hello?" he said anxiously.

"Hey, Caleb. This is Bryant Wheeler."

"Hey yourself, Doc. What's up?"

"I had a follow-up appointment scheduled with your brother. That arm had a little infection in it, and I didn't like how it looked. He didn't show. I had no way to reach him, so I thought I'd give you a call."

"What time was he supposed to be in?"

"Ten this morning. I know he understood that, because I gave him an appointment card. Anything wrong?"

"I'm not sure. I'll try to track him down, maybe give you a call later."

"Please do. Burns are nothing to mess with."

Caleb hung up the phone and glowered at it. Well, that news sure didn't help his mood. He wasn't sure exactly what could.

CHAPTER TWENTY

He needed to talk to Sam. If Mohammed didn't go to the mountain, or, for that matter, even return the mountain's calls, then the mountain would hunt up Mohammed.

He slowed his truck as he approached Sam's studio, spotting Laquanda and Marcus tossing a large ball back and forth on the sidewalk leading to Sam's front door. Caleb eased the truck into the driveway and climbed out.

"Hey mister! Remember me?"

"Sure I do, Laquanda. How's it going?"

"Sam ain't there. The police came looking for him, you know," she said, tilting her head to the side like she was mocking adults.

"When did they come?"

The little boy came trotting up and threw him the ball. "Just a little while ago. We told them Sam was gone. Mama said we gotta mind our own business, 'specially when the police show up."

Caleb bounced the ball and threw it back to Laquanda. "Did you see Sam today?"

"Not today. Yesterday I helped him in his workshop. He's been working a lot." A proud, dimpled grin spread across her face.

That was good news, he supposed. If Sam was working, maybe his physical–and mental–health were improving. "You know when Sam will be back?"

"No. He might have gone for some varnish, 'cause he was 'bout out. But he didn't say nothin'." Her brother snatched the ball and Laquanda tried to swat him, but he was fast, despite his chubby size. "Marcus ain't nothing but a pest," she said to Caleb.

"My big brother used to say the same about me."

"Sam?" she asked. "He too nice. You must have been bad."

He grinned at her, and she took off after Marcus. Caleb looked at the studio, deciding he'd leave Sam a note. He walked behind the studio to the porch where Sam hid his key. He let himself into the house, found a sheet of paper, and left a simple note on the kitchen table: *Sam, call me! C.*

As he locked the door again, he thought about what Laquanda had said. Since Sam had been back at work, it might be interesting to check out the new work. Caleb took the key around the back and opened the door leading to Sam's workshop. The unmistakable scent of fresh sawdust permeated the room. He hit the light switch and fluorescent lights splashed pools of light on piles of pale oak timbers and assorted tools.

It was only four years ago when Sam made a marginal living as a carpenter and cabinetmaker; building furniture was a hobby that filled his evenings and weekends. Then one summer, he entered into what Caleb referred to as Sam's "berserk period," producing a series of abstract furniture pieces that all resembled punctuation marks. A glass-top coffee table with legs that made quotation marks. A round dresser with detached mirror, together forming an inverted exclamation point. A question-mark halltree. Each piece was clever and wild and beautifully crafted, and a local gallery owner bought the entire series. He arranged for Sam to exhibit in a few local shows, and his career took off. Now, Sam sometimes worked in a functional medium, but his sculptures sold faster than he could complete them.

Caleb crossed to the center of Sam's worktable where a new structure was being born.

It was maybe nine inches wide at its base. It curved upward then swelled out to delicate points, about two feet apart, with a rounded knob between them. Subtle contours were emerging where a face would be. The head was bowed, the chin perched delicately on the long fingers of praying hands. It was a gentle, mournful-looking piece that reminded Caleb of the Gabriel, except in this raw state, it looked even more surreal.

He couldn't imagine Sam attempting another Gabriel, especially since his last effort had become a murder weapon. Yet the lithe lines leading to the points were the shape of wings, and the ethereal mood of the work reminded him of an angel. What would bring Sam back to this form?

In the Bible, Gabriel appeared as an angel, but when? Caleb's religious knowledge was embarrassingly lacking. He thought he remembered that Gabriel appeared to the Virgin and told her she would give birth. That made it even more bizarre, given Anne's pregnancy.

The first Gabriel was a gift for Stewart. Maybe he wanted to try it again, for his friend. Still, it made no sense. Given Stewart's grief over Anne's death, he didn't need this grim reminder.

Maybe Sam was grappling with some deep religious questions. Maybe this new sculpture was an attempt to resolve them. And maybe he could get answers to some of these questions if his brother would call him!

He moved to switch off the light when something else caught his attention. A sketch pad rested at the back of the worktable, propped against the wall. He noticed a series of rough drawings and looked more closely.

Each sketch was of a tall, emaciated figure, with long arms stretched out above its head. The exaggerated hands were cupped together, the disproportionately long fingers grasped a shape that looked to be a heart. In the center of the elongated torso was a hollow space.

He flipped the page and found detailed drawings of the figure's head, at various angles, all with the same desperate, contorted face. At the bottom of one of the sheets Sam had scrawled *Self-portrait.*

"Jesus, Sam." He studied the image, which made more sense than the Gabriel did. Caleb hoped sketching this had been therapeutic for his brother. The heart had been ripped out, yet he held on to it, lifting it high over his head. Caleb wondered if he was holding the heart up to God; if Sam was pleading for relief from his pain, or if it was a bitter, sardonic gesture.

He started to turn the page when a noise outside caught his attention. He heard the door squeak open, then heavy footsteps. He glanced out the window, expecting to see Sam's van, but instead noticed a huge silver Cadillac nosing against the back bumper of his truck. Before he could turn around, he heard someone opening the door. He maneuvered behind the door just as Monroe Farrell made his entrance. "You here, Knowles?" Monroe's voice boomed out.

"Is Sam expecting you?" Caleb stepped in front of him.

"Your brother here?" Monroe glanced around the studio.

"No, he's not."

A look of disgust spread over Monroe's face. "So. This is where he works."

"Yes."

Monroe crossed over to the worktable and peered down at Sam's newest piece. "I suppose you call that art," he smirked.

Protectively, Caleb stepped in front of the sculpture. Monroe reached for the sketchpad. He held Sam's drawing up to the light. "He drew this? Looks like he's one sick puppy. You know where he is?"

"No. Do you?"

"I thought he'd be here."

"He isn't ready to see you. This has been a tough time for him."

Farrell gestured with the sketch pad. "So I see. Guess his conscience is getting to him." His sarcasm had an ugly edge.

"Sam loved Anne. He didn't kill her," Caleb said, keeping his voice even. "Seems to me you'd want to know who did."

Farrell didn't say anything for a long moment. He seemed to be measuring his words before he spoke them. "That was my grandchild," he said. "Anne would have been a good mother, too. If Sam didn't want the baby, we'd have helped her out."

Caleb sighed. "Sam didn't know about the child. Hell, he's devastated. He's always wanted kids."

"Elaine said Anne was planning on having an abortion." Farrell spat the words out, as though the taste of them sickened him. "We raised her better than that. We raised her to be a Christian." He glanced at Caleb, who didn't respond. "I saw Captain Bentille today. He said he thinks Sam's jumped bail."

"No. He just needs some time on his own. To work things out."

Monroe came a step closer to Caleb. He was silent, as though mulling over what to do next. Finally, he spoke. "I know you're protecting him, Knowles. But it isn't going to help. Captain Bentille has assured me the police will bring him in. That the courts will lock him away for the rest of his miserable life. And I promise you this: If they don't take care of him, I will."

He glanced around the room again, then left. Caleb didn't bother seeing him to the door.

Caleb switched off the light and closed the door behind him. He waited until Monroe's car left the driveway before locking up the workshop. As he headed back to the studio, he noticed a light on upstairs in Sam's apartment. He unlocked the door adjoining the workshop and stepped inside.

Upstairs, he looked in the bedroom. The king-size bed Sam had constructed early in his furniture-building days was unmade. A swing-arm lamp suspended above a computer had been left on. He wondered if it was the same computer from the studio's tiny office, but when he approached it he realized it was a laptop. Probably Anne's, from her work. He switched the lamp off, then left the room.

Downstairs, he used Sam's kitchen phone and called the office. Janice said she hadn't heard from Percy Elias since the call earlier that afternoon. She put him through to Matthew, who was scheduled to be on call that evening.

"I'll be home, so I'll forward the calls directly there," Matthew said. "That way if Percy calls, he won't have to deal with the answering service."

"Thanks. And give me a call if you hear from him. I want to put him straight in detox, if it's okay with you."

Caleb arrived at the office that next morning with a throbbing headache, so he begged two aspirins off Janice and downed them. As she handed him his morning messages, she wasn't smiling.

"I'm afraid I have some bad news," she said.

Caleb braced himself. The way his life was going, who knew? "Okay."

"Percy Elias was picked up by the police yesterday."

"What?"

"I don't know why they arrested him. They kept him in a holding cell overnight. He didn't have his medicine with him."

"Shit."

"The police finally called us a while ago. They say he's in bad shape. Matthew told them to bring him in."

"All right. I'll see him as soon as he shows."

***

The police escorted Percy into Caleb's office. Chains connected Percy's cuffed hands to his manacled feet. Percy kept his head bowed and moved in faltering shuffles.

"Are those necessary?" Caleb asked the two officers, pointing at the restraints.

"Yep." The younger officer escorting Percy helped him into a chair. "He's been a wild one, I tell you."

"What's he charged with?"

"Possession of cocaine. Resisting arrest."

Caleb dropped into his chair and cursed under his breath. Eighteen months, he'd held Percy's hand. Eighteen months, he'd coaxed and supported and guided him through tenuous recovery. He hoped his irritation wasn't evident on his face. "Percy? Can you talk to me?"

Percy's head tilted up slowly until his green eyes locked on Caleb. They didn't flinch or do their usual dance around the room.

"What's going on, Percy?"

"We can't talk now," Percy whispered.

"We need to talk. Tell me what's going on here."

Percy leaned forward and said conspiratorially, "I think you know, don't you?"

"Know what?"

Percy turned his head so his chin touched his right shoulder, then pivoted it to the left, in an odd, jerky movement. His eyes never relinquished their paranoid fix on Caleb. "He knows," he uttered. "The truth is revealed in the fire."

Caleb wiped his forehead. Percy looked as out of it as Caleb had ever seen him. "Percy, where did you get the cocaine?"

"God revealed this to me, through his messenger of death."

"Was it Snake?"

Percy lifted his shackled hands, spreading the fingers in the air. "I am the Son of God," he announced.

"How much crack did you do?"

"I am the Son of God. I alone can save you." He laced the fingers together, but left the forefingers extended. Slowly, he lowered them until they pointed at Caleb's face. "I alone can save you."

"Jeez, Percy. You're scaring me here. Tell me what you took."

Percy held his face to the light pouring through the window. "And the truth is revealed in fire. I am the Son of God. The truth is revealed in fire. I am the Son of God." Percy began a chant of these words, over and over. His body rocked back and forth, in rhythm with the chant.

Percy's neurons were firing haphazardly now, reality and delusion and hallucinations all stirring around in some casserole of madness.

Caleb turned to the older officer and asked, "What can you tell me?"

"I can tell you he's crazy as batshit," he said, circling his index finger close to his temple.

"And I appreciate your expert assessment. Now, can you offer anything helpful?"

The younger officer said, "I picked him up, a while before dawn, yesterday. He was in an alley off Huger street, in the warehouse district where they're doing all that restoration. One of the warehouses is a nightclub now. Private. For, you know, gay people." He looked down at Percy as if worried he'd offend him, but Percy was on a far and distant planet from the others in the room.

"I spot three men clustered together in that alley. Four a.m., so I know they're up to something. I pull up, the other two take off. So many nooks and crannies in that maze of warehouses, I couldn't find either of them. Mr. Elias here, he just sort of leans against a wall, muttering something to himself. I search him, find the cocaine rocks, and when I take them off him, he starts fighting me. And honestly, it wasn't much of a fight. I don't think he had a clue as to who I was or what I was doing. He was high as a kite."

Caleb shook his head. This was what he feared. Percy was brittle before, precariously teetering on the edge of his illness. Cocaine had hurled him over, into the abyss. And the outlook was far from promising. He'd go to the hospital, where they'd zap him with large doses of medicine. It would be days, or weeks, or even months before his thinking normalized.

And then he'd start again the long, tenuous road to recovery.

"Look," the officer continued. "He didn't have but two hits on him. The cocaine worked its way out of his system twelve hours ago, and look at him. He isn't competent. You take him off our hands, get him some help. I think the solicitor will ease up on the charges."

Caleb nodded, grateful for his kindness. He reached over and touched Percy's manacled hand. Percy recoiled, shaking. "Easy now, Percy. Look at me." The face that turned toward him was foreign. The eyes flared huge, fixed, and leery. "You're in bad shape, Percy. We need to put you in the hospital, get you started back on your medicine. I'll do the papers, then these officers are going to drive you to the Westville General. Do you understand?"

The older officer nudged Percy's elbow. Slowly, Percy rose and turned to Caleb. "I am the Son of God. The truth is revealed in the fire."

As the officers escorted him out the door, the phone on Caleb's desk buzzed. "Patrice Dutton's here. Shall I send her back?" Janice asked.

"I guess. Can you start the admission papers on Percy?" Caleb asked, massaging his temple. The thudding headache had worsened during the session with Percy and he wondered if it was too soon to take more aspirin. But before he could budge, Patrice appeared in the doorway.

"It's all over, Caleb." She wore a denim dress and a very solemn frown. In her hand, she clutched a thin manila file.

"What do you mean?" Caleb asked, gesturing for her to sit.

She dropped heavily in the chair. "I mean I turned the files over to Marie. She went ballistic, especially when she saw the cover-up. The CarolinaCorp account came to us through Elizabeth Skolnick, Marie's partner. Elizabeth was very close to the Edinger family, so she personally handled the account. And since Elizabeth detested computers and never learned to use one, Edinger's books were all done by hand until this year. And nobody touched that data until Anne inherited the account." She thumped a knuckle against her lips and gazed down at the file in her lap.

"Yesterday, Marie called Elizabeth, who admitted everything. Edinger had been embezzling for years. It started because Edinger was having some expensive family problems, so he 'borrowed' from the business, planning to pay it back. Of course, he just dug himself in deeper and deeper. Since Elizabeth covered for him at the beginning, she didn't know how to set things right. So she took early retirement to escape, I guess. When Anne e-mailed her last month, she knew everything would surface. Marie said she was relieved that it would finally be over with."

"What happens now?"

She brushed her hand over the file like she was gathering grains of sand. "The dominoes start to fall. Since we've also done Edinger's taxes for the past ten years, we've sent fraudulent information to the IRS. Marie's already called them. They're sending in an investigator tomorrow."

"That doesn't sound good."

"No, it isn't. The IRS has already called in state law enforcement. We're going to close up shop."

"Does Bill Edinger know?"

"Yes." She opened the file. "This is a letter Marie faxed to him this morning. The IRS will be knocking on his door next. I thought you'd want to know."

Caleb took the sheet from her and scanned it. In obtuse legalized wording, it told Edinger the company would make all files available to investigators. He handed the sheet back. "How about you, Patrice? You gonna be okay?"

A ghost of a smile appeared on her face. "Is it too late to rethink that acting career?"

"Maybe not. Or maybe you could start your own accounting company."

She stood, reached toward him, and shook his hand. "I hope everything turns out okay with Sam."

"Me too. And thanks, Patrice."

Caleb didn't drive straight home that evening. Instead, he found himself pulling into the long drive leading to Stewart's cottage. He rang the doorbell and after a few moments, Stewart answered. "This is a surprise. Everything okay?"

"No big crisis. Got a minute?"

Stewart showed him in. He was dressed in black sweats that almost looked priestly. He directed Caleb into the small living room where strains of saxophone jazz wafted through the air from an expensive-sounding stereo. Caleb sank into an overstuffed leather sofa and leaned back, letting the supple leather enfold him.

"You look like you could use a drink." Stewart didn't wait for an answer. He disappeared into the kitchen and returned with two stemmed glasses. The claret-colored wine tasted dry and went down with unexpected ease.

"What's going on, Caleb?"

"I'm not sure. I don't even know why I came over here." He took another sip of the wine and thought about downing the rest of it. Common sense prevailed, however, and he set the glass down on a table beside him.

"Any new developments?"

Caleb filled him in on Patrice's findings about Skolnick and Bagardis. Stewart listened intently, his own glass untouched in front of him.

"That's good news, isn't it? If this turns into a federal investigation, they'd surely find out if Bill Edinger killed Anne."

"Yeah, that's just it. I should be feeling relieved, but I don't. In my gut, something just doesn't feel right."

"Your gut, huh?" Stewart grinned. "I understand what you mean. You and I both rely on our intuition in our work. So what's disturbing you?"

"Damned if I know. Aside from my brother disappearing. You haven't seen Sam, have you?"

He shook his head, looking alarmed. "Not in a week or so. I've sent about a dozen e-mails. Haven't heard back from him."

"Me neither. I don't think he's left town or anything, he's just in his own form of seclusion. But I really need to talk to him."

Stewart leaned forward and eyed Caleb with some intensity. "Do you think your instincts are questioning Sam's innocence, Caleb?"

"No! Jesus, no. I have no doubt Sam is innocent. Do you?" he asked, not hiding his shock.

"Of course not. Just making sure we're on the same page."

Caleb picked up the wine glass and held it up in front of his face. Light refracting through the cabernet gave it a purple hue. "I don't really know what page I'm on, Stewart. That's just it."

"What's bothering you?"

"One thing. The way Edinger took the money was pretty obvious. Anne discovered it right away. Surely, someone else would have, too. If Edinger killed Anne, was he going to murder everyone who figured him out? He'd wind up with a long trail of bodies."

"I doubt he 'planned' anything. From what I hear, Anne's murder was quite brutal. Maybe she confronted him unexpectedly. He panicked and attacked out of desperation." Stewart picked up his glass and took a quick swallow, the subject of heinous murder clearly uncomfortable for this man of God.

"Maybe." Caleb shook his head in disgust. "So it was all over money. Anne and her baby murdered. Another life nearly destroyed."

"You mean Sam."

"Yes. He lost a whole family that afternoon. I can't imagine how he'll ever make sense of it." A somber silence fell between them. They nursed their wine while a Winston Marsalis CD provided background music. The music was meant to relax, but tonight, it felt mournful. "I keep finding myself thinking about Anne's baby. That child was Julia's cousin, you know. Julia would have loved that baby." Caleb finished his wine and stared into the empty glass.

Stewart thrust a clenched fist against his lips. "Why didn't Anne tell us about the pregnancy, Caleb?"

"Because of the abortion, I guess. That's Elaine's theory, anyway."

"She was going to kill the child?" Stewart's face flushed red and his voice rose.

Caleb nodded, surprised by his strong reaction. He'd never

figured Stewart for a pro-lifer. "She was considering it. She probably felt overwhelmed by everything. Problems with her job—bad problems, as we now know. Plus getting married is stressful enough. Maybe she thought a baby was just too much to take on."

Stewart looked like his mind was far away. Caleb held up his empty glass and finally caught his attention.

"Sorry. Let me get you a refill," Stewart said, still flustered.

"I'd prefer some water."

Stewart headed to the kitchen, then returned with a tumbler of ice water for Caleb and more wine for himself. He still looked shaky.

"This is all getting to you, huh?"

Stewart sighed, studying his wine. After a long moment, he said: "You've been generous in sharing private information with me. I think it's my turn. Anne used to come to me for counseling. When she first moved in with Sam, it was a confusing time for her. She felt guilty about leaving her folks and she had some fears of commitment. She worried that she couldn't give Sam what he needed. But she and I both knew that she was exactly what Sam wanted in his life.

"When she finally agreed to marry Sam, I saw that as real growth for her. But Anne stopped coming to see me. I thought that was good, you know, maybe she was talking to Sam about her fears. But now I think I should have pursued it. I should have gone to her and reminded her that God is ready to listen, whatever the problem is. If only she had told me about the baby, I could have helped her work through it."

"Aren't you doing some Monday morning quarterbacking here, Rev?"

"One of the dangers in my profession, I guess. Yours too."

"Elaine came down the other day," Caleb said. "She and her

husband had seen Anne the day before she died, trying to talk her out of the abortion. The strange thing is, Anne lied to them—she said she'd already had it. I guess she was desperate. And maybe even a little afraid."

"Of what?"

"Maybe Edinger. Or her father. Elaine threatened to tell him about the abortion. We both know he can be a force to reckon with." Caleb stretched and stood up. He felt drained, and sleep was what his mind and body needed. "Sorry I put you in this depressing mood."

Escorting him to the door, Stewart said, "It's okay. But you let me know when you find Sam. I'm worried about him, too."

Back at his house, Caleb unlocked his front door and entered quietly. In the kitchen, he found a note from Shannon: *NO. Sam hasn't called. Claudia Briscoe phoned twice. She'll try you in the morning. Phillip Etheridge, too. I couldn't wait up any longer. Love you.*

A wet nose nudged him in the butt. He reached behind him and stroked Cleo's head. She leaned into him, her weight forcing him to her empty food bowl. "Still got that herding instinct, huh, girl?" He obliged her with a cup of dog ration before turning off the kitchen light.

He climbed the stairs, took off his clothes, and carefully slipped into bed. Shannon rolled over and curved into him; he leaned over and kissed her dark, chaotic curls. He knew he might have trouble sleeping, but for now, just lying with her was what he needed.

He was lucky to have her, to have this. Stewart didn't. Leaving the pastor's house, he'd been struck by how lonely the place was. Stewart had built himself a quiet life, surrounded by his books and his work and his music. But he had no wife or lover. No children. Not even a pet. His home felt empty and sterile.

And, for the first time, he'd seen the same emptiness on Stewart's face.

Caleb remembered what Sam had said, that Stewart was burned-out from trying to meet everyone's needs. Tonight's talk of Sam and his losses must have triggered Stewart's own regret. Caleb wondered how many glasses of wine Stewart poured before getting into his empty bed.

He rolled over and nuzzled his face into Shannon's soft, sweet-smelling hair.

CHAPTER TWENTY-ONE

"Well, well. You've certainly been a busy boy." Claudia Briscoe's tone was berating.

"Good morning, Detective." Caleb looked beyond the phone at his alarm clock. 6:20 AM. Cruel.

"Two things. One, I thought I warned you against playing detective. I heard about your little investigation into CarolinaCorp. We got an FBI agent stopping in at nine. Captain Bentille is ready to shit bricks, he's so mad at you."

"He probably could shit bricks. The man looks terminally constipated."

"Number two. Your brother was supposed to check in with us yesterday. He didn't show. Anne Farrell's father stopped in, demanding to know what Bentille's gonna do about it. Bentille's having him picked up again for skipping bail. You know where he is?"

"No. Did anyone talk to Phillip?"

"I did. He's a slick lawyer, mumbled something about his client misunderstanding the terms of his bond. Played up his being deaf and all. But he and I both knew that Sam understood real well what his situation was. You'd better get him in here, Caleb."

"I'll do what I can. Let me know what happens with the FBI."

Caleb hung up the receiver and stared down at it. He wasn't sure what to feel—anger at Sam for not meeting his obligations, or fear that something had happened. Maybe Monroe Farrell had found Sam and carried out his threats. Somehow, Caleb needed to get some answers.

He mentally reviewed his appointment calendar. He planned to go by the hospital and check on Percy. He had an intake at 10:00. There was an inter-agency meeting he could skip that afternoon, and Janice had scheduled a few paperwork hours for him later on ... good. He'd leave work at lunch, spend the rest of the day combing the city for his brother.

He eased out of bed without disturbing Shannon, who was still sound asleep. He ran a hot shower and let the water beat down on him, firing up the sleeping synapses of his nervous system, melting the knots in his tense shoulders and neck.

He stepped into the foggy bathroom and as the mist on the mirror slowly cleared, he studied himself. The bruise on his chest had faded to a greenish yellow. The tenderness in his lungs had subsided, and he'd gone through the whole night without a single cough. Good. His body, at least, had healed from the fire.

He had lost some weight, though. He noticed the outline of ribs he couldn't see before, and the waist of his jeans fit loser now. He'd always been skinnier than his brother–it had been a sore point growing up. But now he was looking downright scrawny. Maybe when all this was over he'd start an exercise program. Join a gym. Start running. When all this was over ... somehow, that seemed light years away.

Downstairs, he made coffee, let Cleo out, and buttered a few slices of toast. He'd finished an uninteresting breakfast by 7:30 and decided he'd go into work. It would help to get an early start on his day, since he planned on cutting it short. He wrote a note to Shannon, grabbed his keys, and headed out the door.

A light fog lent a mysterious air to the morning, muting colors and blurring the contours of the city. Soon it would lift as the sun poured out its relentless, unquenchable heat. August was on its way, promising to turn Westville into a kiln.

He pulled his pickup into his usual parking spot. Curiously, the small gravel lot wasn't empty. A beige-colored car that looked new was parked under an oak in the rear of the parking area. Someone must have left it there yesterday, probably someone with car trouble. In heat like this, engines were failing all over town. He glanced through the driver's window, but he didn't see anyone. He rolled his own window down an inch or so, locked his door, and stepped out of the truck.

Someone grabbed him from behind. One hand clutched his shoulder as the other squeezed the right side of his neck. A wave of fear lunged through him, paralyzing his muscles. He felt hot breath behind his left ear and tried to pivot, but the grip on his neck tightened.

"Don't move," the words spewed out in a hoarse whisper.

"My wallet's in my back pocket." Caleb tried to still the tremor in his voice.

"I'm not going to rob you, Knowles." The man leaned into him. Their heads touched. "You know who this is?"

And all at once, he did know, the realization sweeping over him like a chilling wind. "Edinger," he muttered.

"Good. I thought we'd take a little ride together." He pinched Caleb's shoulder and guided him to the other side of the truck. As they reached the passenger door, Caleb jerked his arm free and swung against Edinger. But his assailant was quick–he plowed into Caleb, hurling him against the door. He braced his forearm against Caleb's chest and growled, "You don't want to do that. Let's keep things easy so no one gets hurt. And by 'no one' I mean you and me and the rest of your little household, Knowles. Including your little girl. We understand each other?"

He nodded. The force of Edinger's weight against his chest aggravated Caleb's ribs so that breathing started to hurt. "So what now?"

"We take a drive. Get in."

"I don't have much gas." It was an obvious stall but Edinger didn't drop a beat.

"We'll take my car then." He dug one hand into Caleb's neck while the other reached into his pocket. Slowly, he pulled out a small handgun. He pressed it into Caleb's ribs and Caleb stiffened. Nudging him with the gun, Edinger guided him to the beige sedan, opened the passenger door and shoved him in. He ordered Caleb to slide over to the driver's side and pushed his own mass into the passenger seat. He dangled keys in front of Caleb's face. "Start her up, Knowles. And head south on Lake Street."

Caleb's hand trembled as he put the key in the ignition. It seemed a stupid thing to do, letting Edinger force him into the car. But what were his options? He glanced over at Edinger, who had put the gun back in his pocket. It was too risky to chance fighting him ... not after his threats to Julia.

They drove for a long time. They followed Lake Street until it merged into Highway 331. They took the highway out of town, through the cotton fields and peach orchards of rural Cherokee County. Caleb knew he was driving in the direction of Lake Mullen, but wasn't sure why.

Edinger was a tough read. He leaned his head back against the window, but his face stayed fixed on Caleb. His expression was a void. No panic, no sweaty desperation. The small, dark eyes maintained a steely, casual calm.

He gestured for Caleb to turn onto Shore Road. Most of the fog had lifted, but mist still lay in scattered patches of gray at the crests of hills on the serpentine road. He drove slowly, feeling his tight fingers gripping the wheel, just as the fear gripped his chest. He tried to keep an eye on Edinger, on that hand frozen in his pocket.

As if Caleb knew anything about revolvers. The only gun he'd ever touched, other than Ellen's water pistol, was his uncle's hunting rifle. He didn't even like seeing them on TV.

Think ... think! If Edinger's plan was to drive to an isolated spot and then shoot him, Caleb would need to escape, no matter what. He needed to know more. He needed to get Edinger talking.

"It looks like you're holding all the cards here. So why don't you let me in on your plan?"

"What do you want to know?"

"Well, first off, are you going to kill me?"

Edinger grinned a wide, sick grin that made Caleb's stomach churn bile. "No. I don't plan to kill you. I told you I wanted to talk, and that's what I plan to do. Of course, you have to decide whether or not to believe me." He cocked his head to the side with this last statement, as if trying to be playful.

"You want to talk. I'm listening."

Edinger pointed to a dirt road that veered off to the left. Reluctantly, Caleb obliged.

His mind drifted away, sifting through the possibilities like cards on a Rolodex. He couldn't stop it: Edinger aims the gun, fires. Does Caleb feel the bullet? Is it hot, searing into his flesh? Does he feel the life seeping out of him?

Caleb's mind detoured to a bleaker track. Edinger had threatened his daughter, and after what he had done to Melanie ... What if Edinger got his hands on Julia?

Be calm, he commanded himself. Be calm, for Julia. At her birth, he had promised to love her, to keep her safe and happy. Whatever sacrifice needed to be made, he'd keep that promise. Be calm.

"Turn it off." Edinger pointed to the ignition, and Caleb obeyed. They sat beside each other in a long, heavy silence.

Caleb channeled his energy toward readying his reflexes. The chance would have to come for him to flee.

Edinger seemed to be working on something else, something deeply internal. Finally, he said, "Do you know what a mess you've made of my life? And for no reason. For no fucking reason at all."

"Seems to me the mess is your own doing." Caleb said it without thinking, and prayed it didn't inflame Edinger.

"Maybe you're right. I took the money. I knew that would catch up with me eventually. After Elizabeth retired, it was just a matter of time. Hell, I was almost relieved when it finally happened." Edinger wiped his face with the back of his hand. "Anne. She was so damn smart. Didn't take her any time to figure it all out. She handled it well, too. She was ... respectful. She truly was one of a kind."

Caleb stared at Edinger, trying to fathom his meaning. He needed to ask, and fought hard to keep the terror out of his voice. "How do you mean, she was respectful?"

"She came to me, gave me a chance to explain. She suggested that I go ahead and make contact with the IRS, turn myself in, if you will. She said she'd give me a few days to make up my own mind about how to handle things. I liked that. She didn't back me into a corner. I knew what I had to do and made plans to do it."

"And so you killed her?" Caleb asked.

Edinger leaned his head back, his neck making cracking noises. "No. You're wrong, dead wrong about that. I cared about Anne. I would never have harmed her.

"The fire was a bad idea. After Anne's death, I realized I had another chance. Maybe I could delay exposure until I had a chance to set things right. I could sell my house, liquidate some stock. Then I would reimburse the feds, pay off the IRS.

But I remembered about the files Anne was working on. I called Marie Bagardis and she said you had them at your office. When she said your name, I wanted to scream. I'd met you at the hospital, I'd seen that cocky gleam in your eye. Knowing you had the files did something to me that's hard to describe. I hated you, Knowles."

"So you manipulated Harold Carson into burning the clinic?"

"I told him he needed to burn all the records. I did not tell him to burn the entire place down. And I certainly didn't tell him to hurt anyone."

"What about what you did to Melanie?"

He lowered his head for a brief moment. "I found out Melanie accidently got hold of the wrong set of books. She could find out everything."

"So you tried to stop her?"

Edinger leaned his head back again, eyes narrowed into tiny slits. "You don't understand about Melanie. I wanted to protect her."

"Protect her? You molested her. She was terrified of you."

He raised his hand. It now held the gun. "You convinced her that I was some kind of monster. You made her remember things best kept buried. And Melanie didn't even know about your own personal agenda–you used her, Knowles. You abused your power and took advantage of her."

Caleb swallowed hard. "I had no agenda with Melanie. Except to keep her safe."

"You wanted to nail Anne Farrell's murder on me, and you used Melanie. But it didn't work, Knowles. It didn't work because I didn't kill Anne. Hell, I even have an alibi. The afternoon she died, I was with my attorney. We were going over my situation, planning out a strategy to deal with the fucking IRS."

Caleb felt his reality shifting, shaking at his core. Trembling, he said: "You hired someone. Like you did for the fire."

"You don't know me, Knowles. I don't travel in circles with hit men. Harold Carson did the work for me out of love for his daughter. But I knew he didn't have the balls to carry it out by himself. I needed someone else. Ironically, another one of your fans helped me out there. Percy. One of his faggot friends stopped by, begging for work. Now and then we hire him on as casual labor. I knew he had a colorful criminal history and a nasty cocaine habit. He was hurting and desperate, willing to do absolutely anything I asked for quick cash.

"So this prick and Carson started the fire. They had nothing to do with Anne's death. Neither did I. You see, I have no reason to lie to you now. I want you to know the truth because I want you to realize, fully realize, that the devastation you have reaped on me has been pointless.

"Your brother killed Anne Farrell. I don't know why he did it. But he will go to prison." Edinger's eyes widened, as if punctuating this statement. Then they released their fix on Caleb, roaming sideways to stare out the windshield. "I suppose that's my only consolation, really. That you'll see your deaf brother behind bars. Tossed among rapists and murderers to spend the rest of his life. Not likely to be a long one, is it?"

A surge of nausea climbed up Caleb's throat and he could taste it. He wanted to fight Edinger, fight those words and their terrifying meaning. But there seemed to be no fight in him. He'd been emptied out.

Edinger shifted in his seat, shaking the car noisily. "So what do I do now, Knowles? You've ruined my life. It looks like I'll go to prison. The IRS has already confiscated my books, frozen my accounts. My office got a call from a newspaper already. I'll be in the headlines soon. There's no way to avoid it."

Caleb studied his face. The eyes held no venom now. Instead, there was a deep sadness behind them. Edinger was a man grieving for his own life. "I guess you face what you have to face, then put it behind you."

"Put it behind me? How the fuck do I do that? How does my family? We've been in this town for five generations. How can I put them through this?" Edinger stared out at the vast, empty woods.

"Maybe your family will understand," Caleb said, knowing he didn't sound very convincing.

Edinger shook his head. "No. Not this. This is too much."

Caleb could think of nothing else to say. He no longer felt afraid. He no longer felt anything. Through the trees, he could see the water. Dark green, mossy looking. No whitecaps, not enough of a breeze to penetrate the still surface.

Edinger opened his door and climbed out of the car. He turned back to Caleb, staring at him for a long moment. "I think our business is done. You can drive my car back to town now." He slammed the car door shut.

Stunned, Caleb watched as the man lumbered down the dirt road. He reached for the ignition key, but his eyes couldn't leave the isolated figure of that man. He'd seen Edinger's desperation. And he'd seen the gun. Caleb wanted to drive away, to put as much distance as he could between them, but leaving Edinger out here didn't feel right. It was hard to know what to do. Somehow, his thinking had gotten foggy.

Edinger didn't move fast. His walk was a slow stroll, like someone window-shopping. His hands stayed buried deep in the pockets of his jacket.

Caleb couldn't just leave him. He opened the door, climbed out of the car and moved in Edinger's direction. He picked up his pace to a slow trot and was soon within a dozen yards of him.

Edinger must have heard him, because he turned to face

Caleb. His eyes looked softer now. He regarded Caleb for a long time, then raised his right hand and waved. It was a friendly gesture, curiously out of context. Caleb stared at him, trying to decipher his intent. Edinger turned and started walking again.

"Wait! Where the hell are we? Maybe I should drive you back to town," Caleb beckoned.

Edinger turned again, this time his face taut and wary. Slowly, methodically, the right hand slipped out of the pocket. It held the gun.

Caleb froze, unable to think, unable to breathe. Edinger lifted his hand, stretched out his arm, and pointed the small gun directly at Caleb. "Leave here. Now."

Caleb nodded. Panic thwarted his body, but gradually, he got it moving. He walked briskly, wanting to turn around to see what Edinger was doing but he dared not. By the time he got back to the sedan, Edinger was out of sight. He opened the door and stared down the empty gravel road. He waited.

He jumped when he heard the gunshot.

Two hours later, Caleb sat across from Detective Claudia Briscoe in an interrogation room. He couldn't stop shaking. She handed him a cold soda, but he didn't trust his trembling hand to carry it to his lips.

He'd driven to a pay phone and called her. It felt like years later when she arrived, legions of squad cars in her wake. She drove him up the gravel road so he could lead them to the body.

Edinger lay splayed out on a grassy hill. Little blood oozed out of the small hole in his forehead. His eyes, wide open, held an odd, wondering expression. Claudia had leaned over and closed them.

The image wouldn't leave. It was all he could see inside the fog that swirled through his brain. He could scarcely answer

Claudia's questions. He couldn't concentrate to even hear her.

"Caleb!" she shouted. "You've got to talk to me!"

He looked over at her and sucked in a deep breath. She was right, of course. He needed to tell her what happened. Did she think he killed Edinger? He should defend himself, but the words just wouldn't come.

"Listen to me," she was saying. "What took you out to Lake Mullen?"

Shivering, he reached for the soda and took a sip. The ice-cold liquid sent a jolt through him.

"What happened, Caleb?"

He wanted to tell her; she would certainly understand. If only the words would form in his mouth.

He heard a gentle rap on the door and Claudia opened it. Matthew Rhyker looked frantic; he rushed over to Caleb and looked him over. "Thank God," he uttered. "Are you all right?"

Caleb tried to smile, but it wouldn't hold. He felt disgusted with himself.

"Could I talk to Caleb?" Matthew asked Claudia. She nodded and motioned for him to follow her out of the office. Through the window in the door, Caleb watched them talk. Claudia gestured in her usual animated style, with Matthew nodding back at her. A moment later, Matthew returned and pulled a chair over beside Caleb. "You need anything?"

Caleb shrugged, hoping his battle for self-control didn't register on his face.

Matthew laid a hand on his shoulder and said, "You're okay, Caleb. Just take it easy. You don't have to say anything until you're ready."

The words were soothing. Caleb reached for the soda and took another swallow that went down easier.

"How about I talk? I got to work today and the phone rang.

It was Shannon. She said you'd come in early, but I didn't see you. And your truck was in the lot. That didn't make sense. Then your nine o'clock appointment came in and you still didn't show. By ten, I knew something was up. I hoped I wasn't overreacting, but with all that had been happening lately, I decided to call Detective Briscoe. She was at the office when your call came in."

His hand squeezed Caleb's shoulder. "You gave me a few gray hairs today, my friend. But damn, it's good to see you."

"Does Shannon know?"

"No. She thinks you're at the office. Can you tell me what happened?" Matthew's face was kind and expectant. Why was it so hard for Caleb to open his mouth and talk? Why were the words so far away? Bill Edinger's lifeless face appeared again, from a back closet in his mind.

Matthew was in no hurry. He sat there, close, reassuring. And gradually, the words started coming together and spilling out. Caleb recounted the entire experience without stopping. Matthew listened, nodding slowly, taking it in. Caleb stopped when he told him about Edinger's body, stumbling over the image freeze-framed in his mind.

"Dear God, he could have killed you. Okay if I tell all this to Claudia?"

"In a second." Caleb held up his hand to stop him. His thinking was clearer now, but a grisly truth hung suspended before him. "It's all for nothing, Matthew. I thought that if I went after Edinger, I could clear Sam. But Edinger didn't kill Anne."

"That's what he said. Who knows?"

"Why would he lie? Especially since he planned on killing himself. He also said he had an alibi. Jesus. All this was for nothing."

Matthew let out a heavy sigh. "Do you want me to tell that

part to Claudia?"

Caleb blinked at him. With Edinger gone, he could lie. He could say that Edinger confessed to the murder, and Sam would be cleared. God, if it was only that easy. But he couldn't live with himself. He couldn't live with the unanswered questions. "Get Claudia. We'll both tell her."

Claudia was a good listener. She asked a few questions that helped Caleb provide as much detail as possible. She scanned his hand with an ultraviolet machine which verified that Caleb hadn't fired the gun. Then she excused herself, saying she'd need to advise Captain Bentille of Caleb's statement.

Alone again with his boss, Caleb said, "You don't have to stay here and babysit. I'm okay."

Matthew grinned. "I'm very glad that you are. I'll give you a lift home. I do need to make a few calls, though." He slipped out of the office, leaving Caleb alone with his new grim reality.

Fifteen minutes later, Captain Bentille made an entrance with his usual flare. He towered over Caleb and said loudly, "I'm bringing your brother in, Knowles."

Caleb stared up at the man's eyebrows, deciding they looked like silver caterpillars preparing to mate and was grateful for the distraction. "Do what you have to do. That should include finding Anne's real murderer."

"Come off it, Knowles. After today, I should think you'd accept it. Somewhere deep down, I think you know your brother did it. Hell, today you pretty near proved it."

Caleb wanted to retort, but the fight had left him. He closed his eyes, aware of his fatigue. And his mind's eye looked again on the bleeding body of Bill Edinger. It seemed that image was a new, permanent companion.

***

When Matthew drove him home, he accompanied Caleb

inside. He suggested that Caleb take a shower to clean himself up before Shannon got home. It wasn't until then that Caleb noticed the brown splotches of Edinger's blood on his shirt, his pants, and even his skin. When he finished the shower and went back down twenty minutes later, he found Shannon in the living room with Matthew. He stood in the doorway; his sweat pants had no pockets and he couldn't think of what to do with his hands. They felt exposed, dangling there by his sides.

"Come over here, honey," she said. He obeyed, glad to have instructions. He sat beside her and she slipped her arms around him. He could barely feel it. Again, he found himself shivering, as if in some private, icy winter.

"Matthew told me everything. I know you're still in shock, but I promise that you will be all right. Do you need anything?"

"I could use something to eat," he said. It was a lie, of course. The idea of food repulsed him. But if it gave her something meaningful to do, it was worth it. She squeezed him again, then headed for the kitchen. Pots and pans were soon clanging in there.

"Still babysitting?" Caleb asked Matthew, trying to sound jovial.

"I promise to leave you alone soon. But first, I want to say something to you. You've been through a serious trauma ... the kidnapping, then Edinger's death. Which followed a long list of very stressful events, one that nearly killed you. So you feel a bit out of control right now. That's to be expected."

"If you plan on telling me how my clinical skills will benefit from this experience, I'm afraid I'll have to kill you."

Matthew smiled, but his expression wasn't one of relief. "There's something I need to tell you. I should have talked to you earlier. If I had ... maybe ... that doesn't matter, really." There was a hint of sadness in his voice. "I knew Bill Edinger."

"A client?"

He nodded. "I consulted with a therapist running a perpetrator's group a few years ago, as a favor to social services. There were seven men; all had pleaded down from family court for incest charges. They were first-time offenders. Edinger had molested a niece, about fourteen years old."

"Jesus."

"He was a piece of work. Most of the others had boundary problems and addiction. Molested their daughters or whoever when their lives got stressful, and usually when they were drunk. Not Bill Edinger. He was controlled, manipulative. Antisocial."

"He stick with the group?"

"After a few sessions, he dropped out. I thought the judge would slap his wrist, maybe court-order him into some private therapy. But nothing happened. Money talks, I guess. I wish I'd told you all this when you first mentioned Bill Edinger's name."

Caleb shook his head. He doubted that it would have made a difference. "Where's the niece now?"

"He did some sick shit to her. He also introduced her to drugs. Last I heard, she was a runaway. Sixteen years old and living on the street."

Caleb thought back to his conversation with Edinger. He'd put his family through some tough times, he'd said–that may have been an understatement. He walked Matthew to the door and opened it. "I appreciate you telling me this stuff. It'll helps me get a better handle on things–maybe not this afternoon, but ..."

"He was a miserable man, Caleb. The world won't suffer from his death."

CHAPTER TWENTY-TWO

That next morning, Caleb awoke with the strangest hangover. The clock by his bed read ten o'clock, which meant he'd been close to comatose for twelve hours. He sat up and looked out his window on a cloudless, still day. Untangling himself from the sheets, he stepped over Cleo and made his way down the stairs.

He found Shannon in the kitchen. She gave him a long hug and motioned for him to sit. She poured his coffee and refilled her own mug, her ice-blue eyes studying him up and down.

"You looking to see how my nervous breakdown's coming along?" he asked.

She reached over and squeezed his hand. "If you need to have a breakdown, it's okay by me."

"I could use one. But I don't have time right now." He took a sip of the coffee and savored it.

"So you must be feeling better," she said.

"Yep."

"Good. Then I think I should give you this." She handed him an envelope. "It came in the mail yesterday. It's from Sam."

He stared at the letter. The postmark was from Asheville, North Carolina, which was a bad sign. He tore it open and read:

Caleb.

Sorry, I haven't been in touch. I had to get away. Don't know when I'll be back. Leave things alone, Caleb. Anne is gone. There is so much more to her death than you know. I, myself, am only beginning to understand it all.

Please take care of yourself and Shannon and my Julia. I love you guys. Sam.

Caleb stared at it for a long time and then handed it to Shannon.

"So he left town?" she asked.

"Yes. I guess he jumped bail."

"But why?"

Caleb shrugged. He had no answer for her, no answer that was palatable.

Shannon's fingers stroked the lip of her coffee mug. Finally, she said, "I hesitate to even ask you this, but I hope all this isn't going to make you wonder about Sam's innocence."

A silence fell between them. He thought about yesterday and the trip with Edinger. Edinger had been so convincing about his innocence. He'd admitted to the embezzling, but nothing else. Why wouldn't he admit to killing Anne if he was going to kill himself anyway? What would have been the point of keeping that a secret?

She reached for his hand again. "What is it, honey?"

He shook it off. Don't go back there, he told himself. That way madness lies.

"You don't have to talk about it if you don't want to," she said, ever the therapist.

"It's okay. I'm still just a little weirded out. To answer your question, no. I can't let myself believe that Sam killed her. But things don't look good for him." And there seemed to be nothing he could do to help. This realization cast a dark veil on this new world of his. He sipped at the coffee and felt the silence pull him down.

The doorbell rang and Shannon hesitated to answer it. "You up to seeing anyone?"

"It depends, I guess. How about I hide out in here and you see who it is?"

She nodded and headed to the living room. A minute later she returned, Phillip Etheridge in tow.

He sat down across from Caleb and shook his head. "I just got back from the police station. I think you and I need to talk." His right hand groped the pocket of his crisp blue shirt and pulled out a pack of Winstons. "Mind?"

Caleb shrugged, and Shannon retrieved an ashtray from a cabinet.

"I innocently pick up the paper this morning and there's this interesting headline with your name in it. So I read on, get pretty damn curious, and pay a visit to the police station. Detective Briscoe was gracious enough to fill me in on your doings. Pretty damn stupid, my friend. And I can't for the life of me figure out why you didn't clue me in on your suspicions. I am Sam's lawyer, remember?"

Caleb watched as Phillip lit up and fingered the cigarette. He couldn't think of what to say. The phone rang and Shannon motioned that she'd take it in the other room.

"So you thought this guy Edinger killed Anne to cover up his embezzlement, right?"

"Yes."

"And he got your client's father to torch your office. He hired this bum, Dargon Lyles, to help."

"You know him?"

"Yeah. I drew him on a public defender case a year or so ago. A real pig. Deals drugs, pimps, a few B and E's. Looks like the scum that he is, too. Head's all mis-shaped, like one of those forceps-delivered babies. Big tattoos shaped like snakes over both hands. Edinger hired him because Dargon will do anything, absolutely anything, when he needs a fix. Piss poor protoplasm, you ask me."

Caleb thought back to the fire and the man who almost killed him. He felt indifferent about it.

"They picked up Dargon outside some gay bar an hour ago," Phillip went on. "High as a kite. Heroin, probably. He'll do five years or so."

Caleb leaned forward and asked: "You mentioned snake tattoos. You know if he ever went by that nickname?"

"Yeah, he goes by Snake. Why?"

Caleb thought of Percy. In his mad ramblings the other day, Percy had said, *The truth is reavealed in the fire.* But now, maybe Snake would be gone for a few years. Maybe that would be long enough for Percy to get back on track, permanently. At last, something good might come of this.

"So, Mr. Investigator. Where are we now?"

"Now?" Caleb sighed. "We're nowhere. Edinger didn't kill Anne. I don't know who did. My brother's jumped bail, and it looks like he's out of state. And I, myself, have had about all I can take."

"You've sure been through it. I wish it had worked out like you wanted. But listen, Caleb. I need to know about Sam. Do you know where he is?"

Caleb reached over, picked up the letter, and handed it to him. Phillip took a long time reading it. Then he folded it, and gave it back to Caleb. "So. What are you going to do?"

"Find him. There are several places up near Asheville where he likes to camp; I just have to figure out which one."

"You going to bring him back here?"

"Yes, if I can. And I want to hear what he's learned."

"That would help. It would also help if he clued his lawyer in. Or is that against the Knowles's religious beliefs?"

"Okay, Phillip. Whatever I find out, you'll be the first to know. Anything else?"

"Just this. I tried to stall the police, but they're pissed right now. Especially Bentille. That asshole congressman, Cal Moultrie, is really working him. Good friends with Monroe Farrell, you know. Anyway, when Sam gets back, he'll go to lockup. Bail's revoked. So we need to move fast to get him cleared." Phillip ground out his nub of a cigarette and stood. "Take care of yourself, Caleb."

Shannon came back in the kitchen in time to say goodbye, then told Caleb Stewart had called. "He heard what happened on the news."

"Terrific." He wondered who else knew. His clients? Julia?

"Stewart said he was sorry and I should keep you out of trouble. I said fat chance."

Caleb drained his coffee cup and planned the day ahead. He had to find Sam, even if he had to go to North Carolina. But first, he needed to figure out what Sam had meant in the letter. Did his brother know who killed Anne? And if he did, what was he going to do about it?

Caleb showered, dressed, fed Cleo, and was downing breakfast when the phone rang again. It was Matthew, checking on him like he had promised. Caleb assured him he'd slept well and felt better. Matthew said he'd call later for another progress report.

"Okay, Mom," Caleb replied, and hung up.

By then Shannon had dressed in faded jeans and a blue work shirt which perfectly reflected the tint of her eyes. She found Caleb in the kitchen and slid her arm around him.

Caleb stroked her cheek. "Do me a favor?"

"I can deny you nothing. Unless, of course, it involves housework."

"Take me to pick up my truck. I left it at the office."

"Don't need to. Claudia had an officer bring it by last night. The keys are in the living room. Where are you going?"

"To find Sam."

"But he's in North Carolina!" she exclaimed.

"I know. I should only be gone a few days."

She leaned her head against his chest. "I'll go with you."

"No. You stay here and take care of Cleo."

She looked up at him, looked through him, tears forming. "I don't like this, Caleb."

He kissed her. "Tell you what. I'll call you every hour or so. If I don't find him by Monday, I'll come home. How's that for a compromise?"

"It sucks. When will you leave?"

"This afternoon. I'm going to Sam's first to see if I can figure out where he's staying. I'll call you before I leave town." He clung to her for a moment, then she pulled away.

"If you need me, I'll be there in a flash."

"I know you will. I've seen you drive."

The street in front of Sam's mill house looked abandoned. Laquanda and Marcus must be watching cartoons. Pulling to the back of Sam's drive, he parked in Sam's spot and climbed the steps to his back porch.When he found the key in its usual place under a potted plant, he opened the back door and stepped inside.

He immediately noticed the scrubbed kitchen counters and empty sink, which meant that Sam had cleaned up before leaving. Caleb walked through the living room and saw that it had also been straightened. The light over the stairs had burned out, but enough sunlight filtered through the round porthole window over the landing. He took the steps two at a time and entered Sam's bedroom.

The sketchbook lay open in the center of Sam's bed. Caleb turned on the light and moved in closer, noticing that Sam had been busy sketching. Again, he had worked on the emaciated figure of the man, with long arms reaching high, hands cupped around a heart. Caleb flipped the page and found a detail of the man's head. Anguish registered on the contorted face, the open mouth seemed to scream out silently. Around the thin, wrinkled neck dangled a cross shaped by crude, rusted nails.

It didn't look like Sam's mental health had much improved.

Caleb glanced around the room for some hint of where his brother was, but found nothing. He crossed over to the small desk and noticed that the laptop computer had been left open. A screen-saver flickered; the machine had been left on. Caleb touched the keyboard and rows of text flashed up on the screen.

For the next half hour, his eyes didn't leave the screen. He read every letter, understanding the words they formed but struggling to fully comprehend their meaning. Dark reality crept in close now, filling his consciousness. Numbing him. It was all too much.

Edinger's lifeless face appeared again, from the back closet of his mind.

He almost didn't hear the phone ring. But the light signal flashing overhead caught his attention and he reached for the receiver, disconnecting the teletype.

"Caleb?" Shannon said. "I'm glad I caught you. Let me come get you. I'll take you to North Carolina."

North Carolina. He'd forgotten. He had to get to his brother. "No, I'm okay. I will be, anyway."

"Listen. Stewart called again. He got a card from Sam. He

said Sam's camping up at Crabapple Falls. He asked Stewart to come up there. Stewart's on his way now."

Jesus. He opened his mouth to speak, but his voice came out in a whisper: "When did you talk to him?"

"Right after you left. About an hour ago." She paused, then said, "You don't sound right. Please let me come with you."

He heard the love in her voice, and couldn't think of what to say. After a moment, he muttered, "I'll be okay. I promise I'll call soon. 'Bye, Shannon." He hung up before she could say anything else, before she could pierce through the brittle veneer that barely kept him from buckling. He switched off the computer, turned off the lights, and headed for his truck.

He made it halfway down the steps before he saw her.

Claudia leaned back against her squad car, arms folded, watching him. She'd parked behind his truck, her front bumper nosing his tailgate. There was no way he'd be able to get past her.

"Your brother in there?" she asked.

"Nope."

"Any idea where he is?"

"Nope."

"Would you tell me if you knew?"

"Nope." He retrieved car keys from his pocket and eyed the truck.

Claudia unfolded her arms, then propped them on her hips, defiantly. "No. I didn't think you would. I guess I could have you followed."

"Don't, Claudia. Just leave it alone." Something in his voice caught her attention.

She looked closely at his face and it made him uncomfortable. "You okay, Caleb?"

"I think you know the answer to that."

She nodded, a glimmer of sympathy flashing across her face. "We got Harold Carson talking. He didn't take Edinger's suicide too well. We also arrested Dargon Lyles, a local street punk, and charged him with the arson. So I think you and your family are safe now."

"My family includes Sam."

She pursed her lips like she wanted to chastise him but thought better of it. "I'm sorry you know. For how things are working out. I haven't had a chance to tell you that we finally got the results of the DNA test, from the fetus. The baby wasn't Sam's, Caleb. Bentille says that's even more motive. Me, I'm not so sure."

"Me either, Claudia." He looked back toward the mill house, remembering the secrets there.

"We'll make it as easy for him as we can, I promise. But Sam needs to come in."

He thought about telling her. He could open his mouth and let the truth spill out, but she wouldn't believe it. She'd say he was deranged, she'd say the idea was preposterous. And, in a way, she'd be right. Reality often turns out that way.

"I need to get going," he said simply.

"And you have no intention of telling me where." She opened her car door, then hesitated. "Whatever you're doing, Caleb, be careful."

CHAPTER TWENTY-THREE

The drive to Asheville took three hours. Crabapple Falls was twenty minutes beyond the city, up the serpentine Blue Ridge Parkway. The torrid summer had brought throngs of tourists eager for the cool breezes and restful air of the mountains and it seemed like most of them were on the highway, taking their time, gawking at the scenery, blocking Caleb's passage. He did his best to weave around them, keeping the truck at fifty, though his foot ached to press harder on the accelerator. A speeding ticket would only delay him more.

The day was cool and crisp and mostly clear. But when he least expected it, he'd climb a steep grade and plunge into a patch of fog creeping across the highway. Caleb knew the road well enough to be cautious of both the weather and the less experienced drivers.

He passed the Spruce Pine exit. Crabapple Falls would be next. Soon, he saw the small brown sign and slowed to make his turn. His truck wound through dense woods where tall oaks and maples blocked out the sun and cast cool shadows over the narrow road. A half mile later, the road turned to gravel. Caleb slowed down and heard the loud crunch of rock beneath his wheels. When he started up a sharp hill, he saw the sign for CRABAPPLE FALLS CAMPGROUND and turned in.

No one manned the small gatehouse. He drove past it and followed the drive as it curved into a giant circle from which campsites protruded like spokes on a wheel. He eased around, scanning the tents and vehicles, hoping to spot Sam.

He almost missed it. Sam's van was obscured by a large maple tree, and he'd staked his tent far from the drive, in a cluster of wild dogwoods facing the river. Caleb pulled in beside the van, and noticed the other vehicle. A black Bronco. Stewart's car.

"Shit." He climbed out of the truck and looked around for a sign of the two men. He trotted over to the campsite and found the tent empty. Twirls of smoke circled over the last embers of a dying campfire; Sam may have been gone for quite a while. He looked around for a path or trail that might carry him to his brother.

He pushed through the brush and made it down to the river. A narrow trail paralleled it, heading uphill toward the falls and downward toward who knew where. He looked both ways, and opted for the direction of the falls. Sam loved the water, and Caleb gambled that he'd spent most of his time here watching the thunderous torrents. He prayed Sam had no self-destructive thoughts.

The trail was unforgiving. Caleb tried to move quickly, to build up some momentum, but his feet caught on rocks and tree roots, hurling him off balance. He knew a sprained ankle was the last thing he needed. He had to be cautious, even if that meant slowing his pace. He kept one eye on the trail and the other ahead of him, looking for Sam.

Recent rains had left the steep climb treacherously slick. Caleb noticed his endurance had weakened and his lungs still burned from the fire. He felt each breath stretch his chest, and the more he exerted himself, the more his lungs burned. He did his best to ignore the discomfort and continue up the sloping trail.

He heard the falls. At first the sound was faint, like static from a distant radio. But gradually, the roar of the water cascading down the thirty-foot drop swelled through the air like thundering applause in a packed auditorium. He maneuvered himself off the footpath, through the brush, and stood on the river bank to look up at it.

If he had any breath left in him, the view would have taken it away. Pearls of water bounded off the rocks, plummeting down fifty feet, crashing into a turbulent pool of swirling white water. From there, the expanse of water squeezed through rocks and boulders that jutted out of the river like mammoth teeth.

Caleb quickly glanced around and spotted two fly fishermen braving the frigid water downstream. The water was deeper there, a mossy green color, with flashes of mercurial silver. He yelled out, hoping the fishermen had seen his brother, but the grumbling roll of the river would not be upstaged.

He craned his neck upstream again. At the top of the precipice, beside the mouth of the falls, he saw Sam and Stewart face to face, arguing. He wanted to scream, but knew it was fruitless.

The two men faced each other, conversing with flailing hands and arms. He couldn't make out the conversation without getting closer. He returned to the trail and did his best to jog up the steep embankment. Surely Stewart realized that his secret was out. What would he do? And Sam ... Dear God, how must he feel, confronting this man of God who destroyed his life?

The trail ended where wooden railway ties formed steps leading straight to the top. He climbed them quickly, and was soon standing at a split-rail fence that held tourists back from the dangerous embankment. He tried to see Sam and Stewart from his new angle, and finally spotted them off the trail, standing dangerously close to the water.

He climbed over the rail, slid a few feet, then caught himself on a tree root. The bank was steep, and the only way he could get down was to slide on his rear. In a half-controlled tumble, he skidded down, and soon landed within a few yards of them.

Stewart grimaced as his hands signed at Sam. It looked like he was explaining himself, describing his love for Anne and her love for him. His hands said Anne wanted to leave Sam, but couldn't because of her guilt and sense of responsibility. His hands accused Sam of not being what Anne needed. Sam stared back, his own hands stiff beside him.

Caleb approached cautiously and touched Sam's shoulder. His brother looked surprised, then relieved, his eyes filling with grief.

"I know, Sam. I know," Caleb signed. He turned to Stewart. "Why did you come here?"

"To help him. We've all been worried." He tried to smile, to look calm, to don again the guise of innocence. Caleb felt such antipathy toward him that he could scarcely speak.

"Help him? Dear God. You're the cause of everything. You killed her, Stewart. I know it, Sam knows it, and soon the police will." His rage erupted in his words, and he hoped Sam wouldn't comprehend.

But he did. He touched Caleb's arm. "I think you should get out of here."

Caleb stared at him, confused. "I'm sure as hell not going anywhere without you." He turned back to Stewart. The pastor's pewter eyes jerked back and forth between them, as if mentally measuring his chances. Caleb fought a strong impulse to pound his fist into his face. "You son of a bitch. You're gonna make things right, Stewart. I swear, you will. We're going back to Westville, and you're telling the police."

Stewart bit at his lip. "You don't understand. You don't understand how I felt for her."

Caleb inched in closer. "You sick bastard. Anne saved all

the e-mails you sent each other. We know the truth now."

"You don't know anything."

"You stalked her, you bastard. She may have reciprocated at first, because she was swept away by your attention." Suddenly he thought of Patrice. She hadn't recognized Stewart from the newspaper, but from his visits to Anne at the office. The idea sickened him. "But she tried to break it off and you wouldn't let her. She became terrified of you and what you would do. And she had reason to be, didn't she? You killed her. And the child."

"I didn't know about the baby." His voice cracked.

Sam touched Caleb again. "I told you to get out of here."

"No. Why? Jesus ..." He searched his brother for some understanding, and noticed, for the first time, Sam's arm. Bryant Wheeler had warned them about infection, and now the area around the burn was inflamed, crimson-colored and seeping pus. His entire forearm looked nearly twice its normal size. Even his hand had reddened, the swelling extending down to his knuckles. Alarmed, Caleb pointed to it and said, "God, Sam! Look at your arm! We have to get you to a doctor."

Sam ignored him. His physical pain seemed inconsequential to what stirred inside. He looked beyond Caleb, fixing on Stewart Brearly.

"What do you want from me?" Stewart asked.

Sam shrugged. "I don't know."

"Hell, I do," Caleb interjected. "You need to tell the police what you did."

Stewart turned his head to the side and closed his eyes. He looked as if he was absorbed in some internal music. Caleb watched him cautiously.

After a moment, Stewart opened his eyes again. "I would have done anything for her. I would have given up the church, my life, anything."

Caleb heard his brother breathe in a staggered breath and

moved closer to him. "*She's* the one who gave up everything. She gave up her life," Caleb said. "Look, the point is, Sam's the victim here. You have to set things straight."

"The victim?" Stewart laughed darkly. "He destroyed us. He destroyed my life."

Sam moved forward and eyed him intently. "Sign it, Stewart. I want to make sure I understand you."

He obliged. His hands moved in a forced, rageful rhythm. "Do you know what I've learned from this? I've learned what evil is. It isn't the sin that we do. God knows, we all sin. It's the guilt, and what guilt motivates us to do. Anne's guilt about you drove her to desperation. You, Caleb"–he jabbed a finger at him–"your merciless pursuit for the truth killed a man. You stripped Edinger of everything. He stood naked in his guilt, and look what happened. He kidnapped you, then put a bullet in his own head. And you–inside, I'll bet you're still covered in his blood, aren't you? I imagine that won't be easy to shake. He's dead now–was his sin so terrible?"

Sam turned to Caleb, his eyes searching his. Caleb gave him an awkward nod.

Stewart looked at the wild, dancing waters of the falls. "Beautiful, isn't it? You see this, you know the real power of God."

"Strange that you should bring his name into this," Caleb muttered.

"I suppose it is." His tone sounded priestly now, as if sermonizing the currents. "I have spent my whole life trying to live up to the ideal that God set for me. But then Anne falls into my life and I see, for the first time, what God means by the power of love.

"We were so happy at first. Our love grew stronger and stronger. And when we made love, I touched her like she'd never been touched before. She told me so."

Caleb noticed Sam flinching, and he himself felt sickened by this whole conversation. "If you loved her so damn much, why did you kill her?"

Stewart glowered at him, the fingers on both hands angrily kneading the meat of his palms. Then they sprang open and signed: "It happened in an instant. I was with her, in your studio, Sam. She handed me the piece of sculpture and said you had made it for me. She told me to hold it, to feel it, to feel my betrayal." He closed his eyes and tilted his head back, as if inwardly wrestling with the memory. He raised his hands to continue. "I felt it then. The guilt. I looked at the angel in my hands and wished I could burn it. She saw how I felt and she laughed at me. I'd never seen her do that, you know. She never was one who would mock another."

"What happened then?" Caleb asked aloud.

"She said she loved Sam but didn't deserve him. She said she was going away and that I would never see her again. She said her only regret was that she couldn't destroy my life like I had ruined hers. As if she didn't know ... I had no life without her. I reached for her and she screamed at me, balling up her hands and hitting me in the chest. I pushed her back, and she came at me again. She had such fury in her eyes. I begged her to stay with me. But she signed 'No!' and screamed that I disgusted her." For the first time, he looked at them, his expression a strange mixture of madness and wondering. "I honestly don't remember what happened next. But a second later, she was on the floor, and I was holding the sculpture, and it was covered with blood."

Caleb looked over at Sam, whose eyes never left Stewart.

Sam asked, "What did you do then?"

"I bent over her and touched her lips. She wasn't breathing. I wiped off the sculpture and dropped it to the floor. Then I left.

The police called me later, and asked me to come in to interpret for you. I knew then that Anne was dead. And that you would pay for what you did to me." He shrugged, comfortable with that black rationalization.

Caleb had had enough. He couldn't contain his anger any longer. He stepped in front of Sam, screamed, "You sick bastard. I hope you rot in prison, Stewart. I swear, I'll see to it that you do."

Stewart turned toward Caleb, an unfamiliar savagery glowing in his eyes. He moved quickly, with the ease and stealth of a cat, and lunged at Caleb. Caleb hadn't braced himself and Stewart knocked him off balance. Before he could recover, Stewart swung at him again, and Caleb's foot slid out from under him. He tumbled to the ground, clutching a large rock to keep from sliding into the water. Instantly, Stewart came to him, and with surprising strength, shoved Caleb, trying to force him over the edge.

"*No!*" Sam screamed and charged him. He knocked Stewart down and leapt on him, holding him tightly to the ground. Stewart screamed out, his body arching upward in a sudden explosion of primal wrath. Sam toppled over, landed on his bad arm. He groaned in pain.

Stewart pulled himself up. Bowing his head like a bull, he rammed into Sam's side. Sam rolled nearly four yards down before bracing himself against a thin sapling. Stewart, towering above, came at him again.

Caleb threw his legs over the embankment and scooted down as fast as he could—the small tree wouldn't hold Sam long, and there was nothing else to prevent his tumble over the falls. Stewart was more cautious in his approach, and Caleb got to him before he reached Sam. He looked up at Stewart, lifted his legs, and kicked with all his might, his feet catching him at the knees. Stewart swayed. His arms flailed, grabbing at the air. He teetered off the rock and fell into the cascading water.

Caleb gasped as Stewart merged with the thunderous falls. He heard no scream. In a second, there was no trace of Stewart at all.

Sam slid down to Caleb and leaned over the edge. "I can't see him." Sam tugged at his sweater, pulling it off.

Caleb grabbed his good arm. "No, Sam. You can't go after him."

Sam pulled away and started yanking off his hiking boots.

"Shit. Not that way, Sam. You'll kill yourself." Caleb scrambled to his feet, jerked his brother up, and pointed at the trail. "We'll look for him at the bottom," he signed. Sam pushed past him, scrambled up the embankment, and took off down the trail. A few interminable minutes later, they were both at the bottom.

"Do you see him?" Sam panted, scanning the large mouth of water fed by the thirty-foot waterfall.

"No." Caleb pushed past him and went on to a large boulder overhang. Mist from the falls coated their eyes, blurring everything. Caleb blinked away the water and squinted toward the other side of the immense pool. The rapids spilled out and down, splashing around copper-colored rocks and broken limbs, eventually gathering again in a deeper, mossy green river bed. Maybe he'd surface there, where the rapids were more shallow, Caleb thought. He strained to look across the river, as wide as a football field, hoping to spot the red of Stewart's sweater or blue of his jeans.

"There!" Sam yelled. He pointed at a half-submerged cluster of rocks about forty yards away. Stewart's arm draped over one stone as he lay face down in the water.

"I'll get him," Caleb signed, pointing at Sam's injured arm. He tore off his sweater, kicked off his running shoes, and stepped into the rapids.

The frigid water shocked nerve endings in every exposed part of Caleb's body. The deceptively strong movement of the water worked to pull him into the current. Straining with each small step, Caleb felt along the slick, invisible rock bed. His foot slipped, plunging him chest-high into the icy river. He sucked in cold, wet air, pulled himself up and lumbered on, grabbing fallen branches and rocks to balance himself. The fast-moving torrents pushed against him–a strong, unpredictable force trying hard to carry him downstream.

When he reached Stewart, he flipped him over and propped him against a large flat rock. He found a slow pulse, but there was no sign of breathing. He looked toward the other side of the river. It was too far away, which made moving Stewart too risky. He looked back. There was no way to carry Stewart through the rapids without losing the battle against the current.

He climbed up on the rock and tugged on Stewart with all his might until his limp body was half out of the water. Panting, Caleb tilted Stewart's head back the way he'd remembered from CPR training years ago. He blew into Stewart's mouth, but the breath didn't get very far. Caleb repositioned the head, checked his mouth for any impediment, and blew again. He saw the chest rise and fall, but that was it. Three more times, he forced air into Stewart, but still, no response. A hand touched his back.

He turned to find his brother beside him. Sam's arm had opened itself, probably on a rock, and blood dribbled down into the water. "Let me try," he said.

Caleb nodded and backed away, sucking in air that clawed at his own raw, burning lungs. He watched his brother work to save the man who'd tried to kill them. Rhythmically, Sam forced air in Stewart's mouth, keeping a hand on Stewart's chest to measure the heaving up, then down. He waited five seconds, then blew again. Caleb watched, then waved at him to stop and took over again.

A couple of minutes later, Stewart revived. He sputtered and heaved, then threw up the water that had forced its way into him. Caleb pushed him over on his side, and Stewart coughed, regurgitated more, and gasped for air. Caleb slapped his face. “Stewart? Look at me.”

He opened foggy eyes that held no focus. Caleb studied him, trying to compute how long Stewart had been without oxygen. It felt like years, but had probably been only a few minutes.

“Stewart!” he yelled, and struck him again. The pastor’s eyes moved toward Caleb, then looked over at Sam, then squeezed tight.

“Oh, God,” Stewart uttered, and started to cry.

“He’s okay, Sam,” Caleb said.

His brother nodded, relieved. “Are you?” he asked.

Caleb took a quick mental inventory. “Yeah, I think I am. How about you?”

Sam shook his head. “You never do anything I tell you to. I wrote and told you to leave this alone. You show up here, I told you to go back. You never listen to me.”

Caleb tried to read Sam. There was no humor in his eyes. “And your point is?”

Sam shook his head again. “You should have done as I asked. You could have been killed, Caleb.”

Caleb looked over at Stewart. He lay there, eyes closed, shaking. He seemed to be alone in a hellish world of his own making. He’d probably spend the rest of his life there.

Caleb slid over to Sam and sat on his haunches in front of him. He signed, “I don’t know what you had planned here. The fact is, you are my brother and your problems, no matter how fucked-up they are, are my problems. So I had no choice, really, but to come here. You can argue all you want, but if our situations were reversed–" He shrugged at Sam.

Sam watched him intently, the anger dissolving from his face. He looked over at Stewart, then up to the top of the falls. "The cavalry's here," he said.

Caleb looked up, spotting Claudia and about a half dozen officers making the slow descent down to the river bank. He should have known she would follow him here and actually, he was relieved she had.

Caleb waited for Sam to look at him again, and said: "I can't imagine how this all feels to you. Why did you come here, Sam? And why ask Stewart?"

Sam turned and looked back at the river. "I don't know, really. I read the e-mails Anne had saved on her computer. I couldn't believe it. I felt so stupid, so empty. It all seemed so sick, you know? Anne sleeping with my best friend. I guess I hoped to get some answers."

"Did you?"

"Yeah, oddly enough. I loved Anne. I don't think I'll ever feel like that again. But I had a history of other lovers before I chose to spend my life with Anne. She had no one before me, I was her first. Of course, she was curious. Of course, she was swept away by Stewart's attention, by what he aroused in her." He looked over at Stewart, who stared with fearful, haunted eyes.

"I do think she regretted the relationship. And I know she loved me. There's some comfort in that," Sam said, his voice breaking. He swallowed, then turned his face toward the water.

Caleb looked over at the river, too, and was surprised at how calm it seemed. After a moment, he turned back to Sam. Caleb grinned and reached for him. Sam slid his good arm around Caleb's neck, and they held to each other tightly.

"Thanks, brother," Sam whispered.

CHAPTER TWENTY-FOUR

The invitation read: HIGHBURN GALLERY PRESENTS THE NEW WORKS OF SAMUEL ARLEDGE KNOWLES.

Caleb waved it at Shannon. "This means I need a tie, right?"

"You can wear that bolo Julia made you at the arts and crafts camp."

"Don't you dare mention that when she gets here. I had to wear it for a week after she made the thing. Only person I know who owns a tie made out of macaroni."

"Any idea who's coming to this opening?"

"The usual artsy-fartsy crowd, I guess. Sam sent an invitation to Claudia Briscoe. And to Captain Bentille, if you can believe it." Caleb relished the thought of toasting champagne to his brother's success in front of Bentille. "And I told Matthew to bring his checkbook."

"I swear, I can't believe Sam's doing this. After the past six months, you'd think he'd take some time off."

Caleb nodded, but he understood Sam. His brother had immersed himself in his work for six months, even through the eight weeks that his arm had been bandaged. It was his therapy, and each piece of wood that he shaped into a new form represented a part of himself, of his pain, and his recovery. Whatever anger Sam had harbored seemed to dissolve into wood chips and sawdust. He'd visited Anne's parents, offering silent forgiveness to a man who had wanted to kill him. He'd been with

Stewart at his sentencing, and had even visited him twice in prison. Caleb himself had no sympathy for Stewart, and marveled at his brother's compassion.

"Have you seen any of these sculptures?"

"Yep. They're pretty amazing. One is a commissioned work for the church, if you can believe it. A Madonna and Child. The bishop requested it, and Sam jumped at the chance. I thought he'd lost his mind, given all that's happened." But when Caleb saw what he'd done with the piece, he understood. He remembered the soft lines, the gentle, loving face of the abstract Virgin Mary as she looked at the child. The baby's hand clutched a cross, a premonition of his destiny. But the baby's face glowed with joy and life and newness. It was Sam's goodbye. To Anne, to the child, to Stewart.

Caleb looked over at Shannon, who wrestled with her unruly hair, trying to gather it in a clasp. A rebellious strand escaped and fell over her clear blue eyes. "Oh hell," she said.

He stroked the curl from her face and pulled her to him.